I0682408

This is a work of fiction. Apart from the well-known actual people, events and locations that figure in the narrative, all names, characters, places and incidents are the products of my imagination or used fictitiously. Any resemblance to current events or living persons is entirely coincidental.

ISBN: 9780692706732

Jericho Road Press

Library of Congress Control Number 2015908390

Printed in the United States of America

Suggested Retail Price (SRP) $11.95

Cover Design by Tugboat Design

This is a work of fiction. Apart from the well-known actual people, events and locales that figure in the narrative, all names, characters, places and incidents are the products of my imagination or used fictiously. Any resemblance to current events or living persons is entirely coincidental.

ISBN: 9780692706732

Jericho Road Press

Library of Congress Control Number 2015908390

Printed in the United States of America

Suggested Retail Price
$12.95 (USD)

Cover Design by TdjbdEsign

2

## Dedications

**Guessing at Normal** is dedicated to all of you for whom 'normal' has been a goal to achieve, a final destination as it were. You might have been told your whole life that it's what you should aspire to, being 'normal'. I don't want to burst your bubble, but honestly? Normal is just a setting on a washing machine. I heard that somewhere. Wish I could claim it as my own, but I can't. From my perspective, if you are happy, have people around you that you love and who love you, whether or not you are related by blood or by marriage, and you are doing or have done something that makes you feel good, you're probably about as 'normal' as you need to be.

I would also like to thank my husband and best friend, **Deane Olmsted**, for lovingly taking this journey with me. I have heard that the single biggest determinant to happiness in life is the person you choose to spend it with. I wholeheartedly agree!! Thank you, sweetheart for your faith in me, your support and your love!

## Acknowledgements

To my early readers, I can't begin to thank you enough for your suggestions, questions, criticisms and enthusiasm for *Guessing*. **Barbara Wurtzel**, how did I get so lucky to have a friend and colleague like you? You are the most well-read person I know and you like my books. That's huge!! **Donna Lukenbill**, working with you again is the greatest. Your support and attention to detail made *Guessing* a better read. Thank you for all your time and talents! **Karen Jordan**, you rock my world, my friend. I am dying to hear your 'voice'! **Louise Corcoran**, thank you so much for your input and valuable suggestions. **Eve Kinne**, you are such an excellent emotional barometer. Thanks for understanding Jill, and me too! **Diane Sabato**, what can I say? You're the best friend a girl could want. I always feel like I'm one of the cool kids when I'm with you. **Laurie Cain**, my oldest friend! Thank you *mille fois* for your friendship, your love, and all your freakin' commas!! **Hayley Olmsted**, my friend who just happens to also be my darling daughter, your suggestions and feedback were so valuable in making Jill the most authentic main character I could possibly hope to write!! I love my girl. **Conor Olmsted**, my son, thank you for your humor and your love. Neither of my main characters in **JEEP TOUR** & **Guessing at Normal** have had a son. If they did, I would want him to be just like you!

To my biggest fan, my late mother **Anne Brennan Ward**. Someday, Mom, I'll write a main character lucky enough to have an amazing mom like you. In the meantime, you're the gold standard!

To my late, great cousin **Kathy Ward Barry**. Love you more, Kath!!

# Guessing at Normal

## a novel by Gail Ward Olmsted

**"I have always believed I had something to say and I said it."**

Lou Reed

**"Don't you ever say I just walked away. I will always want you."**

Miley Cyrus, "Wrecking Ball"

**"We'll sing in the sunshine. We'll laugh every day."**

Gayle Garnett, "We'll Sing in the Sunshine"

**"I've been waiting for you, darlin'. C'mon and dance with me."**

James Ryan Sheridan, "Dance with Me"

## 2009

## Preface

I met James Sheridan in a motel lobby almost twenty years ago. When I gave him change for cigarettes, I cautioned him about the perils of smoking, but I was just messing with him. What did I know? It was a fluke- I should have gone home almost an hour earlier, but the guy who was supposed to relieve me was late, so there you go. Those cigarettes changed the course of my whole life and James' too! A few years later, his hit song *Jericho Road* (from the bestselling album *Guessing at Normal*) climbed the charts on its way to the #1 song on America's Top 40 for a record 23 weeks. At the time, there was a great deal of speculation about the title of the song and its origin. I'm here to finally set the record straight, because I wrote the damn thing. *Jericho Road* is *not* a song about salvation. I'm sorry if the title was misleading. For some, 'Jericho' is where the Israelites returned from bondage in Egypt, but for me? It just happens to be the name of the street where I grew up and lived until I was eighteen years old. They say you can't go home again, but I wouldn't know. I never really tried.

Carly thinks I should share my story, so here goes.

**1990**

## Chapter 1 - *What I Got*

"Those things will kill you." Those were the first words I ever spoke to James Sheridan. He was waving a five-dollar bill as he asked, "Can you change this? I need quarters to buy some smokes."

I wasn't surprised by his sudden appearance in the deserted motel lobby that night. I'd heard the hum of the elevator just moments before he appeared. I worked behind the front desk from 3:30 p.m. to midnight Monday through Friday. I was supposed to get two fifteen-minute breaks and another half-hour for dinner, but there was rarely anyone to cover for me. It was a pretty boring job, with long periods of inactivity, punctuated by a flurry that would keep three people busy. When I wasn't at work, I spent a lot of time reading and writing in my journal. I usually slept late on weekends and hung out with my best friend and her new baby. That was me, livin' the dream!

So yeah, I heard this guy approaching before I looked up. We got some pretty sketchy folks most nights, and at first glance, he fit right in. Tall and lean, he had longish dark hair that looked like it could use a good washing. I pegged him to be in his mid-20s, but it was hard to be sure. He was barefoot (yew!!) and was decked out in a pair of baggy knee-length gym shorts and a black wife beater. As he got closer, I could see a number of tattoos up and down his pale arms. He had a pair of bright blue eyes that were probably his best feature, but they were ringed in red and featured bluish shadows. He was a really good-looking guy, but probably a stoner. I was more attracted to the preppy types with short blonde hair and golden tans from days spent on the golf course or tennis court. The kind of guy who would never give me a second glance.

This guy was definitely glancing. From the corner of my eye, I could see him checking me out as I hit the buttons and rang a 'no sale' to get the cash register to open. That's when I uttered my snappy line. I hadn't said a single word out loud for more than two hours and I croaked it out, so I think all he might have heard was "kill you." He held his hands up in protest.

"Hey, sorry. I can't sleep and I'm out of cigarettes. So sue me." *Yikes, touchy!* But something about him was vaguely familiar. I had heard that voice before. It was deep and rich and almost velvety. Maybe...

"It's no problem," I assured him. "I was just messing with you. Smoke all you want. I just want to get out of here." I placed four singles and four quarters on the counter in front of him.

"What time do you get off?" the blue-eyed mystery man asked me.

"Gee, if I had a dollar for every time one of you guys asked me that," I said with a smirk. He slid a dollar bill back towards me.

"You're way too cheap," he told me with a grin and wandered off to the far corner of the lobby in search of his cigarettes. Moments later with his mission accomplished, he disappeared down the hall. It would bug me. I knew it would. I'm lousy with names, but faces and voices usually stick with me. Lost in thought, I jumped when Fran the night auditor came rushing up to the desk. He was in his early thirties, a big hulking guy who sounded more like a middle-school girl when he recounted his ongoing problems with his long-suffering girlfriend. I had never met Doreen, but she would have to be part saint to put up with Fran.

"Christ, Fran, you're late," I complained. "Again."

"Come on. Don't you bitch me out too," he whined. I slipped into the adjoining office and opened the door that led out to the lobby. The damn thing locks automatically when it closes, and I can't even count the number of times I had to shimmy over the counter to get back into the inner sanctum after sneaking out to the bathroom off the lobby. I can drop trou, pee and rinse off my hands in less than a minute, which was a good skill to have when nature called and I had to leave the registration desk unmanned.

"Oh, you big baby," I volleyed back at Fran. "Are you two fighting again?"

"Yeah," he told me with a hangdog expression on his flushed face. "She's really pissed that..."

"Save it for someone who cares, Fran. I'm off the clock." I grabbed my car keys, my bag and the journal that I carried everywhere and took off through the lobby. *Oh, wait. Don't be such a bitch.*

"Good night, Fran," I called out. "Full house tonight. See ya."

"Jill, I'm sorry," Fran called after me. "I'll come in a half-hour early tomorrow night. I promise."

"Make it forty-five minutes," I hollered back and raced out the front door and smack into the blue-eyed smoker himself.

"Christ, you really do want to kill me," he protested.

*Oh man, I do not have time for this.* Actually, I did have time as I had nowhere to be for the next fourteen hours or so until my next shift began. But still. "Sorry. I don't really want to kill you," I assured him.

"Well then, why don't you come to my room and make it up to me somehow?" he teased.

"Now I *do* want to kill you. Hey, it's been real. Got to go." I race-walked across the parking lot towards my car. I was supposed to park out back and leave the prime spots for the paying guests, but I'd run late that afternoon and the back lot was pretty creepy in the early morning hours when I got off work. The mystery man quickly caught up to me, as his long strides easily outdistanced my short ones.

"Do I have to call security?" I threatened, only half-seriously.

"No, I'm actually pretty secure," he assured me. "But thanks, anyway." *Hmmm, cute and funny.* "So do you have a name? Do you want a cigarette? Fresh pack." He wiggled them at me.

"Yes, I have a name. No, I don't want a cigarette. Any more questions?" I wiggled my car keys at him. "Good night, okay?" He dropped back and let me pass. I tried to unlock my car door, but the lock sometimes caught and you had to fiddle around with it. He came up from behind me and placed his hand over mine, steadying me long enough to actually accomplish the task.

"I'm James," he told me. "I'm in a band." *Okay, loosen up, girl.*

"I'm Jill. Wait, you're James? James Sheridan from Nomad? Oh my God, I love you guys," I gushed. I might have liked my guys preppy, but I like my rock music hard-core with a hint of grunge, just like Nomad delivered on their first album.

His eyes lit up. Maybe it was the well-lit parking lot, but they actually glittered. "You like us, yeah, really?" He grinned at me, and I was finally able to place his good-looking face. It had been staring out at me from the cover of the album I'd purchased nearly six months before.

"You're staying *here*?" I asked. "Well, of course you are. They never tell us anything." Like management should have sent out a memo or something.

"Yeah, we played the Palace. Tonight was the first of *three big nights,*" he added sarcastically.

*Hmmm. The Palace for three nights.* That couldn't be a good sign, touring to support a newly released LP, playing at a second-rate venue in a second-rate town like mine for not one, but three nights. I tried to work up to my earlier enthusiasm, but failed.

"Cool," I responded weakly.

"Yeah, the tour has been pretty tough," he admitted sadly. "Ticket sales are slow and getting airplay is nearly impossible. We had to reschedule..."

I cut him off. He did not need to apologize or explain himself to me. He was a musician and a good one. "Well, I bet you guys stormed the Palace tonight. Did you have them rockin' out in the aisles?" I asked tentatively.

"Yeah. They liked us, I think. We got called back for an encore."

"What song?"

"*Over You.*"

"Oh, I love that one," I told him.

He started humming the opening chords, and then broke into the chorus. "I'm already over you." *Oh my God! James Sheridan of Nomad is singing to me in the parking lot at one in the morning. Wait till I tell Beth! This is amazing.* I could be in big trouble here, I realized, if I didn't have a hard and fast rule about not fraternizing with motel guests.

## Chapter 2- *Say My Name*

Rules are meant to be broken, I assured myself as I did the walk of shame through the parking lot to my car the following afternoon. For once, my car door, which had been left unlocked the night before, didn't stick and I was able to start the old beater up and pull out onto the main road without attracting any attention. I was humming *Over You,* I realized as I pulled into the drive-through line at Mickey D's. It was too late for breakfast, so I settled for a chicken sandwich and a coffee, light and sweet. After collecting my order and parking in the nearly empty lot, I wolfed down my sandwich and pulled the cover off my coffee to let it cool. I realized I was facing the entrance of an adult bookshop that doubled as a head shop selling rolling papers and all sorts of drug paraphernalia. What a dump! Catching sight of myself in the rear view mirror, I saw that I was smiling. And looking really good, kind of flushed and rosy-cheeked. I blushed at the thought of the sexy guy I had spent the night with. Things had happened pretty fast. After James started singing to me, I pretended to swoon. He took my arm, pretending to steady me, and slipped his other arm around my waist.

"Christ, you're tiny," he murmured, and then he started singing one of my favorite songs, *Tiny Dancer.* We ended up dancing around the parking lot, his hands circling my waist and my hands locked together behind his neck. It was amazing and very romantic. "Hold me closer," he sang into my ear. I responded by kissing his neck and up along his jawline. He stopped singing entirely and our mouths just connected. I kissed him like I've never kissed anyone, and he kissed me back with more enthusiasm than I had ever known was possible. *This guy has some serious moves*, I realized as he swung me up and carried me through the door that he had left open into his room.

What can I say? James wasn't the first man I had been with. Although, contrary to my reputation in high school, I wasn't all that experienced either. But I know what I know. And I know how I felt the morning after our amazing night together. My mouth was swollen from all that kissing, and I was sore, but in a good way. I wanted to curl up in the warm bed that I had just gotten out of and lie next to him forever. We must have fallen asleep at some point in the early morning hours, because we awoke to the sound of someone from housekeeping knocking on the door.

"I'm all set," James called out from his position lying on the bed wrapped around me, and they finally gave up. We spent the morning cuddling, talking and dozing. I finally realized that all good things had to come to an end, and that I needed to sneak out quickly in order to grab some food and a shower so that I could be back at work in an hour and a half. James let me go only after I promised I would figure out a way to show up at the Palace that night for his last set and spend the night with him again. I was thrilled.

"I'll leave you a ticket," he told me, "but I don't even know your name."

"It's Jill," I reminded him. *Christ. He doesn't even know my name.*

"Your last name, darlin'. I don't know what it is."

"It's Griffin. Jill Griffin," I told him.

"Okay then. Until tonight, Jill Griffin." He kissed me on the lips and watched me leave with a smile on his face. So there I was, half a mile away from him and I already missed him. I could smell him on my shirt, I realized. Kind of a smoky, tangy scent that could probably be quite unpleasant under different circumstances. James Sheridan, wow! He had seemed sincere and all, but even if he remembered to leave a ticket in my name that night, what was next? I mean, he and his band would be leaving in another couple of days. What then?

Lost in thought, I drove home and pulled into an empty space on the street in front of the multi-family dwelling I called home. I'd rented a room with a shared bath and kitchen privileges there for the past eight months. Compared to my previous apartment with my psycho roommates and the house I grew up in with my nutty family, it wasn't so bad. Sort of cramped, though, so I frequently escaped to the comforts of my best friend Beth's house where she lived with her parents and her six-month-old baby boy, Jesse. Beth's boyfriend dumped her when she started to show at five months along. He was a dick, and she and her baby deserved better, but her parents were supportive and welcomed her home. Sometimes, hanging out in her childhood home, I almost felt like we were back in high school, watching TV with her dad or baking cookies with her mom. Then Jesse would start to fuss, and Beth would fumble with her top, whip out a monstrous breast and start feeding him. So *not* like back in high school. Things had definitely changed.

I trudged up the two flights and let myself in. My message light was blinking furiously, and I was soon listening to the string of messages from that morning. Three of them were from Beth, who got increasingly pissed off with each message that she left.

The first was pleasant. "Where are you, Jill? I'm waiting for you at the diner." *Whoops!* Her second message was kind of testy. "Hey, my mom is watching Jesse, so you and I could have breakfast together, so hurry up." I won't repeat what she said on her third and final message, but she would just have to understand when I had the chance to explain myself.

I mean, don't get me wrong. I felt terrible. I have never been *that* girl who neglects her girlfriends when a new guy enters the picture. And I knew how precious a couple hours away from Jesse were to her these days. In between Beth's calls, there was a hang up and a message from my mom. She sounded sad and anxious, and she ended with, "Call me, Jilly. Okay?" Living with my dad was stressful enough, but my older sister was off her meds again, and I knew firsthand how upsetting that could be. I vowed to call my mom back really soon. But first I needed to call Beth and explain why I had been MIA that morning. It only took her a minute to go from hurt to thrilled. We were both romantics deep down, me and Beth.

She told me to keep her posted and ended with "Have fun, you slut." Next, I needed to call Fran to remind him to come in early that night, so that I could get to the Palace in time. *Hey, I'm Cinderella!* Then, phone calls made, I rushed through a quick shower and surveyed my closet. I found a clean pair of jeans and my favorite Candie's platform shoes and a light blue button-down. I shoved a sparkly tank top to change into later that night into my bag and raced back down the hall to the bathroom. I took stock of myself in the steamy mirror. Gone was the rosy glow of an hour before. My pale skin looked quite sallow in the unforgiving fluorescent light. Dark circles had appeared under my hazel eyes, and my hair was not cooperating either. I really needed a haircut to give some style to my longish layers, but not today. With no time to spare, I piled on some blush, patted concealer under my eyes and lined them with a dark pencil. A couple coats of mascara, and that was about the best I could do under the circumstances. I worked a huge dollop of mousse into my light brown hair and trimmed my bangs with cuticle scissors.

"You look like shit," I told myself as I glanced at the clock and realized I could only get to work right on time if I'd left ten minutes ago. Crap. For once my shift flew by and eight hours later, I hurried up to the will-call window at the Palace Theater. Fran had come through for me, and I was going to be able to catch more of the concert than I had hoped. What if James had forgotten me, I wondered as I greeted the girl behind the glass window. Should I buy a ticket and just go in? Or say screw it and head home?

"Okay, Jill Griffin. Here you go. Well, look at that? A backstage pass, too. What did you do, win a contest on the radio or something?" she asked me. I smiled at her.

"Yeah, something like that," I told her, and took the ticket stub and laminated pass. *He remembered*, I thought happily. I pushed my way through the heavy doors and into the crazy madness of a rock concert at the Palace. The venue was about two-thirds full, with most of the concertgoers crowded up front near the stage. Everywhere you looked, young adults were gyrating, dancing, cheering and singing along with James and his band. From my vantage point, I could see each of the band members quite clearly. James was front and center, singing into the microphone. He looked amazing and sounded really good, although I didn't recognize the song he was belting out.

The lead guitar player who was backing James up on vocals had to be Alex, his twin brother and cofounder of Nomad. Talk about identical! A longhaired guy was on the keyboards and a husky redhead who looked a little older than the rest of his band mates played the drums. But I only had eyes for James, as he sang song after song, dripping with sweat and moving like a jungle cat across the stage. Shirtless, he was again barefoot and clad only in a pair of low-slung faded jeans. I was almost breathless with excitement. *I'm with him*, I thought. *In another hour, he'll be singing to me, kissing me, loving me.* My sexy thoughts were interrupted when one of the bouncers bumped into me as he dragged a stoned concertgoer behind him, and tried to fend off the blows of what could only be the guy's girlfriend.

"Let him go," she wailed. "He's not hurting anyone." This was true, as I think the guy being ejected had actually passed out. I let out a chuckle, causing the girlfriend to snarl at me, "What the fuck are you looking at?" *Yikes.*

I decided to move closer to the stage, and I really got into the music for the next half hour or so. Right before the encore song, *Over You*, James spoke for the first time, addressing the wasted crowd directly. He thanked them for a great night, briefly introduced the rest of the band, and then dedicated the last song of the night to a special girl. "My tiny dancer," he announced with a large grin. The crowd cheered, and I thought I would burst with joy. Five minutes later, I was being pushed along with several hundred tired sweaty rock fans toward the exit. But I had a magic ticket—access to the backstage that only a select few people would get to experience. I was *with* the band.

## Chapter 3 - *Friday, I'm in Love*

"No, you don't understand. *I'm* tiny dancer," I protested to the large bouncer blocking the door backstage.

"Sure you are, sweetheart," he sneered. "You're all tiny dancers." I will admit that I probably wasn't very convincing, and there were at least thirty girls ranging from early teens through their late 20s, all trying to gain access backstage. I figured some enterprising entrepreneur with a copier and a laminator had sold fake backstage passes to most of these fans, as there were only four band members. Not nearly enough to go around, I reasoned. I hoped my pass was legit. A few of the wanna-be groupies appeared to be giving up and were abandoning their posts. I was seriously considering taking off as well when the redheaded drummer from the band appeared and whispered something to the bouncer. He nodded, and the drummer turned and left. The next thing I knew, I heard the bouncer calling my name.

I hurried over and told him triumphantly, "That's me! I'm Jill Griffin."

"Wow," he said sarcastically. "And here I thought your name was Tiny Dancer." He jerked his thumb in the direction he apparently wanted me to go, and I wasted no time. I quickly slipped through the door and found myself literally in the dark until my eyes adjusted to the dim light. The first thing I saw was a group of at least a dozen girls and young women crowding the hallway. How many girls got the same offer as me? Were they *all* here for James? I was feeling less than special, when the murmur of voices around me grew louder and very excited.

"There he is," one of them shrieked, and I looked up just in time to see James coming through the doorway, pulling a faded Ramones T-shirt over his head. "James, James, James." The chanting grew louder, and I wondered what my chances were of ever connecting with him that night, when he saw me and moved quickly through the crowd.

"You made it," he whispered and pulled me close. I was kissed soundly, then released long enough for him to look me over. "Christ, you look great. You're even prettier than I remember." I just grinned back at him. Then, putting his arm around my shoulders, he murmured, "I want to introduce you to the guys. Excuse me, ladies," he said genially and led me through the crowd.

A collective groan was heard as one by one, each of the hopefuls realized that the object of her desire was leaving. Leaving with me, I thought gleefully. This wasn't an experience I had ever had before. I didn't usually 'get the guy'. I happily followed James down a dark hallway into a large lounge area.

The smell of pot that had permeated the concert hall was much stronger back here, I noticed. There were probably close to a dozen people backstage, talking, drinking beer and passing around a couple of joints. James brought me directly over to a tall, longhaired guy lounging in the corner, strumming a guitar. Alex, the twin brother. They might have been identical, but I could see a few subtle differences, even in the dim haze of the room. Alex's eyes were not as blue as his brother's, and his nose seemed a bit more prominent.

"Jill," James said proudly. "I want you to meet Alex, my brother. Alex, this is Jill. The girl I told you about. Remember?"

Alex looked up at me and smiled widely. "Sure. Motel girl. How's it going?" *Wow. Really? Motel girl?*

"Great concert," I offered. "You guys really rocked tonight."

"Gee, thanks, motel girl. We do it all for you," he assured me. "I'm outa here, bro." And with that, Alex Sheridan made his exit.

"Don't mind him. He's been fighting off this cold that's going around. He's usually much friendlier," James told me with a sheepish grin. *Uh huh. Yeah, he's a real charmer, that one.*

The drummer wandered over and introduced himself. "Hey Jill, I'm Steve. Glad you could join us tonight." Then I met Brian, the keyboard player.

"How do all you guys know each other?" I asked them. At the confused look I got from all three guys, I corrected myself. "No, I mean, you're all in a band together. I get that. What I meant was how long have you known each other?"

"Too long," James told me, shaking his head in mock despair.

"I grew up next door to these jokers," Brian added. "I've been bailing their sorry asses out of trouble my whole life."

"They only brought me in to buy the beer," Steve joked. "I was the only one over twenty-one."

"Well, we sure didn't pick you for your drum playing, Steve-O," James said with a chuckle, as he fake-punched his band mate's arm. I enjoyed the way they teased each other and joked around. There was an ease about them and a genuine fondness that was plain to see. The only awkward moment was when Alex reappeared and announced that he was going back to the motel with the roadies. The laughter died down, and I picked up on the tension with Alex and the rest of the band, especially between the brothers. Believe me, when you grow up in a household as fraught with conflict as mine was, you know a stressful situation when you see it.

No one protested or asked Alex to stay, and seconds after he was gone, the relaxed party atmosphere was back in full swing. I turned down the joint being passed around, but gratefully accepted a bottle of beer when it was offered. I was hot and thirsty and holding the bottle and taking small sips gave me something to do with my right hand. James was holding on to my left hand and kept pulling me towards him for hugs and quick kisses. Standing close to him, I realized that he was almost a foot taller than me. I was getting increasingly excited each time he pulled me close, and I knew I wanted to be alone with this guy. A short while later, the place had cleared out and James whispered, "C'mon, let's blow this chicken joint." I happily let him lead me out through the back door, followed closely by Brian and Steve. Minutes later, James and I were cuddling on the back seat of the beat-up band van, Nomad's primary transport, for the short drive back to the motel. James was murmuring how he couldn't wait to get me alone. Brian, who was driving, was trying to get me to navigate, and Steve was stretched out, riding shotgun and snoring lightly.

"Turn right at the next light," I called out to Brian, while James busied himself with one hand under my sparkly tank top and the other slipping down the front of my jeans. "Stop," I whispered to him.

"Me? Stop?" Brian called out.

"No, you go. You stop," I told James and swatted his hands away. I was not into public displays of affection, and we would be back at the motel in just a couple of minutes, I reasoned. But James was not to be ignored, and just for a moment, I gave in to the thrill of being desired.

Arriving back at the motel, Brian flung open the door to let us out. The cool night air enveloped me as I struggled back into my top and pulled my jeans up. Suddenly shy, I whispered to James that I couldn't let anyone see me. Even at this second-rate establishment, fraternizing with guests was *verboten* and would get you fired. Just ask Rosa, former member of the housekeeping staff. She had changed a traveling salesman's sheets, but rolled around with him on them first. Goodbye, Rosa!

"No problem." James pulled off his T-shirt and covered my face with it. Then he hoisted me over his shoulder and within seconds, we were back in his room and everything felt right and wonderful, and I once again experienced the thrill that was post-concert high James Sheridan, Rock God.

After a second nearly sleepless night, I was dozing and James got up to take a shower. When the phone rang, he called out for me to answer it. Knowing it could be someone from housekeeping or even the front desk, I decided to pick up but not say anything until the caller identified himself. It was Alex.

"James?" he asked.

"No, it's Jill," I told him.

"Who? Oh yeah, motel girl. Put my brother on." *God, what was this guy's problem?*

"He's in the shower," I told him. "Do you want me to have him call you?"

"Yeah, sure, and tell him we're due at the venue for a sound check in 15, okay? Got that?"

"Sure thing," I muttered, and hung up before he could say anything more.

Just then James came back in looking like the cat that swallowed the canary. Wearing a towel around his waist, his long hair dripping, he asked, "Who was that?"

"It was Alex," I told him. "God, he hates me."

James looked concerned. "What did he say?"

I felt foolish. "Nothing. I mean, he just... I don't know. I just don't think he likes me very much."

"He's just jealous," James teased. "He always wants what I have, and I saw you first." He crossed the room and wrapped me up in a hug.

"Wait, no," I protested when his hands started exploring my half-naked body. "You've got to get down to the Palace, James," I told him. "Alex said something about a sound check."

"Oh, bloody hell," he complained. "God damn Alex and his sound checks." And he started to kiss me again. Minutes later, we were rudely interrupted by a pounding on the door. I ran and hid in the bathroom while James opened the door just a crack to talk with Brian. I heard enough of the conversation to know that something was going on with Alex and everyone seemed to be walking on egg shells to avoid pissing him off further. James came back, looking embarrassed, and told me, "I've got to go, Jill. I'm sorry."

"It's okay," I told him. "I've got a lot to do today and before you know it, I need to be back here. At the desk, I mean. Not *here*, here," I explained, gesturing around the room.

"But I want you *here*, here," said James. "Promise. Okay?"

Okay? Yeah, it was more than okay. I told him that I probably couldn't make it to the concert, but that I would meet him after my shift ended at midnight. He kissed me and hurried out and I lay back on the bed with a big smile on my face. Shivering with excitement at the thought of seeing him again that night, I allowed myself a few minutes of daydreaming, then hopped up and prepared to leave. Reaching into my bag for my keys, I suddenly realized that I was stranded—my car was still parked downtown in the Palace parking lot. I peeked out the window to check if the guys had left yet, but I couldn't see the van or the wagon. I would be lucky if my car hadn't been towed or stolen, I realized, as I picked up the phone on the nightstand and called Beth to have her come get me. She said she would, so I hunkered down in the room until I heard her honking her horn twenty minutes later. I would offer to buy her lunch or something. I hoped that she didn't have Jesse with her, as I had a lot to tell her and none of it was rated 'G.'

## Chapter 4 - *Got My Mind Set on You*

I felt such a strong connection to that longhaired rock and roller, and it wasn't just the mind-blowing sex either. I wasn't used to opening up that much with anyone. I had only known James for a couple of days and I'd shared more with him than anyone in my life, except maybe Beth. In between all the screwing and very little sleep, James seemed really interested in getting to know the 'real' me. To be honest, there wasn't that much to tell. I started by telling him how I'd left my family home on Jericho Road on my eighteenth birthday. It was just like any other day, but that night, after my mom's ground beef and elbow macaroni casserole, there was a cake and a $25 check from my folks. So I blew out the candles, and we all made nice for a half hour or so. My father slowed down on his consumption of beer, and my older sister Susan, who came by to drop off a card for me, actually sat still for a short time and didn't pace around smoking cigarettes and ranting about her manufactured crisis of the day. We actually looked like a 'normal' family, whatever that means. But it wouldn't last. It never did.

Later that evening, my dad would land in drunken crazy town and start an argument, usually with my mom, but sometimes with my sister. If Susan wasn't arguing with our dad, she would start up about the government or expound on one of her wacko conspiracy theories. My younger brother Teddy, probably the most normal member of my family, would escape to ride around the neighborhood on his bike or meet his friends at the park down at the end of the street to smoke pot. I waited for what I thought was an appropriate amount of time, and helped my mom clear up the aftermath of the celebration. I shoved the half-eaten cake into the fridge and crumpled up the paper plates smeared with frosting. Then I went to my room, grabbed my backpack, my journal and my car keys. I kissed my mom, waved to my sister and dad, and said something clever like, "See ya." And I left.

"I couldn't wait to get out of there," I confessed to James. Not just that night, but always. For as long as I could remember, I felt stifled and restless in that house, like a caged animal. "Did you ever go to a zoo and see one of those large jungle cats? They just pace around their tiny enclosure, and you know that if they could speak, their first words would be something like, *Let me the hell out of here. Please, I'm begging you. I don't belong here.*"

James was watching me closely as I spoke. He nodded slowly. "Yeah," he told me sadly. "I get that. I mean, my folks were great and all, but I was glad to be gone. Out on my own." He squeezed my hand and I took a deep breath. It felt so good to talk to someone who seemed to get me. Someone I could be myself around. I told him more.

My 'cage' was a tiny grey ranch house plopped smack in the middle of a large lot. My dad had built a huge shed that was half the size of the house, purportedly to store lawn mowers and rakes, but he seemed to get more use out of it as a place to escape the dysfunctional family he and my mom had created. It was the place he went to smoke his unfiltered Camel cigarettes and drink Schafer beer. That shed was where I first smoked a cigarette or two of my own and came close to losing my virginity. Classy, huh?

"Close to losing it, huh? Wish I coulda been a fly on that wall," James chuckled. "If I'd been there, you'd have been begging me for it."

I had to laugh at that. "I was fifteen, you perv. There's a law protecting innocent girls like me from old guys like you."

"Just how old do you think I am, darlin'?"

"Oh crap, is this a trick question? Like if I guess too old, you'll be insulted. And if I guess..." My last words were cut off as my 'older' boyfriend started kissing my neck and then working his way south. *Oh my!* A short while later, we took the van and drove to a diner just outside of town for breakfast. I watched James attack a plate of bacon and eggs and slather butter and jam on a stack of rye toast.

"It's our first date," I informed him after I drained my glass of orange juice.

James looked around the dingy diner and shook his head. "I hope we can do better than this for our second date, darlin'."

As Nomad was leaving town the next day, I wasn't sure just when we would have a second date, but I was pleased to hear that there was a chance we would continue to see each other. But how?

James poured himself more coffee from the carafe on the table and relaxed against the vinyl booth. "What were you like as a little girl? I bet you sat up front in class and were the teacher's pet," he teased.

*No, not me.* I had always been a dreamy kid, kinda spacey, shy and relatively quiet. I sat in the back of every classroom and rarely spoke up.

My sister Susan was the one everyone noticed, I explained. She was well known for her big mouth and erratic behavior. She served more detention in high school than anyone and had zero impulse control and no respect for authority. Nowadays, she would probably receive a proper diagnosis and a daily regimen of meds to keep her in line, but this was the 70s. My mother figured she just wanted attention. Even as a toddler, Susan would toss all her toys out of her playpen, even if it meant she would have nothing left to play with. Mom would sign the notes and detention slips brought home almost daily and threaten, "Wait 'til your father gets home." My father would spank her and for a while poor Susan would appear to be toeing the line, behaving. But it never lasted.

As she got older, the spankings grew less common and the groundings began. The list was endless... too much makeup, caught smoking, drinking, ditching school, topless in the back of some older guy's pickup truck. Susan was the original wild child and sucked virtually all of the oxygen out of any room.

I dreaded the inevitable moment when a new teacher would be taking attendance and stop at my name. "Griffin?" they would ask suspiciously. "Any relation to Susan?" I would blush furiously and nod, and then spend the rest of the year proving how unlike Susan I really was.

"Did you go on any family trips when you were younger?" James asked. He shared a story about a trip to Disneyworld, and how he and Alex had ditched their folks and went off exploring on their own. The whole family was reunited hours later in the First

Aid office, after both boys got sick from drinking too much orange soda right before riding on a huge roller coaster. "Boy, was my dad pissed at us," James recalled with a huge grin plastered across his face.

Family trips? No. Pissed-off dad? Now *that* I could relate to. "We didn't do much as a family," I explained. My parents had enough going on in their crappy marriage and had no energy left for me and Teddy after dealing with Susan and all her drama. I'm not complaining, although I'm sure it sounds like I am. I really didn't mind being forgotten about and actually spent most of my time trying to remain *out* of any type of spotlight.

But Teddy? Man, he got the short end of our family stick. He is the smartest person I have ever known. Tested off the charts. Reading at the age of three and writing full sentences in pre-school. He probably should have skipped a grade or maybe two, but he was small for his age and my father said he'd be picked on for being an 'egghead'. My mother was concerned that people would think we were putting on airs, trying to be too fancy, so an alternative education plan was never seriously considered. Poor Teddy floundered along like the rest of us in the public school system: bored, unmotivated and unchallenged.

Caught between a cyclone like Susan and a brain like Teddy, you could say I failed to thrive. I was cute, but not particularly outgoing or popular. Besides Beth, I had a few other friends, and we managed to stay solidly in the middle of the high school hierarchy, bound together by our lack of a discernible identity. We weren't the jocks or the brains or the nerds (unpopular brains) or the band geeks, the stoners or the drama kings and queens. But there were enough of us who defied stereotyping, so there was always a party or a group going ice-skating or to the beach.

"What do you do when you're not working?" James asked me with interest. "Any hidden talents?"

*Hmm. Something I'm good at?* "Memorizing song lyrics." I giggled. It was the only thing I could think of. You could always count on me to know what was being sung on the radio. "Oh, and parallel parking. Honest, I'm great," I told James as he started laughing. "But seriously, I like to write. I have this journal, you know?" Now that got his interest.

"Really, you write? I suck at writing. Those songs on our album? Torture, babe, pure torture. '*Over You*' was the only one that came easy," he confided, with a twinkle in his eye. "Maybe you'll let me read your stuff someday, huh?"

Not likely. No one *ever* read what I wrote. "It's just silly," I protested. "Teenage girl stuff. Nothing you would be interested in." But writing was actually very important to me. For years I had been carrying small notepads around and, as I grew more confident, larger journals. I jotted down phrases that came to me, expressions and words I wanted to know more about. Halfway through my freshman English composition class, I realized that I could write poems and even short stories.

I never figured I would do anything with this hobby of mine. But it relaxed me and kept me from reaching for a second piece of cake at night or zoning out daily to the soap operas that so many of my classmates adored. Writing gave me a purpose, and I wrote about everything. Teenage shenanigans, family arguments, crazy Susan, brilliant Teddy, my bully of a dad and my doormat of a mom. I wrote about struggles and relationships, love and friendships. Nothing was out of bounds. But I was *not* willing to share. It was just too personal, too private. I needed to get everything down on paper to prove to myself that I wasn't crazy. To find some clue to help me live a normal, happy life. But I was always just guessing at what a 'normal' life was supposed to be. Honestly, I didn't have a clue. But sitting with James in that diner? I was really happy. Exhausted, but happy.

I felt normal.

## Chapter 5 - *I'll Be Missing You*

True to his word, Fran showed up on time on Nomad's third and final night in town, so it was just a few minutes after midnight when I slipped into James' room with the passkey that I had 'borrowed'. I had packed my bag carefully that afternoon and after refreshing myself with a quick shower, I was able to apply some makeup and slip into a tank top and fresh panties. I unearthed my journal from the depths of my backpack and had just started jotting down some thoughts when James came rushing in.

"You're here. I'm so glad." He was positively beaming at the sight of me. *Me!*

Relaxed and happy, I could be seductive. I slipped the journal back into my bag, stretched languidly and purred, "Really? How glad? Show me." So he did, and he was quite convincing, I can assure you. Much later, we lay on top of a pile of tangled sheets, James' head resting on my chest, his arm circling my waist. I was tired but couldn't turn off my brain in order to sleep. How I was going to say goodbye to James in just a few more hours? I felt him stir against me.

"Jill? You awake?"

"Yeah," came my soft reply.

"We'll work something out. I promise."

"You don't owe me anything, James," I protested as he pulled himself up on his elbows and peered at me, his blue eyes glittering in the predawn light.

33

"I want this," he told me solemnly. "I want you."

God, did I ever want to believe him. He kissed me lightly and rolled over on his side. Moments later he was sleeping quite soundly. I curled up against his back and told myself that if I didn't close my eyes, this time we had together would last forever. But sleep must've overcome me because a few hours later, I woke to a banging on the door. It was Alex.

"C'mon, James. We don't have all day. Say goodbye. Wheels up," he shouted. *What a freakin' buzz kill!* I stumbled around, searching for my things and trying to hurry.

"Keep your shirt on, Alex," James called, and tossed me my top from a heap of clothes on the floor. "We'd better go," he told me as he shoved everything into a green duffle bag. In the light of day, James' face was drawn, pale. He looked exhausted.

"It's okay, James. I'm ready," I assured him, and we walked out into the bright sunshine. *It should be raining*, I thought sadly. It's too nice of a day to feel this crappy. The guys were loading the van and stowing their instruments in the roadie's wagon. And as if I wasn't already aware, Alex kept reminding everyone that they needed to get going. I wished that he would just shut up or disappear, along with everything else that was taking James away from me. My whole life, I've pretty much kept my emotions in check, bottled up, as it were. But not that day. I was on the verge of tears, and the lump in my throat was only growing bigger. I wanted to believe James and his assurances that he would see me soon, and that he would 'send for me' as if I were a war bride or something. So I tried hard not to cry as James hugged and kissed me for what I imagined would be the very last time. Suddenly I panicked.

"It's Griffin, James. You know that, right?" James looked down at me and brushed the hair back off my forehead.

"Yeah," he said with a smile. "I know that, Jill Griffin." After a final kiss, James turned and strode toward the van. "Come on, guys. I'm driving. Let's go." Alex called shotgun and hurried after his brother. I hoped he wouldn't, but he turned and smirked at me.

"Ta ta, motel girl," he said. "It's been real."

I hoped he saw me flip him off before he jumped into the van. I blinked and they were gone, leaving a large space in the parking lot and an even larger one in my heart. I didn't care who saw me that morning as I walked over to my car. I had nothing to do for several hours before my shift began. Since I was in no shape to see or talk to anyone from work, I got in my car and hit the drive-through, just like I had not even forty-eight hours earlier. Too upset to eat anything, I ordered a coffee and parked again by the adult bookstore. I felt sad and totally adrift. How was I going to go back to my everyday life when the man I loved— yeah, loved—was gone? I pictured the dozens of groupies, girls much better looking than me, throwing themselves at James night after night. Although he hadn't said that he would, I hoped he would resist them because of his feelings for me. Did he even have feelings for me? I knew that even if I never saw James again, it would be a long time before anyone would touch me the way that he had. Sadly, I made my way out of the nearly empty parking lot and drove to my best friend's house.

"I'll never see him again," I cried to Beth as we sat in her parents' kitchen. I turned down her mom's offer to make me some eggs, and after noticing my tear-streaked face, she took Jesse upstairs for his nap so we could be alone. Beth held me against her and let me cry. Despite the number of times that Beth had been dumped, she remained hopeful for me.

"You don't know that, Jill," she told me. "He could be the one, right? I mean, why not? Maybe it's your turn. Maybe it's your time."

I had my doubts. I'd never been particularly lucky in love. In high school I'd had a couple of boyfriends, one of whom I'd even talked into taking me to the prom. Despite my penchant for preppy golden boys, the only guys I seemed to attract were longhaired stoners or social deviants. But by the last few months of my senior year, I actually looked like I had it all together. I was dating Tom, a pink-cheeked honors student who was satisfied with a chaste peck on the cheek at the end of our movie dates.

He either believed the wholesome virgin act I was putting on, or was too afraid to rock the boat. Either way, I usually would sneak out shortly after he brought me home so that I could go meet Gary down at the park at the end of my street. Gary was sexy and a bit dangerous, with a reputation for being a bad boy. Gary thought the whole thing was pretty funny, I guess. I mean, some other guy pays for the movie and a fast food burger, and he gets to have sex with me at the end of the evening. I was starting to have second thoughts about the whole arrangement when Gary started to get really cruel.

"Bring me a burger next time," he sneered one night. "Hold the pickle, extra ketchup. Why not? He pays for you. Why shouldn't he pay for me, too?" *What a jerk!*

Things started to fizzle with both of them that fall when Tom took off for college, and Gary just took off. Over the next three years I had a handful of relationships, if you can call them that, including one fairly intense one with Sean, a bartender, who worked nights in the lounge adjacent to my motel. For a few months, I would wander next door after work every night and drink for free while he wiped down the bar and announced last call. Some nights we would drive to the diner and talk and drink coffee until the sun came up. Sean was a romantic, a real storyteller. He had a faint brogue that I never questioned, although I knew for certain he had never once traveled to the Emerald Isle. He lived with his sister, and their relationship seemed rather complicated. So most nights we would end up at my apartment. When my own roommate situation got out of hand and I was looking to move, I hinted to Sean that perhaps we could get a place together.

That's when he told me that his 'sister' was really his wife, and that moving in with me wasn't such a great idea. I was pissed. I mean, I was no innocent, and I'd done a lot of crappy things in my life, but sleeping with a married man just wasn't on my to-do list.

"Lose my number," I spat at him, and when I moved the next weekend, I threw away a couple of his T-shirts and a lame silver-plated shamrock he had given me for my key ring. I never got really close to another guy for almost a year. Until James.

"I don't know what to do," I cried to Beth, as a fresh wave of tears left me blubbering. "I've never felt like this before. This isn't me. What am I going to do?"

My best friend watched me over the rim of her tea mug as I cried and moaned.

"Don't worry, Jill. Something will work out," she told me and I wanted to believe her. I really did. If the depths of my emotional outburst surprised her, she didn't let on. For years, I had been the stoic one, listening to Beth and all of her struggles with the opposite sex. I always held back with the guys I dated, and never let myself get too close, while she was the one that was frequently getting dumped by some jerk, or occasionally doing the dumping herself. Getting knocked up had not been part of her plan, but after Jesse was born, Beth really stepped up to the plate. Demonstrating her newfound maturity, she listened patiently as I tearfully told her how my last night with James almost hadn't happened. Following a late afternoon phone call with Ron, Nomad's manager, Alex was convinced that leaving immediately after the show was a wise move in order to get to the next venue. Somehow James had talked him out of it by promising to leave first thing in the morning. I wanted to believe that James chose to stay because of me, but maybe it was the idea of being cooped up in a van after performing on stage for nearly three hours. Whatever! It gave us more time, another night of sexy fireworks and some very tender moments. Pillow talk. Time with James. The only thing I wanted was more.

Jill's Journal

1. Johnny
2. Gary
3. Ed? Ned?
4. Sully
5. Sully's brother
6. Sean
7. James

Is there like a magic number or something?
If you reach it, do you just have to stay
with whoever it is for the rest of your life?
At what point do you go from 'friendly' to
'slutty'?

Letter Never Sent

*Tuesday 1AM*

*Dear James,*

*I hope you remember me. It's been a couple weeks and I haven't heard from you, so I figured I would write you and let you know that I'm good. You know, keeping busy. I am looking at taking a creative writing class at the community college. Did I tell you that I like to write? Other than that, I am still holding down the fort at the motel. One of the day people is going to be on vacation soon, so I may be able to pick up some extra hours. Some overtime would come in really handy, you know?*

*So how's the road treating you? Is it going well? How are the fans? Is "Over You" still your encore? I play your album a lot. Say hi to your brother Alex for me and the other guys too. I know Alex hates me, but let him know that there's no hard feelings. Just kidding! Well, that's all I wanted to say. If you're ever in the neighborhood, look me up. If I'm not at the motel anymore, maybe they could tell you how to find me. I would like it very much if you were to find me.*

*So, that's it. Bye for now.*

*Luv,*

*Jill*

*P.S. I hope you know that I don't sleep with every guy that stays at the motel. If I did, I would sure be busy. But seriously, you are the first guy I ever slept with at the motel. I just want you to know that, okay?*

## Chapter 6 - *Baby, One More Time*

Somewhere a phone was ringing, I realized. It sounded far away, but as it was my phone ringing in my tiny room, it couldn't be *that* far. My senses were dulled since I had collapsed on my bed fully clothed and totally drunk only a couple of hours earlier. Shit. I stumbled across the dark room to dig my baby blue Princess phone out from under a pile of clean and dirty clothes. Anything to stop that incessant ringing, which was aggravating what I already knew would be a doozy of a hangover.

"Hello. Hello," I mumbled into the phone. I realized it was 3AM once I was able to see the digital numbers on my VCR. Nothing good ever happens at 3AM.

"Will you accept a collect call from James Sheridan?" Her tone may have been quite nasal, but the operator's enunciation was perfect. James!

"Yes, yes I will," I screeched.

"Okay, sir. Go ahead," the operator commanded.

"Jill? It's me, James." At the sound of his voice, I nearly wept with joy.

"Hiiiiii!! Where are you?" His voice was as clear as if he was calling from next door instead of all the way from....

"I'm in Iowa. We just finished a gig in Des Moines. Wait, what time is it there? Did I wake you? You're two hours earlier, right?"

41

"No," I told him. "It's two hours later. I don't care. How are you? I've missed you like crazy." It had been two and a half weeks since our goodbye scene at the motel. Seventeen long days and nights. I was almost giddy with relief.

"It's good. We're opening for The Blues Gang now. Long story. Crowds are picking up and we've done some radio promos for a couple of the stations here in the Midwest. It's going good. How are you? What have you been up to?" It was our first phone conversation, I realized, and I hardly knew this guy, but I already felt like I couldn't live without him. I didn't *want* to live without him.

"Just work," I admitted. "Oh, and Jesse? Remember I told you about my girlfriend Beth's little boy? He rolled over yesterday for the first time. It was so cool." I was rambling, nervous. *God, what a dork he must think I am.*

"Sounds great," James told me. "So do you think you could make it to Detroit this weekend? We have a few days free after three nights there. I was hoping you could join us."

*Detroit?* Christ, might as well be the moon. Just where was Detroit anyway? Would I have to fly? Of course I would. How much would *that* cost? My MasterCard still had a little wiggle room, so maybe...

"Sure. I'll do it," I told him. "I'll figure something out."

"I wish I could buy your ticket Jill," he told me sadly. "But at least you'll have a place to stay and we'll cover your meals."

"Don't worry about it," I reassured him. Surely I could dig up enough money for airfare. "Okay if I can get there on Saturday, maybe middle of the day?"

"Yeah. Call Ron with your flight info. You still have his number, right? He'll get it to me and I'll meet you. Oh, and ask for an open return," he added.

"A what?" I asked.

"Ron says it lets you decide how long you want to stay. Maybe you could come on the road with us for a couple of days. After the break, I think we head to Indianapolis."

"The road? Me?" I squeaked. Where was Indianapolis?

"Yeah, it would be great," he assured me. I racked my brain. Did I have any vacation time? Did I care? If I just took off, would there be a job waiting for me when I returned? What was I thinking? I hardly knew this guy!

"Yes, yes. It sounds great. I'll call Ron tomorrow."

James let out a whoop. "Awesome. Wow, Jill. I'm psyched. You'll love it. Well, not Detroit, maybe, but we can drive up to the lakes from there. It's supposed to be beautiful."

"You're beautiful," I told him.

He gave a low chuckle. "Hey, this call is costing you a fortune," he warned. "I better say goodnight."

"Good night, James," I told him. "See you in a few days." Slowly, I returned the phone to its cradle. Too excited to sleep, and now wide-awake and fairly sober, I spun around my little room. I needed to call Beth, get a plane ticket and let them know I'd be taking some time off work. I should call my mom too, in case she tried to get hold of me while I was gone. What would I tell her? That I was taking off to visit a friend? Depending on the level of crap she was dealing with from my dad and sister at the time, her response would range from an absent-minded 'Have fun. Send me a postcard,' all the way to a semi-hysterical 'But your job? You can't afford to lose it. Don't go.'

Maybe I could invent some former classmate that had moved away. I would be all "Mom, I know you remember Lisa, don't you?" But I was actually a terrible liar, despite all the practice I'd had. I would wait until early afternoon when she would be out for a walk with Helen from next-door. Let the machine pick up, I figured. And wait till later in the week, so there's less chance for her to call me back.

"I'm going to see James," I told myself. He had sent for me. Kind of. I hoped that I could locate Ron's number in all this clutter. Still too keyed up, I found my journal and filled a couple of pages with happy thoughts for a change. For the first time in months, I couldn't wait for the weekend.

"What's the catch?" Teddy asked suspiciously. It was Friday afternoon, and I had asked my brother to stop by on his way home from school. He was a senior in high school, but lacking a car, he usually relied on the bus or rides from friends.

"No catch, Mr. Suspicious," I assured him. "You can drop me off at the airport tomorrow morning and then keep the car while I'm gone." Anything would be better than paying for airport parking, I figured. "I'll even leave you with a full tank," I promised.

"Who's the dude?" he asked. *What?*

"No, I told you. It's my friend Lisa. She moved to Detroit a couple of..."

"Yeah, right. Mom may have bought it, but you and I both know there's no Lisa. Who's this guy that you're quitting your job and going into hock for?" My brother's tone was firm and his jaw was set. He had lent me $50. It was time to come clean.

"I'm not quitting my job and, Ted, you can't tell, okay? Besides Beth, you're the only one who knows." My brother was a great secret keeper. He'd had a lot of practice. I could trust him.

"It's James. James Sheridan, the singer from Nomad. You heard of them, right?"

"Yeah. Where did you run into him?" he asked suspiciously. I filled Teddy in with the details of my new relationship. It didn't take long. There really wasn't much to tell.

"I'll give you his manager's number," I told him. "He can get hold of us. If anything comes up, you know. But only for something big, okay?"

"Yeah, big news. Like if Dad wraps the car around a telephone pole, or if Susan actually shuts up for once," Teddy drawled sarcastically.

*When did my little brother get to be such a cynic?* I wondered. "Yeah, like that. Okay, Ted? Thank you." It felt good to confide in a member of my family. I didn't have to be at work for my last shift for a while, so I offered to drop him off at home on my way. He was silent during the short ride.

"Tomorrow morning. 8 a.m., okay? I'll wait out here. I don't want to have a big scene inside," I pleaded.

"I'll be here, Jill. Stop worrying. But, just one thing? Tell me he's not an asshole, okay?"

"He's not an asshole, Ted. I promise." I hoped I was right. With a quick wave, Teddy was gone and I drove to work. My shift at the motel really dragged that night. A few of the housekeeping crew came by to wish me well, but my last minute trip was really a nonevent. People came and went at the motel all the time, and I barely knew most of my coworkers. Fran showed up twenty minutes early and gave me an awkward hug.

"Have fun with your friend," he called out as I sailed through the lobby. I guess he meant the fictitious Lisa. I actually had forgotten which story I told him.

Before I knew it, I was back home, trying to figure out not just what type of clothes to pack, but how much? I didn't want to scare James off by appearing with three weeks' worth of luggage, so I stuffed and rolled as much as I could fit into a giant duffel bag that Beth's brother let me borrow. My carry-on bag was a black backpack I'd had for years. Some make-up, a few books, an assortment of gel pens and my journal. I was done. I finally fell asleep and was shocked when my alarm went off just a couple of hours later. I stumbled down the hall to take a lukewarm shower and brush my teeth. I would have to do some damage control with my makeup at the airport while I was waiting for my flight. Minutes later, I grabbed my bags and rushed out to my car. 'Please start,' I begged silently. Maybe it was my lucky day, because it started right up despite the cold. I drove back to Jericho Road and found Teddy already out on the sidewalk waiting for me. *These are good signs,* I told myself, and we drove to the airport with no delays.

A short while later, we were double parked in front of a huge sign that said 'Departures, No Parking'. My brother beat me to it and shifted my bags from the trunk onto the sidewalk.

"God, Jill," he asked me. "What did you pack in there, rocks?"

"Yes, Teddy. I packed rocks," I said with a smile. He wasn't much for physical displays of affection, but I went in for a hug anyway. My little brother. The smart one. The only member of my family whose company I actually enjoyed. Ted towered over me (how long had *that* been the case?) but he returned the hug.

"You be careful, Jill," he mumbled in my ear. "If he turns out to be an asshole, come home. Or call me. I'll come get you," he promised. The tears I had been holding back all morning finally let loose, and I sobbed into my brother's shoulder. *What was I doing?*

"I'm kinda scared, Ted," I told him in a strangled whisper. Grasping my shoulders, he pushed me away so he could look into my eyes.

"Don't be scared, Jilly," he said lightly. "It's only rock 'n roll, right?" I had to smile at that. Freakin' Teddy.

I made my way to the gate, clutching my ticket and dragging my bags behind me. Once again, luck was on my side and moments later, my duffel was checked, and I was waiting in a short line to buy a large coffee and a bear claw. Breakfast of champions! I was able to doze during the three-hour flight and before I knew it, I was walking off the plane. The area was crowded, and a few of my fellow travelers must have been pretty important, because there were a handful of uniformed drivers holding up signs stating 'Sullivan' or 'West Electronics'. I looked around, and then I saw it. In a sea of people, I could spot my tall, longhaired boyfriend holding up a huge sign of his own. It looked like it was a ragged side of a cardboard box. In black marker, it simply said 'JILL.' I rushed over to him, and he swept me up into a hug.

"You made it," he whispered. "I've missed you."

It felt good to be missed. I felt happy and relieved, and I could tease him. "Just Jill?" I questioned. "Did you forget my last name again?"

"No chance. Jill Griffin," he assured me. "C'mon, let's get your bags and get out of here." I happily grabbed his hand as we made our way to claim my bag. True to his word, James had borrowed the roadies' car and with the windows open and the radio blaring, we drove into the city. The hotel where we would be staying for the next couple of days was a definite step up from the place I worked. And before I knew it, we were alone in his room.

"Two beds," I joked. "Great, we each get our own. That's terrific." I suddenly felt shy as I once again realized that I barely knew this guy. James seemed a bit nervous too, as he paced around the room.

"Do you want a shower or should we grab some food? You tell me what you want. I aim to please," he added with a wink.

"That's easy." I walked into his arms. "I just want you."

By mid-afternoon, only one thing was clear. Okay, two things, the second being James was the sexiest, most passionate man I have ever known. What that man could do! And get me to want to do! But the first thing? A bear claw does not a substantial breakfast make. As we were lying close together, the growling sounds my stomach was making were unmistakable.

Pulling himself up on his elbows, he peered at me closely. "Hungry? Of course you are. Let's fix that." A two-minute shower would have to suffice, and feeling somewhat refreshed in a clean top and my travelling jeans, I followed him out the door and down to the parking lot.

"Is a burger okay?" James asked me. "There's a drive-through right around the corner, and you probably want to save your appetite for later anyway. The spread they put out is unreal."

"That's fine," I assured him, and we drove a few blocks to the Golden Arches. I quickly dug into my burger and downed half my Coke. Feeling human again, I finally asked him, "Are the rest of the guys okay with you taking the car all day like this?"

James gave a low chuckle. "Yeah, for the most part. They're pretty cool, except for..."

"Alex," I finished for him. "Wow, now he'll really hate me." I moaned.

"Alex doesn't hate you, Jill. He barely knows you. You'll see, give him a couple days and he'll come around." *Hmm. Doubtful.*

We drove around for a while, and James pointed out some of the sights. "Here's tonight's venue," he told me proudly, stopping in front of a large decked-out Gothic revival building. The marquee said it all. In big bold letters,

## The Blues Gang. Below that, & NOMAD.

"Wow, impressive," I told him. "What time's the show? Don't you have somewhere to be? I thought you always had a sound check in the late afternoon." What an excellent rock and roll girlfriend I was getting to be! "Look at the time." I extended out my arm so he could read the digital display of my hot pink Swatch watch.

"Aw, hell. I've got to get you to the hotel and be back here in like 20 minutes." Clenching his jaw, he started towards the car, not waiting to see if I was following him. I hurried to keep up.

"That's crazy. I can hang out here. No problem. Well, not *here*, here," I amended as I surveyed the topless bar and pawn shop that bookended the theater. "Can I just sit in the back? I'll be quiet."

James looked a bit uneasy, but agreed with me. "Let's go in then and get you settled, okay?" As he locked up the car, I saw the band van approaching.

"They're here," I called out.

James swore under his breath, but slipped a possessive arm about my shoulders. Quickly he escorted me towards an aisle seat in the back row of the deserted theater. "I'll be back in a flash," he promised. "Gotta get to work." Just a few minutes later, all four band members and Nomad's two roadies filed in, each carrying an instrument or speakers.

"I'll go pull around to the back," Brian said. And with a wave and a "Hey, Jill," he was gone. Steve and the roadies, brothers named Myles and John (although I couldn't remember who was who) surrounded me. I got warm welcomes from everyone, even Alex. It was so nice to see these guys again. But there was still a lot to be done to get ready for the show that night.

"C'mon guys, let's check out backstage and finish unloading the van," James suggested and they started to head out.

"I can help," I called to them. "I'm stronger than I look."

"No worries, motel girl," Alex told me in a loud whisper. "You just sit here and look pretty." Then he ambled down the aisle to join the other guys. I shook my head in amazement. *What a moody fucker he is!* I needed to keep my distance from him.

51

## Chapter 8 - *Two Princes*

After a thorough sound check late that afternoon, we piled into the van for the short drive back to the hotel. Following a shower and some rather enthusiastic lovemaking, James and I were ready to head back to the venue in a shuttle that the concert promoters had provided. Things were definitely approaching the first class status that I thought Nomad deserved. Backstage they had set up an appetizing buffet for us. I filled my plate to the brim with salads, barbecued ribs and mac 'n cheese and found a seat off to the side. It had been a long day, and I was famished.

"Better watch your girlish figure, motel girl," Alex warned with a smirk as he sauntered by, munching on an apple.

"Okay, no worries," I responded cheerfully. What *was* his problem? James and Brian joined me, and we quickly tore into the feast. Conversation was kept to a minimum as we focused on the task at hand. I needed several wet wipes to get myself cleaned up, but the guys had passed on the ribs, chowing down on salads and pasta. James filled a tray with our empty plates and dumped everything on the counter.

"Gotta get to work," he whispered in my ear and kissed me lightly on the lips. I grabbed a Coke and watched him talking to the roadies and going over the set list with Alex. He seemed so relaxed. They all did, moving around backstage getting ready. When they were announced, the guys high-fived each other and walked out to thunderous applause, waved to the fans and started their set. They were in fine form that night, believe me. James sounded great and when backed up on vocals by his twin,

I felt a chill down my spine. Alex's voice was much higher than James', and the resulting harmony was terrific. Nomad was really good. And not just because I was hot for the front man, either. They could really go places. The only question in my mind was a simple one. Would I get to go with them? After a forty-five minute set and a standing ovation, they performed an encore of *Over You*, and trooped off the stage.

"God, you guys were great," I called to them. James hugged me as he reached for a towel. Everyone was ecstatic. They knew that it had been a really great performance. Feeling it was only good form to stay and support the headliners, we headed out and enjoyed their high-energy show from the back of the auditorium. A couple of hours later, we were back at the hotel again, and it was starting to feel like home. I had my own room key and everything. I was ready to crash, but my boyfriend was feeling antsy. He paced back and forth, while I surveyed him from my vantage point, lying on one of the beds.

"We need to be better," he was mumbling, only half to himself.

"What're you talking about?" I asked him. "You guys were great."

James came over and sat on the edge of the bed next to me. "No, Jill. We're good, not great. Not yet anyway," he added wistfully.

"What do I know?" I teased. "I'm just a small-town groupie, hot for the lead singer." That got a smile. With one quick move, James had me pinned down. Seconds later, my tank top sailed across the room after the panties I had been wearing, and James was kissing me.

"And he's hot for you too," he told me. Then he showed me just how much. Afterward we were lying together, and I could see the sun coming up through the partially closed drapes. James was wrapped around me with his head on my chest, my fingers running through his long, dark hair. I was ready for sleep as it had been nearly 24 hours since I had been back home preparing for this trip. But I had to know something first.

"Why does he hate me?" I whispered. James didn't even pretend to not know who I meant.

"He doesn't hate you, Jill. I'll talk to him. Just give him some time." With that, he rolled over on his side and burrowed his head into the pillow.

"Okay, sure," I murmured. A minute later, his deep, steady breathing told me that my boyfriend was sleeping soundly, but I couldn't stop all these nagging thoughts... did I do the right thing coming here? How long was I welcome to stay? Why was Alex so hostile towards me? Why did I care? I finally fell asleep and by early afternoon, felt a bit more refreshed after a long, steamy shower. We opted for a late lunch in the hotel's coffee shop. It was pretty much deserted, and the waitress had just finished refilling our coffee cups when Alex joined us. He greeted us warmly and slipped into the booth next to me. The waitress made her way over, but Alex waved her away.

"Nothing for me, thanks," he told her, and she left us alone. "We sounded good last night, bro. What did you think, er, Jill?"

"Great, Alex," I gushed. "You were great. I love the way you two sound when you sing together."

Alex actually smiled at me, with no sign of the smirk he usually wore. "Years of practice, Jill."

The three of us spent the next half hour or so just talking and joking, sharing stories. Well, they shared. I mostly listened. The connection between the brothers was clear. Each credited the other with coming up with the name for their band, as well as providing the motivation to get it started.

"It was you, Alex," James said, smiling affectionately at his twin. "You were always the restless one. You always wanted more. I would have been content playing clubs in South Jersey, but you had bigger plans for us."

"Don't believe him, Jill," Alex cautioned me. "Your boyfriend was the dreamer. The schemer. He's the one who convinced Brian to join us and recruited Steve. He said we were like nomads, roaming from place to place and it stuck."

"When did you guys first get together?" I really knew very little about Nomad's early days. Alex couldn't wait to answer me.

"We were still in high school, Jill. We didn't even go to our graduation. We had a paying gig in Asbury Park that night."

James jumped in to correct his brother. "No, Alex. Don't you remember? We played there the night *before* graduation, but we met those girls and ended up staying another couple of days."

"Oh shit, yeah. We had to call Mom to tell her that we weren't gonna make it home for the ceremony. She was sooo pissed at us. But it was worth it, huh?"

James let out a whistle. "Hell yeah, it was worth it. They had that little place on the beach. Remember mine had the really big..."

Okay, this was a little too much information. "I'm right here, James. You can see me, right?"

James leaned over the table and covered my hands with his. "I know that, darlin'. And I'm glad you are. We just get to remembering everything. Hell, we weren't even eighteen and they were college girls. It was a big deal, you know? And that gig? That was the turning point for Nomad. We got a taste and that was it. We were hooked."

Alex told me how all four guys had day jobs for a while, but spent their spare time practicing and writing songs. They covered artists like Aerosmith and Van Halen, and eventually starting getting gigs in clubs all over the Northeast. "We'd be gone for weeks at a time those first few years. Then the weeks turned into months. Dad was great about letting us crash at home whenever we were in town. Remember Mom used to make us those sandwiches, James?"

James scrunched up his forehead in concentration, then grinned. "Oh Christ, yeah. She got it in her head that we weren't eating enough, so every time we left to go on the road, she'd make us these huge cheesesteak subs. We'd polish 'em off before we even hit the pike." James shook his head in wonder. "God, what we put her through, Alex. Hey, was it my turn to call her this week or yours?"

Alex assured him that he had called home that morning and that all was good. He seemed impatient to get on with his story. So Nomad was in demand and things were going well for the guys. A couple of their original songs made it into their set and were well received. An agent from a startup record label was in the audience one night and signed the guys later that month. Their contract was strictly boilerplate, but it got them into the studio and eventually out on tour to promote their self-titled debut album, *Nomad*. They had been on the road touring in support of the album for nearly a year when I first met James. The label had recently filed for bankruptcy and sold off their few assets to a more established firm.

The new management team decided to pull the plug on Nomad's floundering tour, but through a stroke of luck had agreed to let them open for one of their more popular bands, The Blues Gang. Both James and Alex credited their manager Ron with getting Nomad the reprieve that kept them out on the road and doing what they loved.

"You're his favorite, James," teased Alex. "Ron did it all for you, and you know it."

"What can I say, bro?" James countered with a grin. "Ron knows talent when he sees it."

I loved watching the two of them, so psyched to be touring and playing bigger venues to increasingly larger crowds. They had high hopes for the rest of the tour, and were enthusiastic about the cities and iconic venues they would be performing in. Their excitement was contagious, and I felt like I was actually part of something big that day. Nomad was going places.

James raised his coffee cup. "C'mon, how about a toast to Nomad? And the fans who love us," he added with his sexy grin. I clicked my cup against his.

"To Nomad," I echoed. "I love you guys," I blurted out. *Oh Christ, not the "L" word.*

James smiled at me and leaned over the booth for a kiss, but it was Alex who spoke up first. He made a sweeping gesture with his arm, taking in the deserted coffee shop. "Hey, what's not to love?" he asked. He pretended to look at a nonexistent watch. "Is that the time? Hell, I have to go. Butterface is waiting for me in my room. Sound check at 5 p.m.," he told James. "Be there or be square." And with that, he sauntered out.

"Who's butterface?" I asked James. He started to chuckle.

"Depends. Where are we again?"

"Detroit."

"In that case, I think it's Carrie," he said. "Or maybe Jen. I don't know. I honestly can't keep track."

"But why does he call her butterface?"

"Well, that's a good question. You see, with Alex? He likes to keep things simple. Not a lot of drama, especially when he's on the road. So he tends to pick girls who are, well, not so pretty. They don't expect as much. Girls with hot bodies, big boobs, good in the sack, everything going for her—but her face. Get it?"

*Oh, hell no!* I thought I might throw up the BLT I had just eaten. "Is that how you feel, too? Is that what I am to you... some groupie to screw?" *Tell me I'm wrong. Tell me I'm your girlfriend*, I begged silently.

"You're kidding, right?" James looked dumbfounded. "I can't believe this. Is that what you think this is? Some kind of game?"

"I don't know, James. I don't even know why I'm here." *And I just said I loved you. Well, you and your brother. But still.*

"Because I want you here, Jill Griffin," James told me softly. "Because I need you here. Okay?"

"Okay," I told him. It was enough… for now. After leaving some cash on the table, we left the coffee shop together, hand in hand.

"And besides," James whispered in my ear. "Your boobs aren't that big."

"You jerk." I swatted him on the arm, and we took off on foot to explore before it was time for another sound check.

The next several days flew by, and the time off that James had hoped for never materialized. The headliners agreed to stay in Detroit for an extra night and to show up in Indianapolis a day early. As openers, Nomad had no real choice but to agree to do the same. We left Detroit in the wee hours after four nights of sold-out shows and drove nine hours to the next venue. The fans were waiting, and the show must go on.

Dear Mom,

I am having such a good time here in Detroit, the Motor City! Lisa and I are keeping really busy and it's real easy to see why she likes it so much. Maybe I'll move here myself. Just kidding! I'll write again soon. Love to everyone,

Jill

Dear Beth,

I am in love!! James is the sweetest, nicest, hottest boyfriend ever. Being on the road is so much fun. I don't want to come home, so maybe I'll have to learn to sing or play a musical instrument. Yeah, right! Kiss Jesse for me.

Your best friend and Nomad groupie,

Jill

## James Tells All

*Jill is a real cute girl. She's a sweetheart and it's cool having her on the road with us. I never did that before. Ask a girl to come out on the road. Neither did any of the guys. Alex says he's fine with it, but I think he's pissed that I'm the one with the steady girl. Usually I like to play it pretty loose, keep my options open. I haven't had a real girlfriend since Leah, I guess. And that was a few years ago. We were together for a while. Leah was pretty cool. The only girl I ever met who could drink me under the table. Whenever Nomad wasn't touring or playing random gigs here and there, I was usually with Leah. When she caught me with that chick Sally from the bar, she told me she was packin' it in. "I'm done, James," she told me sadly. "Don't come after me. I mean it this time." To be honest? It wasn't fair to expect anyone to sit around and wait for me to show up. I didn't blame her one bit. If the situation was reversed and I was the one waiting by the phone... well, that's not gonna happen. Not in this lifetime.*

*But there's something about Jill. I can't explain it. She's pretty, but she doesn't seem to know it. She's got this real sexy grin and these big, sad eyes. She's kinda little. Petite, I guess you'd say. The first time I was with her? Christ, I thought I would break her in two. But she's not all that fragile. She's actually pretty tough. And she gives as good as she gets, if you catch my drift. It's always the quiet ones, you know? We're good in bed. Really good. And I can talk to her too. She's honest. No pretenses. What you see is what you get with that girl. She's a good listener, and she's starting to trust me. Tells me her fucked-up stories about growing up. All about how her dad ruined every holiday showing up drunk or not at all. How her sister acts all* whacko and her mom cries a lot. I don't blame her for wanting out of all that. But she's pretty happy most of the time. Like a little bird, always chirping about this or that and hopping around. When I wake up, she's always there. Wide awake and busy writing in that journal of hers. "Wouldn't you like to know?" she tells me with a big grin when I ask what she's writing about.

Most of the girls I meet act like I'm the best—singer, lover, whatever. But with Jill? I actually want to be the best—for her. I hope I'm not just another one of her fucked-up stories someday.

## Chapter 9 - *Every Rose Has Its Thorn*

Okay, so I guess it was official. It had happened somewhere along the way, somewhere between Detroit and Chicago with a stop in Indianapolis. Or maybe it happened somewhere between 'I'm havin' too much fun' and 'who the hell cares?' The result was the same. I was unemployed, homeless, and totally dependent on a man I had known for only a couple of months. I didn't plan it, but there I was.

Life on the road with James and Nomad had its ups and downs. The venues got bigger, as did the crowds. And the accommodations? Well, let's just say I'd never dreamed I would ever stay in hotels as nice as the one we stayed at in Chicago. In my humble opinion? The main difference between motels like the one I worked at, or used to work at, and the one I was currently staying in? It was all about the sheets and towels. Higher thread counts, Egyptian cotton, whatever. I could lay on those sheets forever, wrapped in one of those towels—and maybe I would. Things were looking up for Nomad, and James had made it abundantly clear that he wanted me to stay on the road with them. The other guys didn't seem to mind too much. I was pleasant and all, and I didn't take up a lot of room. Even Alex lightened up, and was mostly civil around me. And the days were flying by. Knowing that my rent was due, I told James of my plans to ask Teddy and Beth to pool their funds in order to pay my landlord for another month.

"That's crazy," James had replied. "Why pay for a place when you're not even there?" He convinced me to ask them to clean out my rented room and store my things for a while. Using Ron's phone card, I made the calls on a Saturday morning and reached my brother first and then my best friend. Ted was skeptical, but told me that he would do whatever I needed him to do, that the car was running fine, and that my mom had been asking for me. I had sent her a couple of postcards from the road, but had yet to explain what had really caused me to leave Detroit and exactly what the hell I thought I was doing. I asked Teddy to hug her for me and he said that he would. I didn't think Mom needed to know that I was giving up my apartment, so Beth agreed to store my things in her parents' basement. She was a little more enthusiastic than Ted, but still expressed her concern to me.

"Are you sure?" she asked me. "Have you really thought this through?"

"Beats the hell out of me," I replied. "But it's good. Don't worry, Okay? I'll be in touch," I assured her. I had one more call to make, and that was to the motel. My supervisor wasn't around, so I ended up giving my notice to the general manager, a guy I had spoken to only a few times while I was employed there. He agreed to let Beth come in to pick up my last paycheck and even offered to say that I had been let go, in case I ever wanted to file for unemployment. I thought that was pretty decent of him considering the circumstances and thanked him for being so understanding. So that was it. I had tied up all the loose ends and, except for a call to my mom that I promised I would make soon, my old life was over. The fact that I was now totally dependent on James didn't really hit me until a couple of weeks later. I was out of cash and needed to buy lip-gloss and tampons. The money I had brought with me was gone. But where? Oh yeah. A sexy pair of knee-high boots, a couple of tops and a daily ice cream cone while I walked around strange cities during my boyfriend's sound checks. And a blue shirt for

James that made his eyes pop. I had a couple hundred dollars in my bank account back home, but my MasterCard was maxed out, and I was broke.

One morning, James came out of the shower wearing only a towel and that sexy grin of his, and was shocked to find me sobbing facedown into my pillow.

"Jilly, what's wrong? Talk to me. What's the matter?" He had never seen me like this. Honestly, no one had. I was never much of a crier, but I made up for it that morning.

"I'm broke," I blubbered. "I have no money. I need lip-gloss. I got my period. I need tampons. What was I thinking?" James gathered me up in his arms and tried to console me.

"Don't worry," he said. "I'll take you shopping. We'll get everything you need. At least you're not pregnant, right? That was a joke, okay? Please, just stop crying." A bit calmer, I sat up and faced him.

"James," I told him solemnly, "we need to talk." Those dreaded words that strike fear in every man's heart.

He sat back and squared his shoulders. "Okay, shoot."

"Thank you. I mean, I appreciate it and I'll definitely take you up on the offer to go pick up a few things. But what about tomorrow and the next day? I'll need stuff and I can't come running to you every time I do. I've never been dependent on anyone before. It's not fair to you. You guys have been great, but I should be paying my own way, earning my keep, you know?"

James was thoughtful for a moment. "Yeah, I know. I can't expect you to just follow me around without some sort of commitment," he admitted. Wait, what? Where was this heading? He wasn't going to propose to me, was he? How pitiful. Marry me, I'm poor. I stopped him before he could go any further.

"No James, you don't understand. I'm not looking for a commitment. I just need to have a few bucks in my pocket. That's all."

He looked relieved. "Let me talk to the guys and I'll call Ron. He'll have some ideas. Okay? Don't worry, Jill. We'll work something out."

A short while later, we were walking hand-in-hand window-shopping along a row of trendy boutiques in the heart of Chicago. One display really got our attention. Two mannequins posing as rock 'n roll royalty—him wearing leather pants and her in boots and a suede miniskirt.

"That'll be us, Jill," James told me. "That'll be us someday."

I was just happy to have purchased a few necessities at the corner drugstore and was grateful that James had insisted that I keep the change from the $50 bill he had used to pay for them. Crisis averted. I was all set for now. I squeezed his hand.

"Sounds good, James."

True to his word, James came up with a creative solution to my cash flow problem. Somehow he got Ron and the guys to agree to put me on the payroll. For the princely sum of $75 a week, I would be in charge of confirming most of Nomad's travel arrangements. All of the bills would continue to go to Ron for payment, but I had been trusted with a credit card so that I could call ahead and guarantee hotel rooms for us. It was pretty straightforward, really. Each of the band members got their own room, and the roadies shared a room with two beds. Most of the arrangements for the tour had already been made. I only had to confirm the details and coordinate arrival dates and departures. Ron's secretary was happy to have me doing the grunt work and I was fine with that.

I was thrilled to have an official job, and I was a natural, of course, with my previous work experience. Since I was technically a contractor, I kept my entire paycheck each week, but knew that I would need to worry about taxes and other deductions at some point in the future. For now, I was just glad to have some cash in my pocket and not feel so dependent on James. It was like getting an allowance. Other than that temporary setback, I have to say that my life was pretty damn good. When we were travelling, James frequently drove the van, and I got to ride shotgun. Brian and Steve generally sprawled out in the back with some of the equipment. Alex had taken to riding with John and Myles in the station wagon that followed closely behind. There was a little bit of good-natured grumbling about my frequent need for restroom stops, but other than that, I felt like I fit right in. On the rare occasion that James was napping or off checking something out, I felt comfortable alone with the guys and enjoyed their company. It might sound like it could get boring, but I was never really bored.

Sometimes we played silly games like 'I Spy' or 'Name the Capitals', just to pass the time while driving. During the hours between the late-day sound checks and show time, we frequently played Gin Rummy or War. It was all in good fun.

None of the guys were big drinkers, and only Brian and the roadies routinely got high. James had pretty much quit smoking cigarettes at my urging (I told him that he smelled like my dad, which was a real turn-off) and he frequently used the exercise room at whatever hotel we were staying to help him fight off the nicotine cravings. We all enjoyed the lavish buffets provided by the venue each night, and frequently sat around after the show to just catch up and chill. I felt like I was part of a family, but not like one I'd ever known.

I didn't want it to end, but like all good things, an ending was inevitable. Things started to go downhill as we traveled west. James and Alex were having 'creative differences'. They argued over which songs to add to their longer sets and how they should be performed. Roadies John and Myles started screwing up a lot—simple things like not testing amps or putting out the wrong guitar. As the unofficial leader of Nomad, it was James who frequently had to have a talk with them. One night, things got particularly heated.

"It's not rocket science for Christ's sakes, Myles," James hollered. "When I go to pick up my fucking guitar, it has to be there. Right then, not two minutes later."

"I'm sorry, James," Myles whined. "I just…"

"Just nothing, damn it. Just do your fucking job, okay? Maybe lay off the pot, huh? It's killing your brain cells," James lectured.

"Jesus, James," Alex jumped in. "Back off, will you? He said he was sorry. What do you want from him?"

"I want him to do his job, Alex, okay? I need to rely on him. So mind your own business, will you?"

"Nomad is my business, asshole," Alex roared. Before I could stop myself, I added my two cents.

"Alex," I chided him gently. "I think all James means is..."

"Oh, now you're going to tell me what my brother means? Really, motel girl? Who the fuck do you think you are? No one asked you." Alex was practically spitting out the angry words at me.

James jumped up and crossed the room to stand toe to toe with his brother. "You don't talk to her like that, you asshole," he roared. "No one talks to Jill like that. You got a problem, you talk to me, got it?"

The more upset James got, the calmer Alex became. "Hey, chill, bro. I got no issue with your girlfriend." He held up his hands in mock surrender. "I know when I'm outnumbered."

"What's that supposed to mean?" James asked.

"Figure it out, genius. I don't have time for this crap," Alex told him. "C'mon, Myles. Let's go smoke a bone and head back to the hotel. The hot tub is calling my name." He strode out of the dressing room, and Myles and John followed him.

"Sorry, James," Myles mumbled over his shoulder as he left.

"Just do better, huh Myles?" James called after him. He grabbed my hand, and we went back to our room. My heart was racing, I realized. I took a deep breath and tried to match James' long strides.

The next day, we headed to Dallas. Everyone seemed eager to leave the unpleasantness of the previous night behind. The band actually had a night off, which was a rare occurrence. After we checked into the hotel late that afternoon, James whispered that he wanted to have dinner alone with me.

"Just the two of us," he promised. "Ask the front desk to make us a reservation. Whatever you want, steak, seafood, Italian."

I was thrilled. As much as I loved the guys, a night alone with my boyfriend sounded amazing. Reservations were set for eight that evening at a swanky steakhouse that was reported to be the best in town. After showering and lounging in our room, we walked through the lobby to meet the driver.

The concierge had offered to shuttle us to the restaurant, and I agreed. "This leaves both cars for the guys and if you want to have a couple of drinks, you can," I explained to James.

"Good thinking, babe," James congratulated me just as Alex and Brian wandered in.

"What's good thinking?" Alex asked. "Where are we heading?"

James explained how he wanted to spend the evening with me and that I had arranged transportation so as not to inconvenience anyone. Alex looked put out, but just shrugged. "How thoughtful," he drawled. "Wow, Jill, you're really earning your paycheck today. Good job."

James' face darkened as he listened to his brother. Brian tried to pull Alex away. "C'mon, Alex, let's go grab a drink and find a couple of cowgirls. C'mon." he pleaded.

James looked really pissed. "Can it, Alex. I've had it with your crappy attitude," he told his brother, who had already started to walk away.

Alex turned and walked back, shouting in James' face. "My crappy attitude? You smug bastard, your attitude is what's killing us. Everything has to be your way, just so for King James and his queen," he sneered.

"Fuck you, Alex," James responded.

"No, fuck you, James."

The two brothers faced off, and I was expecting one of them to take a swing at the other. Brian stepped in just in time. "Knock it off, you two." He pushed James back and pulled at Alex. "C'mon, Alex. Show's over, folks," he added to the small crowd of hotel guests that had gathered around. "Let's go," he directed Alex, and the two of them crossed the lobby towards the exit.

Alex looked over his shoulder and just shook his head in disgust at his brother as he left.

I didn't want to, but I spoke up. "Maybe we should forget about going out tonight," I suggested to James. "I'm not all that..."

"No way, Jill. Everything is all set. Let's go," he insisted. So we went. The steak might have been as good as promised, but to tell the truth, I didn't enjoy it very much. I had trouble swallowing due to the lump in my throat, and my heart was pounding as the fear in my gut grew steadily all evening. James ordered a double bourbon, then another. His meal lay untouched before him as he proceeded to get smashed. I had never seen him drink more than a couple of beers, so a drunk James was kind of a shock. He refused to talk about Alex, instead grilling me about my family and past lovers.

"So when you say your sister is crazy, just what does that mean? And if Teddy is so smart, why is he still living at home? And what about that Gary?" he pressed on. "What's he up to these days? If he hadn't taken off, maybe you would still be with him, huh? And Sean? You *really* didn't know he was married? C'mon. A smart girl like you?"

"Stop it," I begged him. "I told you those things in confidence. You can't use them against me just because you're pissed at Alex." He was scaring me.

"Who's Alex?" my very drunk boyfriend bellowed at me. "Fuck him."

"Please, James," I begged him. "They're going to throw us out of here. C'mon. Let's just go. Please." I left a whole week's pay in crumpled bills on the table and half dragged him out of the restaurant. I shoved him in the cab that was idling out front.

"Don't worry. He's just exhausted," I told the worried driver, as he realized just how inebriated his passenger was. "He's fine."

When we got back to the hotel, I was relieved to find the lobby was deserted. I'd had a fair amount of practice with my drunken dad, but he was pretty small compared to my long and lanky boyfriend. I dragged James into the elevator and pulled him along the hall to our room. The coast was clear. I was glad to not see anyone as we lurched down the hall. Once we were safely in the room, I pushed him towards the king sized bed, then I pulled his pants off and removed his shoes. Mission accomplished, I collapsed against the vanity in our huge marble bathroom. My hands were shaking and I felt nauseous, like the small amount of dinner that I had tried to eat was not going to stay down. I was sweating, and I needed to catch my breath, so I splashed cold water on my face and tried to breathe deeply. My nerves were starting to settle down but my stomach was rumbling. Confrontation was never something I'd learned how to handle. I looked around, but our combined inventory of first aid supplies consisted of Extra Strength Tylenol and two Band-Aids. Crap.

Ginger ale was the only thing I could think of to settle my tummy. So after checking that James was lying on his side, and therefore unlikely to choke to death on his own vomit (do you know how many rock-and-rollers have died at 27?), I grabbed the hotel key and went in search of a vending machine.

I found one in a tiny room off the lobby, but Pepsi products and orange soda were the only options. *Maybe the bar*, I reasoned. *I can get it to go*. But after claiming a stool in the nearly deserted bar and placing my order, I decided to enjoy my drink there. No point rushing back to the room to watch my boyfriend *not* choke to death. A few swallows and I was starting to relax. The bar was dimly lit, and I enjoyed the relative quiet. What a night! I had just gotten used to being around people who actually got along with each other for the most part. What would happen next? Some horrible things had been said, and I couldn't imagine how everything could go back to normal. But it would have to, right? The band was like family, the brothers *were* family. Lost in thought, I didn't realize that the stool next to me was being pulled out until Alex sat down next to me.

"Hey motel girl," he drawled. "What's up?"

Part of me was relieved to see Alex acting normally. "Hey," I replied." Just having some ginger ale." I pressed my hands to my stomach and made a face.

"Yeah," he answered. "My mom swears by it for an upset stomach."

"Mine too," I told him. "I already feel better. I guess our moms were right."

"Where's your other half?" he asked, looking around for James.

"Uh, he's upstairs. Um, lying down," I told him.

"Passed out drunk, huh?" He nodded sagely. "Yeah, I figured." I waited for him to continue. And he did. "He's got a problem. I mean, you know that, right?"

I felt a chill, and my heart started to hammer in my chest. "What do you mean? I've never seen him drink like that. It's not like it's a regular thing, is it?"

"How long have you been around?" he asked." A month or two?"

"Almost three months," I told him. "Why?"

"It's just that James stays on the wagon for a while, then he slips. Like tonight."

"Then why did you provoke him?" I asked desperately. "If you knew he would react like that."

"Wow, you don't know shit about drunks, do you?" Alex asked incredulously.

"James is *not* a drunk," I told him.

"Yeah he is, motel girl. Sorry to be the one to burst your bubble."

"You're wrong," I told him. "I can't listen to any more of this." I got up to leave, but Alex reached out to stop me.

"I've upset you. I'm sorry, Jill," he told me, and he actually sounded sincere. He grabbed a napkin off the bar and gave it to me. "C'mon, darlin'. Wipe away those tears. It's bad for my image to have a pretty girl crying over me in a bar."

I had to smile at that. "Oh, so what are you? A real lady-killer?"

"Try me," Alex answered, and before I knew it, I was in his arms, and he was kissing me and it was amaz... so freaking wrong!

"What the fuck, Alex?" I pushed him away. "Are you nuts? I'm in love with your brother, you idiot. What's the matter with you anyway?"

He gave me a lazy smile that reminded me eerily of James. "Hey, nothing ventured, right?" He looked like he was about to say more, but I'd had enough. I raced to the elevator and hurriedly pushed the button for the seventh floor. I fumbled with the key and let myself in. The room was dark and very quiet. I leaned over James to make sure he was still breathing (he was) and, stripping down to my skivvies, hopped in bed next to him. I was shivering and completely exhausted, but I couldn't shut off the images whirling around in my brain. Alex grabbing me and kissing me. Me liking it at first. James, stumbling around drunk, shouting and showing me a whole different side of himself. This had to be a fluke, I reasoned. I'd lived with an alcoholic my whole life. I would have known, right? And what about Alex? If I told James about the pass he made, it would only set him off again. No, better to just forget this whole evening had ever happened.

I lay there for a long time, trying to slow down my breathing in tandem with my nearly comatose boyfriend's. Eventually, I did.

## Alex Weighs In

*I wasn't trying to get back at James last night. Grabbing Jill like that? Kissing her? No, it wasn't like that. I actually have feelings for her. That little chick drives me crazy. That smile of hers, the way she's always so into everything. The music, the road, even the chicken-fried steak at the Cracker Barrel on the way here the other day—she gets so excited. The way her eyes light up when my brother walks into the room. Christ, I wish she would look at me like that. Just once. Seeing her with James 24/7 is killing me.*

*Yeah, I'm pretty pissed at James right now. Nomad is finally starting to make it big, but if James can't keep his shit together—man, we're done. I don't think I can handle another one of his meltdowns. For ten years we've been putting all of our blood, sweat and tears into this band and he's gonna piss it all away. He wants it all: being the front man of the band, having this amazing girl at his side, drinking and carrying on all he wants. Something's got to give.*

*But I didn't make a pass at his girl because I'm angry with him. No—I want her. I want to be in her head, in her heart and yeah, in that tight little body of hers too. Write about that in your journal, motel girl! Maybe she'll tell James about last night. Maybe we'll fight over her. I'm not sure if Nomad can survive this. If I could end up with Jill, maybe it would be worth it.*

## Chapter 10 - *Bitter Sweet Symphony*

Several hours later, I awoke to bright sunshine streaming through the window. It was only a couple of seconds before I remembered the night before, and everything that had happened. *Oh, no.*

"You're awake," James called out as he crossed the room to sit on the edge of the bed. He actually looked better than I felt, despite all that drinking. "I got you some coffee. Three creams and three sugars, just the way you like it." Other than maybe acting a bit sheepish, he actually seemed pretty normal. I struggled to sit up and reached for the coffee.

"Thanks, James," I told him. "Light and sweet." James gave me a big grin as he watched me take a tentative sip. *Oooh. Hot!*

"Yeah, sweet just like you," he told me. I put the cup down on the bedside table.

"Hey, James? About last night?" My heart was pounding. *Yeah, what about last night?*

"Yeah, Jill. Hey, don't worry about it, okay? Sometimes, me and Alex? We just need to blow off some steam. It's tough, you know? Being together so much. Once in a while, things just get a little out of hand. But don't worry," he told me. "Everything's fine. You'll see." But this was about way more than just him and his brother.

I reached for my coffee and took another sip. I needed the jolt of energy I hoped it would provide. I was on pretty shaky ground here. "But James," I began slowly. "It's more than just

78

your fight with Alex. Last night you were... so out of it. I've never seen you like that. I was scared. I am scared."

"You don't need to worry about it, Jill. I'm fine. I'm not your dad, you know? Not everyone who gets drunk is an alcoholic," he told me, clearly getting pissed. *My dad?* Ouch, that stung.

I tried to keep the anger I was feeling out of my voice. In a level tone, I continued. "I'm not saying you're an alcoholic, silly. I'm just telling you that I hate to see you like that. Believe me, you're *nothing* like my dad."

The grin that had been missing was now stretched across his face. "Well, that's good to hear, darlin'," he drawled. "I'd hate to think that I was reminding you of your dad, especially when I did this. And this." As he was talking, his hands were busy trying to separate me from my skimpy top and panties. I started to laugh and tried to relax. But first, I had to say one more thing.

"Just promise me," I pleaded. *Don't drink like that again? Don't be mean? Don't leave?*

"I promise," James told me, and we stopped talking for a while.

A few hours later, I opted to stay in the room while James went down to the hotel coffee shop. Nomad's manager Ron was in town, and he wanted to have lunch and check on his 'boys'. I wasn't ready to face the other guys, especially Alex, and I really wasn't up to meeting Ron for the first time.

"I'll be fine," I assured James. "Just go. I think I'll order a sandwich and some more coffee. Maybe take a shower and write in my journal. Go."

James left after I promised to join him later for some sightseeing before the 5 p.m. sound check. As he left the hotel room, he turned to look at me. "I love you, Jill. You know that, right?"

"I love you, too," I assured him. "I'll see you soon." Half an hour later, I was happily munching away on a turkey club sandwich and a mound of French fries, curled up in a comfy armchair and watching some dumb soap opera. Never a big fan of TV, I watched even less on the road, in part due to the fact that I never knew what was on, with traveling through time zones and a different channel lineup in every town. But somehow sitting there, enjoying my room service meal, I started to feel better. More normal. Things would settle down, I told myself. Last night was just one stupid night. All relationships hit a bump some time. Why should the Sheridan brothers be any different? And the pass Alex made at me? That had to be just a one-time thing. Maybe I had imagined it or maybe Alex was just testing me. Anywho, Nomad was opening tonight in the largest venue they had ever played, and things would get back to normal. They just had to, I reasoned.

And things did settle down, at least for a while. Later that day I finally met Ron, who turned out to be much smaller and older than I had imagined, standing just a couple of inches taller than me and well into his late 40s. But he was just as charming and funny in person as he had been during all of our phone conversations. When introduced, I started to shake his hand, but he pulled me in for a hug.

"I'm glad you're with him, Jill. You're good for him," he whispered. I told him how much I appreciated his trust in me and how grateful I was to have some spending cash. I gave him an envelope with all of the hotel receipts I had been collecting since being put on the payroll. Ron gave me a big smile in return. "Anything for James," he told me. "I'm glad it's working out so well."

Since business was concluded for the day, we set out on a sightseeing tour around Dallas. Brian ended up joining us at the last minute, and we hit some of the big tourist attractions. My favorite was Sundance Square over in Fort Worth. I could have spent a whole week exploring all of the shops, but we only had time to pop in a few of them. I bought Jesse a cowboy hat to grow into, but passed on the toy gun and holster set that Brian picked out.

"Did you and Alex get to play with guns?" I asked James. He started to laugh.

"Hell, yeah. My mom was cool with that. Anything to get us out of the house, you know? We could get pretty wild," he added wistfully.

Late that afternoon, we were due for a sound check at the Coliseum, so we drove back to the hotel. I decided to go back to our room to take a shower and lie down for a bit. I quickly fell asleep and woke to find James sleeping soundly beside me. An hour later the call came, and James and I walked hand-in-hand backstage where the catering crew had set up a buffet for us. Not quite as hungry as I frequently was, I scooped some pasta and a bread stick onto my plate and found a seat in the far corner of the room. Halfheartedly twirling spaghetti around my fork, I looked up to see Alex standing over me.

"Hey, Alex," I said. "How're you doing?"

He looked at me before he spoke. "I'm doing okay, Jill," he told me with just enough sarcasm to put me on edge. "Just peachy." And he wandered away to the buffet table. A couple of minutes later, Brian and Steve joined me, and I polished off the food on my plate. I was contemplating going back for seconds when James sat down beside me.

"How're you doing, darlin'?" he asked me. "You okay?" He looked beat as I squeezed his hand and assured him that I was fine.

"What's with you?" I teased. "Your hands are like ice." And kind of clammy too, I realized. "Are you feeling okay?"

"Just got a case of the jitters," he assured me. "I'll be right back." And he disappeared down the hall. Something was off, I knew it. Was it really just a case of preshow jitters? After all, this was the largest audience Nomad had ever played to. Anyone would be nervous, I figured as I considered snagging a bowl of yummy-looking rice pudding from the buffet.

A short while later, I caught up with James as Nomad was preparing to take the stage. I leaned in to kiss him and for the first time ever, he tried to pull away from me. I caught a whiff of something alcoholic, whiskey or something. He mumbled, "Gotta get to work, Jill. I'll be back." And he walked away. I staggered backward and bumped into Ron. *What the hell?*

"Watch out, honey," he teased. He squeezed my arm, and we stood there listening and watching as Nomad started to play. "They're really good," he told me. "Every time I hear them, it hits me just how good they are."

"I know, right?" I agreed enthusiastically. "They really are." We grinned at each other happily, and I waited a few moments before I spoke up. "So Ron," I began conversationally, "What's up with James and Alex? They aren't getting along very well lately."

Ron frowned. "Yeah, those two? They're as close as any two people I have ever met. Maybe that's part of it. I don't think they've ever disagreed about a single thing, until Nomad. They have very different ideas about how the band should work. Alex is all for a democracy where everyone gets an equal vote. But James? He prefers to make decisions on the spot, and fill the rest of the guys in later. Stuff like where and when they'll perform. Or which songs to play and in what order. He likes to control things, James does," he finished with a shrug.

"Does he seem okay to you, Ron? James, I mean. Do you think he's... happy?"

"Happy? James? Yeah, I guess so." He peered at me shrewdly. "I mean, we're talking about James here, right? Passionate? Driven? Moody as hell? All of the above I guess, but yeah, Jill. I think you make him happy."

I pulled away, feeling confused. "I don't understand." *Driven? Moody? James is none of those things. First Alex tells me James is a drunk, and now Ron is telling me he's a control freak and more.* James was all light and breezy, from what I could see. Alex was the one who was always angsty about something or another.

"Everything will be fine, Jill," Ron assured me, absentmindedly patting my arm. "Don't worry." I tried to relax after that, and we stood together silently for the rest of their set. But pleading a headache, I told James as soon as I saw him that I was heading back to the room.

"Stay and enjoy the Gang," I assured him when he offered to come with me. "Don't worry, I'll be fine." He promised me he wouldn't be late, and after showing him that I had my key, I let him hug me, and walked down the maze of hallways leading back to the hotel lobby. It was quite deserted, and I gratefully sank down into one of the plushy armchairs facing a cold and dark stone fireplace. "You look like I feel," I whispered to the massive hearth, and shivered. I told myself that things would get better, and I almost believed me.

April 10, 1990

Dear Mom,

I know it's been a long time and I should call you more but it's just been soooo busy. Honestly, the days just fly by. I know I should have told you about James and being on the road with the band and all. I was going to, but it looks like Beth's mom beat me to it, huh? I'm sorry that you found out like that. But please stop worrying, okay?

We're in Dallas for the rest of the week. Someday, I'll show you on a map all of the places we've been. You would really like James, Mom. I know you would. He treats me like I am made of gold or something. We get along great. And the rest of the band acts like I'm their little sister. We have so much fun.

Speaking of sisters, have you heard from Susan? I can only imagine how hard it is worrying about her and dealing with Dad at the same time. I hope he's doing better. Teddy told me he was sick a lot this month and missed work. I know you've had a lot of sleepless nights over the years and I only wish that you had an easier time of it. Maybe when Nomad hits it big, I can afford to send you on a cruise. Wouldn't that be cool? I want to get a special gift for Teddy's graduation but I can't think of what he would want. I asked James what he would have wanted when he was 18, but I can't tell you what his answer was. It was fresh though. He's so funny, he always has me in stitches.

I will write again soon and will call you when I know when we are going to be back East again. Please don't worry.

All my love,

Jill

## Chapter 11 - *Only Wanna Be with You*

The Blues Gang and Nomad sold out four nights in a row at the Dallas Coliseum. The tour was going great, and there was already talk about Nomad going out on their own again.

"It's all about timing, Jill," Ron explained to me. "It's like love," he joked. "You just can't rush it."

"I'm glad you're looking out for them, Ron," I told him sincerely. "I mean it. You're a great manager."

Ron smiled wistfully back at me. "I love these guys. They're like the sons I never had." James had only told me that Ron was single, so I really knew nothing about him other than his contributions to the band. But now I was curious.

"No kids? No wife?" I asked him lightly.

Ron let out a low chuckle. "No, Jill," he told me. "Nomad and the other bands that I manage? They're my family." The silence was about to get awkward, so I asked him about the other three bands, and he briefly filled me in on them. I could tell how much he liked each one, and how proud he was of them.

"But James and Nomad. They're your favorites, right?" I teased him.

"My favorite band is always the one I'm with at the moment," he assured me with a wink. "Love the one you're with, right?" Sensing I still needed to hear more, he leaned in and whispered, "But yeah, Jill. James is my favorite. Always has been."

It was odd thinking of Ron being this close with his other bands. Knowing him just for a few days, I was amazed at how this dapper little man, old enough to be my father, could manage all these wild, partying musicians so well. I knew he would be leaving us the next day to fly out to Los Angeles, so I asked him when we would see him again.

"Don't worry," he told me. "I'll catch up with you guys soon. You'll be sick of me before you know it." I couldn't even imagine the day when I wouldn't want to see Ron's smiling face, and I told him so.

The next day, we said goodbye to Ron at the airport. Leaving the band van and the roadie's wagon in the long-term parking lot, the seven of us boarded a flight to Nashville. The Blues Gang's booking agent had managed to squeeze in another show and decided to spring for our airfare. I found out later that they had balked at paying for my ticket, so Ron quietly charged the expense to his personal credit card. It felt strange to be traveling without the van and all of our equipment, and to see the now familiar guitar cases belonging to James and Alex disappearing from sight on the airline's conveyor belt. Brian and Steve were assured that instruments comparable to their own would be made available to them that night for the show in Nashville. Waving goodbye to Ron, I struggled to keep the panic that I was starting to feel at bay. Things had just gotten back to normal, or at least as normal as it ever got for us. What was next? Change was good, I tried to convince myself.

Walking hand-in-hand through the airport with James and his band mates, I should have been relaxed and happy, and I told myself that I was just being silly. *Everything will be fine. The guitars will be waiting for us at bag check, and the shuttle will be waiting to take us to the hotel and everything else will be all set. Nashville is the music capital. There's nothing to worry about.*

Turns out, there was plenty to worry about. When we landed in Nashville, Alex's guitar wasn't there. Alex started to freak out, but calmed down a bit when he was assured that it had been located, already loaded on the next flight, and would be delivered to the hotel later that day. James was not as easy to convince, however.

"How can you be so fucking incompetent?" he hollered at the poor attendant. "You only had to do one thing, just get the guitar from point A to point B, and you screwed up. What's wrong with you people?"

Alex tried to lighten the mood. "My guitar just needed a little 'me' time, bro. Not worth getting excited about."

It didn't work. James went ballistic. "Grow up, Alex. This is a business. It's our job and we can't do it right if everyone else keeps fucking up." He turned his attention back to the poor clerk, who looked like she was ready to bolt or faint.

I had been on that side of the desk more than once at the motel, when a reservation got lost or a phone message was never received. I knew just how she felt. "C'mon, James." I tried to calm him down. "Leave her alone, huh? There's nothing more that can be done right now. Let's just get to the hotel."

He shook me off. "Back off, Jill. This doesn't concern you."

I stormed away to the only place I could think of where I would be, if not alone, at least away from James and the other guys.

Locking the stall door behind me, I perched on the toilet seat lid and tried to fight the panic that had been building all day.

"Oh, shit," I told myself. "This is it. It's over." Now what? My breathing finally slowed down and after splashing some cold water on my face, I was ready to leave the ladies' room when the airline clerk came in. Her eyes were ringed in red, and she was still visibly shaken. Poor thing. I decided to reach out to her.

"Hey, sorry about that," I began. "My boyfriend shouldn't have talked to you like that. He's just such a perfectionist, you know." When she looked at me rather blankly, I continued on. "Temperamental musicians, right?"

She finally turned and faced me. "Are you afraid of him? Has he turned on you?" She really sounded concerned. "You don't have to live like that, you know? There are places that..." but I cut her off.

"It's not like that. You don't know what you're talking about." *Stick to your own job, and leave the advice to Dear Abby.* James would never hurt me, I reassured myself as I hurried out to join the guys who were waiting for me.

"Everything okay, Jill?" Brian asked. I was happy to see James looking calm, or at least less upset than he had just ten minutes earlier.

"Everything's fine," I assured Brian. "You know me. My bladder's the size of a pea." James laughed at that and grabbed my hand, and we left the terminal in search of the shuttle that would take us to the hotel. Crisis averted.

Sure enough, Alex's guitar made its way back into his arms just before the sound check in the cavernous auditorium later that day. Normally quite complacent, the guys of Nomad were in awe as they moved around the celebrated auditorium and set up for the show. This wasn't just another venue. Everyone knew that this was the big time. It may have been the Country Music Capital of the world, but Nashville welcomed all types of music, including that of The Blues Gang and Nomad. But the sound check didn't go that well, to be honest. The acoustics were off, and James' microphone wasn't up to his standards.

Assured that all the problems would be fixed in time for the show that evening, we went back to our rooms to shower and relax for a bit. I was feeling anxious and tried to convince James to join me in bed, but he was clearly *not* in the mood. He paced back and forth in our spacious hotel room for so long that I told him he would wear a groove in the carpet. He looked at me, and for a second, I saw anger flashing in his eyes. I half expected him to tell me to shut the fuck up, but then he grinned.

"Rain check, okay?" he assured me, and a few moments later gave me a quick peck on the cheek. "I'll see you there, Catch a ride with the guys, okay? I'm gonna grab a cab over to the venue. I want to make sure that everything is all set."

"I'll go with you," I offered, but James was not to be swayed.

"Just stay here and relax," he told me. "I'll see you soon." And with that, he rushed out of the room. What a day it had been so far! First James goes off like a maniac on that poor woman, and then he turns down sex with me. Now that was a first! I picked up a magazine and tried to read, then put it down in favor of my journal. But my mind was wandering and after nearly a half hour, all I had written was a series of question marks across the page. I decided to run a hot bath. After testing that the water was just right, I was about to climb in when the phone rang.

Realizing there was an extension in the bathroom, I grabbed it quickly.

"James?" I said. There was a long chuckle on the other end.

"No, darlin'," Alex drawled. "Just me, brother Alex." Then his tone got serious. "Wait, where's James?"

"Oh, he's fine," I told him, not very convincingly. "You know James. He told me he was going to check out the venue."

"Oh, shit," he responded, and the phone went dead.

Telling myself that Alex was just being Alex, I tried to relax in the spacious tub. I gave up after ten minutes and decided to focus my attention on my hair and makeup. As we rarely bothered to unpack any more, I had to rummage around in my duffel bag for a top that was both clean and wouldn't require ironing. Satisfied that I looked as good as I could under the circumstances, I wandered down to the lobby to meet the guys. But after twenty minutes of sitting there alone, I knew something was up. I walked over to the front desk. "Can you please ring Alex Sheridan's room?" I asked the desk attendant.

"Certainly," she told me, and after punching in the room number, she handed me the house phone. It rang and rang.

"Pick up, Alex," I begged silently. "Just pick up the phone." But he didn't, and I struck out after trying to reach Steve, Brian and the Anderson brothers as well. I poked my head into the bar, half expecting to see everyone there, sitting around a table, saving a seat for me. But I didn't recognize a soul, so I headed back to the front desk. "Can you call me a cab?" I asked the clerk.

"Sure," she said. "Where're you heading?" I told her I needed to get to the auditorium, and she smiled. "Are you with the band?" When I nodded mutely, she asked casually, "So are those hot brothers *really* identical?" My death glare convinced her to focus on the task at hand. "The hotel shuttle can take you over," she informed me and rang for the driver.

An older guy named Chuck appeared, and we walked out to the van. He eased his considerable girth behind the steering wheel and chuckled when I told him my destination. "That's my third trip there tonight," he chided me gently. "You folks need to get your act together."

"Wait," I asked him. "About an hour ago, did you drive a really good looking, long haired guy over there? Tall and kind of skinny?"

"Sure did," he told me. "And a little while later, I swear he was back waiting for me in the lobby. So I asked him, 'Hey, how did you get back here so quickly? I just dropped you off at Costello's.'"

"What's Costello's?"

"That's what he said," Chuck told me. "Turns out it was his twin brother. Can you imagine that?"

Yes, I certainly could imagine that. "What *is* Costello's?" I asked again.

"Don't tell me you want to go there too, little gal," he said gently. "Costello's isn't the sort of place for you."

"So what? It's a bar?" Despite the cold night air, I could feel myself starting to sweat.

"Now, you listen to me," Chuck said. "That first guy asked if there was a bar in this town where they *didn't* play live music, so I brought him to Costello's. A little while later I dropped his twin brother off there, too. Now why on earth should I bring *you* there?"

"Because I love him. The first guy, I mean. And I'm worried about him." My shoulders shook as I started to sob. "I don't know what else to do."

"All right then," Chuck relented. "I'll take you, but if those guys aren't there, I'm bringing you right back to the hotel. Okay?" I agreed, and we drove silently through the streets of Nashville to Costello's, the only bar in town that didn't feature live music. When we arrived at the dimly lit neighborhood tavern, Chuck insisted on parking and escorting me inside. A quick peek and two things were evident. There was no sign of the Sheridan brothers, and Costello's was clearly a bar for people looking to drink with no musical distractions. Not even a jukebox.

"C'mon, sweetheart," Chuck said encouragingly. "The night's young, and so are you. Nashville has plenty of great places to go to. Maybe your boyfriend just needed some time alone."

"Yeah, maybe. Can you bring me to the auditorium?" I asked him.

"Well, sure," he said, clearly pleased that he had convinced me to leave so quickly. A short while later, he pulled up in front of the main entrance.

"Have a good night, little gal," he told me as he helped me out of the van.

"Thanks, Chuck," I told him with a forced smile, and I squeezed his hand and hurried in to the lobby. I was hoping that my name was on some type of list so I could get backstage, and it was. Sporting my laminated pass on a cord around my neck, security waved me through, and I raced to find James.

I found him. He was already on stage, and at first glance, everything looked fine, but then I realized that everything was *so* wrong. James' deep voice sounded all gravelly, and his guitar, which he normally played during this song, was propped up against one of the amplifiers. *What the hell?* Finally I found Myles and John.

"What's going on?" I asked them. "Why doesn't James have his guitar?"

John rolled his eyes at me, and Myles slowly responded. "He's stinkin' drunk, Jill," he told me. I turned my attention back to the stage where, as if on autopilot, the now all-too-familiar set was progressing, but James was way off. He was lurching around on the stage, a far cry from his normally limber moves. His timing was off, and he apparently forgot his own lyrics more than once. Alex was trying to cover for him, even I could see that, but Brian and Steve were both rattled. There was no encore for Nomad that night, no standing ovation. When the guys trooped off stage, it was if they had been defeated in battle. No high fives, no fist pumps. Alex stormed by me, followed by Brian and Steve, with James bringing up the rear. I ran over to him.

"James, what's going on?" I asked him in a panic. He held up his hand as if to stop me from going any further, and promptly threw up all over my sexy leather boots.

## Chapter 12 - *Torn*

Sleep on it. Things will look better in the morning. That's what everyone always says. But from my perspective, perched on the bathroom vanity the next morning, things still looked pretty crappy. As I unsuccessfully tried to scrape dried vomit off my pricey leather thigh-high boots over the small sink, I could hear James snoring in the next room. *I'm glad that one of us can sleep.* I'd spent the last five hours staring at the ceiling and listening to James on his way through the various sleep cycles. He was currently out cold, lying diagonally across the huge bed. Before he passed out the night before, I was unable to get him to open up after the band's disastrous set. He apologized for ruining my boots, but clammed up when I asked him about what had happened earlier.

I knew that Alex and the other guys had already met with the Blues Gang's manager and their booking agent in an effort to control the damage that had been done during Nomad's disastrous opening act. I had noticed the message light blinking when we made it back to the room. It was Alex, letting James know that Nomad would be meeting at noon today to 'discuss the recent events'. His tone was cold and distant, and barely hid the anger that I knew he must be feeling.

I listened to the message over and over as James slumbered on. What would happen? Could James be fired from his own band? Six hours to go. I kept running through my limited options as I counted the ceiling tiles. I could wake James early, force black coffee into him and get him to shower and shave before the meeting. He could wear the blue shirt that I had bought for him. Or I could wait until the meeting was about to start, wake him up and let him face the guys in whatever shape he was in. I could also walk out the door, find a mall or a movie theater and hide out until this whole mess blew over. I despised any form of confrontation, but I also felt loyalty for my boyfriend. I had to be on his side, right? And no mall would be open for hours, I realized.

In the end, I fidgeted around for a few hours and ordered coffee from room service with a double order of rye toast. I don't think either of us could face eggs right then. I found James' blue shirt and hung it in the bathroom, hoping that steam from the shower would help to get the wrinkles out. *Now for the hard part.* I sat on the edge of the bed and slowly stroked James' arm, tracing the maze of tattoos that covered it.

"James," I whispered. "C'mon. Time to wake up." He mumbled something under his breath, and turned away from me, but I could not give up that easily. "C'mon, sweetheart. You need to wake up," I pleaded.

Finally, he rolled over to face me. He looked worse than he had the night before, if that was even possible. Bloodshot eyes, greyish skin, cracked dry lips. What a sight he was!

"Jilly," he croaked. "Are you okay?" Relief flooded through me. Now this was someone I recognized. We would work this out together. Patiently, I filled him in on what needed to take place in the next hour or so. He seemed to be on board with the coffee and the shower, but when I mentioned the meeting, he scowled at me. "I'll pass on that," he told me. "I don't need to hear from those pricks today."

"But, James," I begged. "You need to face this. The guys are pissed." *And they have every right to be,* I added silently.

James raised himself up on one elbow and, wincing as if in pain, asked me, "Whose side are you on, Jill?" For a split second, I just wanted to slap him. But this was James, after all. He was a great boyfriend. He had just hit a bad patch.

"I'm on your side, you big dope," I assured him. "But it's not about taking sides. The band needs you. I need you. And you promised," I added weakly.

James watched me carefully as he nodded slowly. "Yeah, I get that. And I'm here for you, for them. But last night, things just got a little out of hand. Shit happens. I'm fine." I remained silent. "Christ, what do you want me to say? I'm sorry, okay? I fucked up."

"Just tell me that it won't happen again," I begged him. "Please, promise me." And I wanted to believe him when he looked at me and tiredly agreed.

He gulped down a cup of coffee, swallowing the three Tylenol I gave him. He stripped down and climbed into a scalding hot shower and I was finally able to let go of the breath that I had been holding for hours. He started humming, then actually singing, and I felt a smile coming on. Maybe if today's meeting went well, and James could just last a few more weeks, we could go somewhere warm and relax for a bit. He was exhausted after months of touring, first as a solo act, then as an opener. *Everyone is entitled to an off night, for God's sake*, I reasoned, and started looking for the iron that I thought I had seen in the closet.

Forty-five minutes later, a shaved and sheepish James went to meet up with his band members wearing a freshly pressed blue shirt. I kissed him on the cheek and cheerfully wished him good luck. I kept my tone light, but deep down, I couldn't rid myself of the anxiety that had been building since Alex's phone call before the concert last night. James' apology just had to be enough to convince the guys that he was going to be able to keep up with the demands as front man for Nomad.

There wouldn't be a Nomad without James Sheridan, I told myself as I took my own shower. When he wasn't back after an hour, I started to worry again. I tried to think back to all those crime shows that I used to watch. Was it a good sign if the jury didn't come back right away?

Yes. That had to be it. If it had been pre-determined that there was no chance of staying on tour with the band, James would have been back in the room right away. How long does it take to say, "You're fired"? On the other hand, if the discussion started to drag on, would my boyfriend lose his temper and storm out? I tried writing in my journal, then reading the book on my nightstand, and finally flipping through the extensive channel lineup on TV.

Nothing held my interest, so I was staring out into space, completely zoned out, when James returned mid-afternoon. I jumped up and followed him around like a puppy as he pulled off his shirt and jeans in favor of a pair of baggy gym shorts.

"How'd it go?" I asked, trying unsuccessfully to keep the desperation out of my voice. "Everything good?"

James didn't respond right away, so I was about to repeat myself when he finally spoke up. "It's okay," he told me tersely. "We're good. Stop worrying, will you?" He walked away from me, heading towards the bathroom. He must have realized how sharp he had sounded, because he suddenly turned and came back over to where I was sitting. Taking me in his arms, he murmured softly, "Don't worry Jill. We're gonna be just fine. I promise."

I started to shake, and couldn't stop the tears that had been building up all day. I was so relieved and so tired. Sobbing and quivering, I allowed James to pull me towards the bed and we crawled under the covers. He kept rubbing my back to try to get me to calm down. Finally we fell asleep, and slept soundly for hours, curled up like a pair of spoons.

Alex must have decided to forego the requisite sound check because the first contact he made with us was a phone call at 7 p.m. "You guys up for some dinner?" he asked gently.

"Sure thing," I told him.

"See you in ten," he replied, and he hung up before I could add, "Thanks, Alex."

James was already getting dressed, so I followed suit and we made our way downstairs and joined the rest of the guys for dinner. Everyone was pretty quiet, but the mood overall was relaxed considering the drama of the past twenty-four hours. The show that night went off without a hitch, as did the next two. Leaving Nashville later that week, I felt a sense of relief. It was time to move on, and I was glad to be back on the road. Nothing bad *ever* happened on the road.

May 5, 1990

Dear Teddy,

I wish you would stop worrying about me! James is doing just fine and the stuff that you're hearing about him messing up and cancelling shows is nonsense. That Rolling Stone reporter is just trying to stir things up. That's how they sell magazines!! I mean, James blows off steam with some grass or a beer sometimes. Big deal! You have no idea how much pressure he's under. Only a couple of shows were cancelled. Happens all the time. Oh yeah, and let's start a rumor that the band is breaking up, that there is a lot of infighting. Ooh, that's more like it. It's all garbage, believe me. Besides, you should be spending less time following this crap and more time deciding which of the amazing scholarship offers you are going to take and figure out which college I'll be visiting you at in the fall.

Love from the road,

Jill

P.S. It doesn't look like I will be able to make it back for your graduation next month. Nomad's schedule keeps changing so don't count on me, okay? I'm sorry, but I know you hate that pomp and circumstance shit even more than I do!

# Jill's Journal

J & A are fighting all the time. I sometimes wonder if I'm the cause. That sounds so conceited when I read what I just wrote, but honestly? I look up sometimes and catch Alex watching me with this weird look. Likes he's ravenous and I'm some tasty morsel that he wants all for himself. I don't know if James is picking up on this. Probably not or they would be fighting about more than just Nomad. I sure can't bring it up to James and what would I say to Alex anyway? Um, I'm not sure if you like me or not, but don't. Okay? Crap, I don't know. Maybe this will all pass. Everyone is just freakin' exhausted.

## Chapter 13 - *Hard to Handle*

I wish I could say that things got better after that, but I can't. The arguments between the two brothers started up again just a couple of days after we left Nashville. Creative differences between the two had always been fairly common, but this was different. Slight disagreements escalated into full-on shouting matches, and more than once Brian and Steve had to separate them. It turned out that a nondrinking James was almost as easily provoked as a drunk one. Myles was screwing up more than ever, and James' rants against him became a daily occurrence. His anger spilled over with just about everybody that he came into contact with. No one was exempt, from wait staff to shuttle drivers. Unfortunately, that list also included me.

I thought about leaving several times a day, but kept holding out hope that things would return to normal. The music had never been better. The manager of the Blues Gang was guardedly optimistic about keeping Nomad on for the balance of the tour, roughly three more months. That was good news, but probably way too long for James to go without a real break. Despite the bickering and fighting, the guys managed to keep it together on stage, and audiences were once again cheering enthusiastically and demanding at least two encores at the end of each show. For one hour each day, everyone was at his best. But as soon as the guys left the stage each night, everything broke down.

Gone were the cozy talks and the card games. Battle lines drawn, Alex and Steve usually stayed to watch the headliners, while Brian and the Anderson brothers got high out in the parking lot. James and I usually just went back to our room to shower and watch TV. Well, actually I tried to watch TV, while James paced back and forth on the postage stamp-sized balcony, chain-smoking cigarettes.

He wasn't drinking and believe me, I watched him like a hawk. But he wasn't sleeping or eating much either. I begged him to open up, to talk to me, to tell me what was wrong and how I could fix it. But he wouldn't or couldn't confide in me. On our last day in Cincinnati, I had finally had enough. During the late afternoon sound check, I left the auditorium, scrounged up several dollars' worth of change and found a phone booth. I needed to hear a friendly voice, so I called Beth. I had not been in regular contact with her since she and my brother had packed up my belongings and moved everything to her basement months earlier. I had wanted to stay in touch, but other than a single letter and a couple of postcards, I had not, and of course it was next to impossible to reach me. I had lost track of my family as well. Traveling with James had become my full-time focus.

But if Beth was surprised to hear from me, she didn't show it. After holding Jesse up to the phone and encouraging him to show off his growing vocabulary for his 'Aunty Jill', she must have realized that my call was not entirely of a social nature. After handing off the baby to her mom, she listened patiently as I filled her in on the tour and kept silent when I started to open up about just how stressful everything had gotten. I remained dry eyed while I reported on how dysfunctional and out of control James had gotten, and when I finished, I heard her exhale slowly.

"Wow. Come home, Jill," she begged. "I'll wire you some money so you can take a train or bus. Just come home, please."

"I can't," I told her sadly. "James needs me. Nomad needs me. I can't just walk away." I cut her off when she tried to tell me that it wasn't my job to keep James sober.

"You don't understand, Beth," I told her. "I love him." Looking up, I saw James walking across the parking lot towards me. "I've got to go," I told her quickly. "I'll be in touch." And I hung up.

"Who was that?" James asked me as I rushed over to meet him.

"Just Beth," I answered brightly. "She said to say hi to you."

He slipped his arm around my shoulders and pulled me close to him. "Hi to Beth. Are you up for some coffee?"

"Sounds good," I told him and hand-in-hand we made our way to the hotel coffee shop. For the next hour or so I was almost successful in convincing myself that things would settle down. But I was so wrong. That final night in Cincinnati was the last time that Nomad would ever perform together.

## Chapter 14 - *Everybody Hurts*

I watched in shocked silence as the band van drove away the next day, leaving James and me behind. *This can't be happening*, I told myself. After a disastrous show in Cincinnati that ended with a whole audience booing, and James swearing and flipping everyone off, The Blues Gang's manager told Alex that Nomad was fired. Furious, Alex insisted on packing up and leaving that night, so an hour later, I climbed in the roadie wagon with John and James and we followed the rest of the band in the van. We drove all night, heading east. Around 6 a.m., it was clear that John was too exhausted to drive any further, so at the next rest stop, I agreed to take my turn behind the wheel.

I passed Alex in the parking lot on my way back from the rest room, and he didn't respond to my nervous, "How ya doin'?" I got back to the wagon and tried to familiarize myself with the standard transmission and the driving lights. Looking up, I saw that the van was pulling out, so I rushed to keep up. I had no idea where we were heading; I don't know if anyone did. I just followed along, strangely relieved to be driving again for the first time in six months, with John passed out in the passenger seat, and James nearly comatose in the back.

Close to noon, we pulled into a motel parking lot just inside the Harrisburg, PA city limits. Alex ran in to the office and came out minutes later. Following his instructions, I parked the wagon in front of room 23 and hopped out. Alex spoke briefly to John, but ignored James and me. Myles moved over to make room for his brother, who grabbed his duffel and hopped into the van. Finally, Alex approached James and they faced each other.

Suspicion and fear marked James' tired features while Alex seemed wary and looked sad.

That's when it hit me; the realization that this was the end of the line. The band was going on without us. I still don't know the exact words that were exchanged, but the bottom line was crystal clear. The guys were returning to New Jersey for a much-needed rest and time with family. It was hoped that James would give them some space by staying here for a few days and the room had been paid for to allow that to happen. No plans were final, but it was anticipated that the guys would look to recruit a new lead singer and allow James the time to rest up and get some help.

I was numb with shock, but James seemed to take the whole thing in stride. Steve jumped out and hugged me, and I waved goodbye to Brian and the Anderson brothers. Finally, I faced Alex. James had already walked away and let himself into the room, so it was just the two of us.

"Don't do this, Alex. Please, I'm begging you," I pleaded in a low voice. I did not want James to hear me begging. For a second, I thought Alex was going to relent, but the moment passed, and he was once again resolute.

"It's gotta be this way, Jill," he told me. "He can't have it all. No one can." And with that, he swung himself back into the driver's seat. The van roared to life and seconds later they were gone.

I let myself into the sad little room, a far cry from some of the lovely four-star places where we had been staying. Even my old motel was nicer than this dump, I realized, and for a second I let myself miss Fran and some of the low-rent regulars. But that was in the past, and I was here now. I crawled in the lumpy double bed next to my sleeping boyfriend, and we managed to sleep straight through, not waking up until the next morning.

The next day, I tried to paint a pretty picture from our bleak situation. I blabbered on about how good it would be to relax a bit, get some rest and sample some of the local culture. I omitted the fact that we were in a strange city, jobless and low on cash.

I tried to convince James that together we would be fine, great even, but it didn't matter. He wasn't buying it. He took to pacing out in the motel parking lot, smoking joints and cigarettes intermittently all night long, and sleeping until midday. Pot was always available from the sleazy night clerk in the office, and I paid off one of the maids, convincing her that a supply of fresh towels by the door was all we required each day, no need for tidying up or changing sheets. I was growing increasingly panicked. James made it perfectly clear that he needed space during his nightly jaunts.

"Just let me be, okay?" he would mumble as he shuffled out of the room.

For a while, I would relax. It was actually good to be alone for a bit. His presence had gotten so dark, so overpowering, that time alone was welcome. I would usually take a shower, brew a mug of tea with the little in-room unit and open the sliding door to let in some fresh air. The room had gotten very close with the air fairly pungent, laden with tobacco, pot and sweat.

After a while I would drift off, not really a good deep sleep, but enough to quell my nerves for a while. Around dawn, James would return to the room. Some nights he would creep in silently and crawl into bed beside me without a word. Other times, he would be needy and rough, pawing at my T-shirt and staking his claim to my body with an urgency that I found more sad than thrilling. We would both sleep for most of the morning, and finally stumble across the parking lot to the Denny's that served breakfast all day. We always sat in the same booth and ordered from the same waitress: bacon and eggs for James and French toast for me, washed down with a trough of coffee.

We liked our coffee black. I had learned to drink it that way on the road. A steady supply of caffeine was a necessity, but there wasn't always the opportunity for me to doctor up each cup with cream and sugar. "Hit me," I would plead to whoever passed by, gratefully accepting a few inches of fresh hot brew added to the leftovers in my mug.

But three days after being left by the rest of the band, I knew we couldn't continue to live in this limbo we had created. We needed a plan. We needed money. We needed to get the fuck out of Harrisburg. After watching him wiping up the remains of his eggs with his rye toast and finishing his third cup of coffee that morning, I felt the time was right to talk.

"James?" I began tentatively.

"Yeah?" he responded somewhat suspiciously.

"So what do you think?" I asked.

"About?"

"You know. Us. What are we going to do?"

"Oh yeah, that." He smiled. "I don't know, babe."

"But James? You know I love you, right?" After he nodded, I added, "And that whatever happens, I'll stick with you, right?"

"Yeah, sure."

"But James? We need a plan." I reached over and took his hand, which was drumming nervously on the Formica tabletop. "James, sweetheart. We need to get out of here," I ended with some urgency. For a split second, he looked around, like the threat was coming from inside the restaurant. Then his face relaxed.

"I know, Jill. Don't worry. We'll be fine. I'll think of something." That was the first promising thing he had said in days, so I decided to let it go for the moment.

After breakfast, we ambled down to the triplex cinema a quarter mile down the road from the motel. Darting across the busy road, we escaped into the cool darkness of the theater to view the only film we had not yet seen during our stay. It was quite forgettable, a back-to-the-future, alien adventure mash-up, but two hours passed as we sat there quite companionably sharing a large popcorn and a box of Whoppers.

We left the theater, blinking in the sunlight. Why is it that no matter what time of day you see a movie, when you leave you expect it will be dark out? We got back to the motel and decided to extend our outing just a bit by the deserted swimming pool. It was mid-May, too soon for swimming, so we snuck in and sat on the edge, dunking our feet in the chilly, leaf-choked water. I felt calmer than I had in days. Maybe things were looking up. Something good was bound to come from all of this pain, right?

Well, it turned out I *was* right. Opportunity came knocking. Not in the form of reconciliation with his band, or even a paid singing gig. In fact, at first it didn't look like much of an opportunity at all. Not to James. The next morning, I came back to the room after walking down to the convenience store for cigarettes and a six-pack of Coke. James was finishing up a phone conversation, and from what I could tell, it was definitely *not* with Alex.

"Yeah, well, I don't know. It sounds like a big commitment," he said. Then silence on James' part, followed by, "I'm not sure. Don't think it's in the cards. Why don't you try someone else?"

I assumed that the caller was trying to get James to join an ongoing tour or studio session. I knew for a fact that he had turned down lots of those offers over the last couple of years, staying loyal to Nomad, his band of brothers. But they had moved on without him, so why was he turning down a chance to get back to doing what he loved?

I gestured for him to fill me in, to get his caller to hold on for a moment, but he held up a hand right in my face. "Stop," he communicated, without saying a word.

Frustrated and pissed, I stormed out into the parking lot. *What the hell?* Were we going to stay in this crappy motel forever? Nomad was done, but I was certain that James had more to offer to the music world. I flopped down on one of the benches outside the motel office and watched the door to unit 23. I didn't have to wait long. James came out and sauntered over to me as if he didn't have a care in the world, sitting down next to me on the bench.

"Jill?" he ventured.

"What?" I was still furious with him.

"It's not what you think."

"Oh yeah? What do I think?"

"I don't know... that it's a job? Some music gig?"

"Yeah. It's not?"

"No. It's crazy is what it is."

"Tell me," I begged.

"It's nuts. Ron wants us to housesit for him."

"What? Ron?"

"Yeah. He's headed overseas with a new band and he wants us to stay at his house for a few months. Water his plants and watch his stuff."

"What? Why us?"

"Guess we're the only people he knows with all the free time in the world," he answered bitterly.

"Geez. When?"

"Now. As soon as we can get there."

"Where?"

"Up north," he told me. "Martha's Vineyard."

Well, that was beginning to sound more like it. A summer at the shore? Sand and surf? I could get into that, I thought, as I surveyed the cracked blacktop, rusted signage and the deserted parking lot. I was feeling pasty and pale. Some time at the beach sounded like just the ticket.

"But wait. Even with a free place to stay, there'll be expenses," I argued. Living in paradise had to come at a high price. "Can we afford it?" At some point, even our current budget accommodations would cease to be affordable.

"Yeah, Jill," he assured me. "Ron has accounts all over the island, so we can charge groceries and stuff. And he says he'll wire us some money for gas and the ferry. What do you think?"

I thought it sounded like heaven. But I was still tentative. "I don't know. It would give us a break, you know? Time to figure out our next move. We can't stay here forever," I reminded him.

"Okay, well maybe I'll call him back. We could leave by the end of the week, right?"

"Why not today?" I cried. "Let's get out of here."

So we packed our bags and loaded up the roadie wagon that Nomad had left for us, with the few belongings that we had left, including James' guitar. Next, we stopped at the closest Western Union for the $200 that Ron wired us, filled up the gas tank and began the eight-hour drive to Cape Cod.

## Chapter 15 - *Walking on the Sun*

We arrived at the ferry that would take us to our new home close to midnight. Traffic had been fairly light, and despite a few wrong turns, we found our way without a map. The only thing we hadn't really considered was the ferry schedule. We missed the last one by a few hours, so we had no choice but to spend the night in the wagon. We were down to slightly less than a hundred dollars after paying for gas, tolls and food for the day. Not to mention the fact that we were both totally exhausted. By the time I returned from the public restroom where I relieved myself and brushed my teeth, James was sprawled out on the front seat of the car and sound asleep. I let myself into the back, and after arranging a few of our belongings, fell asleep with my head propped on my trusty duffel bag.

The next morning, we were awakened by the sounds of excited tourists lining up for the first ferry of the day. We quickly moved the wagon into the fast-growing line, and were relieved when the driver of the car behind us was told that his would be the last vehicle allowed to board. I should have been more excited anticipating my first ferry ride, but it had been an exhausting and mentally draining last few months. This past week had been the worst, so all I felt was relief that there wouldn't be another delay.

I lined up at the concession stand, and soon after, returned to the wagon balancing two cups of steaming coffee and a couple of packaged coffee cakes. James was content to sit down below in the car for the half hour trip across the ocean, but I was eager to head up to the main deck. After gobbling down my breakfast, I hugged James before I left.

"You sure you don't want to come with me?" I asked him. "It's such a pretty day."

James convinced me to enjoy myself and told me that he was fine staying with the car, so I climbed the stairs to the top to enjoy the fresh salt air and the gorgeous views. It *was* a pretty day, and I spent my time looking out at the ocean and dodging a couple of the pesky seagulls that seemed convinced that I had food to share. I offered to snap a couple of photos for an older couple who had been taking turns posing against the bow of the boat.

"Where are you staying on the Vineyard?" the woman asked me. I had to admit that I had no idea, just that we were housesitting and had Ron's address written on a scrap of paper. But her husband was not put off that easily.

"If he's a summer resident, it's probably out in Vineyard Haven. Did he say it was Vineyard Haven?" he asked severely, and looked suspicious when I repeated that I had no idea where we were going once we left the ferry. He was shaking his head in quiet disapproval when I said my goodbyes.

I went below, and James awoke with a start when I hopped back in next to him. I chattered on about the couple and the gulls and wondered aloud just where Ron's house might be.

James smiled at me but said little. I could probably count on both hands the number of words he had spoken since arriving at the ferry nearly nine hours earlier. He had been so quiet and seemed kind of shell shocked. I realized again just how traumatic this whole thing had been on him. The band he had started and fronted for the last ten years was gone and his closest friends and his own brother had literally deserted him. If he wasn't a musician, what would he do? Did he have any other skills? *Besides that*, I told myself, blushing. I was used to scraping together a meager living for myself, and had always assumed that I would be trading in one minimum wage job for another every year or so. But James had been dreaming of a career in music since grade school, when a music teacher had plucked him from the choir and given him a solo role in the school musical. I vowed to give him all the space he needed as we got familiar with our new life by the sea.

*Right* by the sea, I noted with satisfaction as we parked in the driveway of Ron's summer home. Situated on the bay in Vineyard Haven, the large weathered grey cottage offered an unobstructed view of the water and a couple hundred yards of white sandy beach. Traffic on the island had been non-existent, and the beach was deserted. It was only 9 a.m., mid-week in the middle of May, so I figured we had beat the crowds. It only took us a couple of trips each to empty the wagon, and we easily found the largest of the three bedrooms that Ron had told us was ours for the duration of our stay. A queen-sized four-poster bed dominated the room, which adjoined a spacious bath featuring a claw-footed tub. I smiled slyly as I pictured a series of bubble baths for two this summer. A little romance was definitely in order! The cottage was furnished simply but luxuriously, in what can only be described as beach chic. In the main living space, soft, muted tones on the walls and cozy fabrics on the bleached oak furniture gave a welcoming feel. The large stone fireplace and the stunning views from the wall of windows facing the ocean were enough to convince me that we would be spending a lot of our waking hours in this room.

Heading into the kitchen, I panicked, realizing that my meager cooking skills would finally be put to the test after months of fast food, room service and catered buffets. I needn't have worried. James had obviously been investigating the stocked fridge and pantry and had already begun preparing breakfast for us. I happily found plates, silverware and glasses and set us up on the terrace facing the beach. The fresh air felt so amazing after months of hotels, elevators and packed auditoriums. I would need some sunglasses and maybe a hat if I planned to spend time outside, exploring the beach and playing in the gentle surf. James soon joined me, balancing a loaded tray, and we quickly dug into the delicious cheese omelet he had prepared, accompanied by links of spicy sausage and fresh fruit.

"Let's eat like this from now on. Home cooked meals! Let's not even step foot into a single restaurant all summer," I urged. I got a deep chuckle from James in return.

"That won't be a problem, darlin'," he assured me. "We can charge all the groceries we want, but Ron didn't say anything about restaurants."

Or bars, I realized. I would have to check out the liquor inventory to see just what I was dealing with. After paying for the ferry, we only had about $50 left. A partying James could blow that in a single night. *Not going to happen*, I vowed.

Ron had saved us. His call came at the most opportune of times. We had been at the breaking point just the other day: James breaking down and me strongly considering breaking up. Life at the beach suited us to a tee. We spent hours each day walking, picking up sea glass and dodging the waves, and James demonstrated his exemplary stone-skipping skills. And we talked, really talked, more than we ever had, even during our first few weeks together. We read on the deck and in the cozy main room, picking out books from Ron's well-stocked shelves, often in front of a roaring fire. There was always a breeze and nights could be quite chilly, but as we moved into June, the sun got stronger and the days got longer. The water stayed cold, but wearing bathing suits left behind by former houseguests, we body surfed and played on the beach like children. We sat out at night, holding hands and counting stars. James was quite adept with the monstrous grill, and we enjoyed swordfish and salmon and other local fish that I had never even heard of.

"I love fish," I marveled. Who knew? My mom's idea of cooking seafood was pushing a cookie sheet full of frozen fish sticks into the oven. I needed to call her, I realized guiltily. I assumed Ron wouldn't mind too much if a couple of charges for long distance calls showed up on his bill. After all this time, it would be awkward to make my first call home a collect one.

"I used to hate it, 'til I ate it," joked James. Growing up so close to the Jersey Shore, he was quite familiar with all sorts of yummy seafood. My culinary repertoire had improved somewhat, and I usually whipped up a salad and some veggies to complete our meal. One day, I got creative and prepared a tuna macaroni dish just like Mom used to make. I presented it proudly to James, who looked askance at the contents of the large glass bowl.

"What is this?" he asked suspiciously. "Macaroni, and is that tuna? But it's cold."

"It's tuna mac," I told him. "Haven't you ever had it?" It was a warm weather staple in the Griffin household. I couldn't believe James had never eaten any.

"It's pretty good," he admitted and polished off two large servings Thereafter, I made it just about every week all summer.

We had been going into town a couple of times each week and quickly got over our shyness at filling our cart with fresh fish, steaks and local produce in addition to the staples like bread, eggs and milk. James never even paused in front of the store's wine and beer selection, and I finally stopped my daily monitoring of the bottles of wine and spirits that Ron kept in his kitchen cupboard. Maybe we were out of the woods. But I tried to stay alert to any signs that James was slipping.

We must have made quite a sight, those first few weeks as we walked through the small town center. We learned the hard way that parking was at a premium and came at a hefty price, plus we weren't at all sure that charge account privileges extended to the town gas station. So most of the time, we walked the half-mile or so into the center of town. Until the swell of tourists more than doubled the population, we must have stuck out like sore thumbs in the conservative and upscale community. James' dark hair was down to his shoulders and he had let his beard and mustache grow as well. Still pale from years of rocking all night long and sleeping all day, his tattoos really stood out. He didn't have any shorts, so I fashioned him cutoffs from a pair of discarded jeans, which he wore with a black T-shirt or a faded grey tank that had probably been purchased from one of the souvenir shops we frequently passed. Oh yeah, and on hot days, James pulled back his hair with a strip of jean fabric leftover from my attempts to even off his shorts. Compared to the golden brown locals who sported pastel plaid shorts and matching golf shirts, James clearly didn't fit in. But people were for the most part friendly, and as James rarely gave a damn about what others thought of him, he didn't give his appearance a second thought.

But I was thinking enough for both of us. I really preferred staying home those days, as it was just us, and James thought I was sexy whether I was wearing someone else's swimsuit, a ripped T-shirt or nothing at all. Getting dressed to go into town was torture. All of the local women seemed to worship at the Lily Pulitzer altar and my skimpy wardrobe, consisting of ripped jeans, spangly black tank tops and a single cotton sundress, was just not cutting it. Then one day, I struck gold. I would have to thank our host someday for having the forethought to have a short, slight female houseguest at some point in the past, because I unearthed a drawer full of shorts and tops in a variety of pinks and greens. I had been rummaging around looking for sheets when I came upon this bounty of upscale summer wear. I shrieked so loudly that James came running into the house.

"Are you okay?" he asked me, then smiled as he quickly assessed the situation and identified the cause of my excitement. I was trying on a pile of used clothes with tears streaming down my face.

"I'm so happy. The shorts fit me," I exclaimed happily, as I pulled on pair after pair.

"I'm glad, Jill. I really am," he told me. "But you always look good. Why is what you wear so important?"

What could I say? That growing up, I never could afford to wear the same labels as the cool, popular kids? That all I ever wanted was to fit in, to blend? That I was embarrassed that I didn't look like I belonged here or anywhere? That so much of my puny self-esteem focused on my physical appearance? All of the above, okay? But how do you tell that to someone who has always stood out, yet always fit in? Someone who will never be just a face in the crowd? You don't. So I lied.

"I'm just so sick of all my clothes. I can't wait to wear something that hasn't been in my duffel for the last six months." I jumped up and hugged James tightly. "Let's make this the best summer ever," I whispered in his ear.

"Sounds good to me," he answered, then swept me up and carried me out of the unused bedroom into our um, well-used one.

## Jill's Journal

I love living at the beach. Maybe when James makes it big someday, we can get our own place here!! We wake up every morning to a hazy mist that burns off by mid morning and we fall asleep listening to the crashing waves. The gulls, the salt air, the pounding surf....it's the best place I could ever imagine. I could definitely get used to living like this. I know James misses the road, but every day he seems a little more relaxed. I just don't want this summer to end. I am trying to live in the present and most days, I actually am.

Be here now

Seize the day

Carpe something

## Chapter 16 - *Right Here, Right Now*

One night after dinner and a moonlit walk on the beach, we came back into the living room and instead of reaching for a book or the TV remote, James disappeared upstairs and returned carrying... his guitar. It was the first time I had seen it since the day we arrived on the island and James had shoved the case under our bed. It felt faintly nostalgic, seeing him looking so comfortable as he perched on the edge of the sofa, cradling it in his arms. I was thrilled, but kept my tone light as I asked, "How does it sound?"

He responded by playing the opening chords to *Over You*, and I had to smile. *He's still got it*, I realized happily. He spent the next half hour or so picking away and experimenting with different chords and I put down the book that I had been half-reading and picked up my journal. I had continued to write in it over the last few weeks, and I smiled as I read over the last few entries. Such happy thoughts! I looked up and realized that James was watching me closely.

"Wanna share?" he asked with a sly grin.

"Why not?" I responded. I had never shared the contents of any of my journals with anyone, but I figured there was no time like the present. We had no secrets left between us. Hmm, where to start?

"Okay," I told him, "but if you laugh..."

"I would never laugh at you, Jill," he told me soberly.

"All right. Well, here goes nothing." I found a poem I had written a few months back about growing up, and I started to read it out loud. After a few stanzas, I looked up to see James staring at me in amazement. "What?" I asked him, once again feeling very self-conscious. "Is it really that bad?"

"No, Jill. It's really that good," he assured me. "What's it called?"

"*Jericho Road*," I told him. "Where I grew up."

"Read it again," James commanded and as I started, he began to strum on the guitar, a haunting melody that I couldn't identify. As I read the last line of my poem, he ended the song with a flourish.

"Wow. I love it. What's it called?" I asked him.

"*Jericho Road*," he responded with a smile. And that's how we began our songwriting collaboration. I unearthed a few of my older journals and started piecing together some of the random phrases and snippets that I had been jotting down for years. Who knew that I could actually write a song, or two or eleven? You write what you know, right? Well, apparently what I knew was pain and the isolation that comes with always feeling like an outsider. If James was surprised at the extent of my angst, he didn't let on. But he did ask lots of questions to make sure that he really understood the lyrics he was singing.

"I don't understand why you would do that," he told me one night, after we fine-tuned a song about how I cheated on a boyfriend with a one-night stand with a co-worker. That one act totally sabotaged our fledgling relationship. "That doesn't even sound like you."

But in my defense, it wasn't like I had firsthand knowledge of any healthy relationships that I could try to copy or anything. "I was just guessing. I never know what 'normal' is supposed to look like, so I just guess at it," I admitted.

"Hmmm. Guessing at normal, huh? I love that."

James spent hours each day writing music, and within a month or so, we had the makings of nearly a dozen songs. James played each one of them again and again for me, and I even tried to accompany him on the vocals.

"Too bad Alex isn't here to sing with you," I blurted out one night. At the sound of his brother's name, James grimaced and shook his head.

"We're fine without him," he assured me. But still.

Trying to inject a little levity, I added, "One more song and we can turn this into an album. Twelve is a good number, don't you think?"

"I started writing one a few nights back," he told me sheepishly. "I've been turning it over and over in my head since the night we met." Had James Sheridan written me a love song? Yes, yes, he had. With a little prompting on my part, James sang it to me.

*Dance with Me* was the sweetest ballad I had ever heard him sing. "I never knew what I was missing, until you said you'd dance with me."

Tears streamed down my cheeks as I hurried over to hug him. "It's our first night," I marveled. "We danced in the motel parking lot and you sang to me." And we hadn't danced since, I realized, unless you counted jumping up and down during the Blues Gang's sets.

"Dance with me," James whispered in my ear, and so we danced around the living room with him singing the song he had written only for me. I wanted to write a poem about how happy and cherished I felt right then. The next day I did, and I called it *Normal*.

A couple days before Labor Day, James got a call from an old friend who had tracked him down through Ron's office. Lenny was a sound engineer in Nashville who had been trying to get James into the studio for years. Apparently, a band that was going to be recording their second album in a few weeks was looking for a solid guitar player who could be counted on for backup vocals as well. It was a far cry from fronting your own band, but we couldn't afford to be choosy. Summer was nearly over, and we needed a plan. Ron assured us that our duties as house sitters were winding down and even offered to arrange for airfare for both of us. We decided to drive, however, so a couple of weeks later, we took the ferry back to the mainland and began the drive to Nashville. Lenny had wired James' first week's salary to him in advance, so we were feeling pretty flush. At the last minute, we took a detour to my hometown. It had been about nine months since I had been home, and who knew when I would get the chance again? It was only a couple of hours out of the way and anyway, how bad could it be?

Pretty bad, I quickly realized. Everything in my hometown, including my parents' house, seemed so small and dingy compared to the island paradise we had just left behind. My mother greeted us warmly, but I could tell she was anxious. My father barely acknowledged us. I guess I could understand. I mean, we showed up late that afternoon, after calling from a pay phone only a half hour away. Although we were tanned and healthy looking after three months on the island, James' long hair and tattoos must have been a real turnoff to my straitlaced parents.

"You're so skinny," my mother kept fretting. "Haven't you been eating?"

I assured her that I was fine and that I wasn't 'on the drugs.' She was shy around James, who normally could charm the pants off of just about anyone, especially women. Teddy came home in time for dinner, so we crowded around the kitchen table, with James sitting in Susan's old chair, and ate meatloaf, green beans and roasted potatoes. James happily agreed to seconds, and my mom jumped up to serve him.

"I'd like more too, if anyone is interested," my father remarked loudly, and my mom stopped in mid serve and hurried over to scoop the remaining potatoes onto my dad's plate. Nothing had changed with my folks, but why would I imagine that they would have? I offered to help my mom with the dishes while my dad returned to his recliner, popping a can of beer on the way. James wandered outside with Teddy, and I could see them talking down at the edge of the driveway. Teddy was almost as tall as James, I marveled. I was anxious to hear what my little brother thought of my boyfriend. I hadn't brought anyone home since my prom date in high school, so this was a really new experience for me.

"Is he nice to you?" my mom whispered to me as we stood side by side in front of the sink, with her washing and me drying.

"You don't have to whisper," I told her. "But yeah, he's really nice. The best, Mom."

"You seem different somehow," my mother said.

I patted her hand. "I'm happy, Mom." *Wow, what a concept!*

"Well, okay then," my mom replied and that was the end of our bonding moment. I asked about Susan, but my mom hadn't heard from her in weeks, so there was nothing much to report. We were never much of a dessert family, so when I suggested going out for ice cream, my mom looked confused. "Now? So late?" As it was almost 7:30, I had to smile.

"Yeah. C'mon, Mom," I answered. "Take a walk on the wild side. You love the strawberry ice cream at Knudsen's Dairy Bar."

"Well..." I could see her wavering when I caught the menacing look my father gave her. "No, I'd better not," she said slowly.

"I'll bring some home for you," I promised. "Dad, how about you? What's your pleasure?" His return grunt could have been interpreted as anything from "I'll pass," to "Vanilla, please," so I decided to take it as the latter. "Coming right up," I told him with a tight smile, and I went out to my old car and squeezed in between James and Teddy. We decided to enjoy our ice cream there, and found a corner table in the old-fashioned ice cream parlor. James and Teddy were really getting along, I realized happily. The conversation ranged from cars (mine was running fine) to music (we all agreed that The Rolling Stones were the best rock band of all time and that The Who were highly overrated) to the cities James and I had traveled to. Ted was particularly enthusiastic about our upcoming trip to Nashville.

"Come with us," James offered. I could see Ted was tempted by the idea, but he reluctantly turned it down. He was starting his first semester at the state college and didn't want to jeopardize his scholarship. "Yeah," James told him. "Stay in school."

My brother responded with a sly, "Don't do drugs."

James smiled and offered, "Just say no."

I decided to join in the fun, but was laughed at when I came up with, "Only you can prevent forest fires." All in all, it was a pleasant hour away from Jericho Road, and I was not very anxious to return, but we finally did. My mom was happy with the ice cream we brought her, but as my dad had already turned in by the time we got back, I put his cup of vanilla in the freezer.

Not wanting to rock the boat, I agreed that James bunking in with Ted made the most sense as there was a second twin bed in the room. I slept alone in the childhood room that I had shared with Susan. The comforter and curtains were the same as back in the day, and I recognized the paint color on the walls as 'peach sherbet'. Beth and I had painted my room right after Susan left for the first time. We made a real mess, but got most of the paint on the walls, while my dad offered sage advice of the 'you missed a spot' variety. *Ah, good times!* I had convinced Ted to take the second bed so I could squeeze in a table that I had dumpster-dived for, and that had served as my writing desk for a few years.

That night, I half expected James to pay me a midnight visit, but I woke up alone hours later, with sunshine pouring in. I lay still, and it took me a few moments to realize just where I was. After being on the road for so long, I had really enjoyed waking up each day in the same place on the island. It was only the day before at about this time that we had left, but it already felt like an eternity. I could hear a low rumble of voices coming from the kitchen, with one high-pitched one. *I know that voice*, I realized and raced out in my T-shirt and bikini underwear to find Beth and Jesse at the kitchen table with James and Teddy. My mom was bustling about pouring coffee and offering everyone more juice. Beth shrieked at the same exact time I did, and we hugged it out, best friend style.

"Wow, James. He's awesome," she whispered. "And you... You look great, but don't lose any more weight."

"I've missed you," I told her. "And look at that little man of yours!" I knew he wouldn't remember me, and I've never actually been a kid type person, so I approached the toddler with caution. But Jesse had other ideas. As I knelt down in front of him, he turned and burrowed himself back into James' lap. Lucky kid!

"He's shy," James told me, ruffling his blond curls. "We need to have one of these," he added with a grin. Yeah, no.

"Yeah, Jilly. I want to be an uncle," Teddy teased and high-fived James.

"You guys are a freakin' riot," I told them. *A baby, just what I need.* Looking around, I noticed that the plates covering the table had remnants of maple syrup.

"What's cooking?" I asked hopefully.

"James made the most delicious pancakes," my mom trilled, smiling happily at my lover. James grinned back at her. Cuddling Jesse, hanging with Ted, charming my mom and Beth... it was obvious that James was fitting in better than I was.

"There's some batter left, dear," my mother began, but I cut her off.

"I'm not hungry. Besides, we need to get going," I said for James' benefit.

He looked surprised. "We don't have to rush, Jill. Lenny isn't expecting us until the end of the week." If he noticed the glare I sent him, I wouldn't know because my mother clapped her hands with glee.

"Well, it's settled then. You're staying." The next hour featured embarrassing tales of my misspent youth narrated by Ted and Beth, ending only when James agreed to get his guitar and play for us. As soon as he walked out to the car, patiently holding Jesse's chubby little hand in his, I turned on everyone left in the room.

"Knock it off," I hissed. "I'm not enjoying being the butt of all your jokes."

"But Jilly—" Mom started.

"But nothing. I mean it. James already knows what a fuck-up I was growing up. You don't need to make it worse," I growled. My mom winced at my choice of words and shrank back in her seat.

"Take a joke, Jill," Ted warned. "We're just kidding, for Christ's sakes."

Beth just shook her head at me and turned to smile at her son as he walked in, still holding hands with James. Great, everyone was disappointed with me. Some things just don't change. I used up the remaining batter on a single large pancake and started a second pot of coffee as James played all of the songs we had written. Ted simply gazed in admiration at his new best friend, but my mom and Beth were more vocal in their approval, especially when James told them that I had written the lyrics.

"You wrote these, Jill?" my mom asked in amazement. "I never knew that you..."

"Could put two words together? Actually accomplish anything?" I asked heatedly.

"Jill..." James' tone was disapproving. "They like the songs you wrote. Just say thank you." 'Who are you?' he was clearly thinking. I was not used to being happy here, I realized. Jericho Road was never a place where I could relax and have fun. I hadn't thought anyone could.

"Sorry," I told everyone. "I'm just tired." Beth hopped up to fill everyone's coffee cups, and the conversation turned to more neutral topics like Ted's course load at college and Beth's new part-time job in a dental office.

I began to relax and tried to enjoy myself, but was glad when Beth announced that she had to get Jesse home and down for his nap. I walked her out to the car as she held the sobbing toddler in her arms. "James, James," he cried, trying to escape from his mothers' arms.

"James is great, Jill." Beth fastened Jesse in his car seat. "Don't fuck this up," she warned.

"I'll try not to." I waved as she drove away. "Stay in touch," I mumbled to myself as I wandered back inside. *Time to go*, I vowed. My father wouldn't be home from work for a couple more hours, but it probably wasn't worth our waiting for him anyway.

I went back to my room and gathered up the few things I had left lying around. I wished that Beth had thought to bring me some of the clothes from my stash in her basement, but decided against calling her. I found a couple of sweaters I had left behind a few years ago and went back into the living room, where James was in a lively conversation with my mom and brother.

*Everyone's so freakin' chatty*, I thought bitterly. *We need to get out of here.* My mood couldn't get much worse. I hugged my mom and promised that I would be better about staying in touch. Ted's parting words really pissed me off.

"Don't be an asshole." He shrugged at my look of surprise. "You know what I mean, Jill," he told me cryptically, and shut the passenger door as I settled in. I fumed silently as we drove through the crumbling mill town where I had grown up. Once we got on the Interstate, I looked over at James.

"What were you guys talking about just now?" I asked him suspiciously.

James wrinkled his brow and confided that Ted had offered to switch cars and allow us to take 'my' four-door sedan to Nashville. Although it was a beater, it was slightly newer and in considerably better shape than the wagon we were riding in.

"Why didn't he ask me?" I asked in amazement. "It's my car. I would have said yes, for Christ's sakes."

But James was adamant. "Your brother needs a way to get back and forth to school," he told me. "He can't afford to be without a car or pay for any expensive repairs."

"Neither can we," I said heatedly, and then lapsed back into silence as James drove south.

A few minutes later, he turned and looked at me, grinning. "Did we just have our first fight?"

I looked at him in amazement. "Our *first* fight? You're kidding, right?"

Chuckling, he reached over and pulled me close, and I leaned stiffly against him. "Okay, our second fight," he allowed, and for the first time since I woke up that morning, I was really able to relax. We drove in companionable silence for a while before James spoke up. "You can't let' em push your buttons like that, darlin'."

"What do you mean?" I questioned lazily. I had been on the verge of nodding off.

"Your family. Beth. You know what I mean. You were kinda pissy this morning," he told me.

I was about to get heated again and defend myself, but I wasn't in the mood to argue. "Yeah, I guess you're right," I admitted and then slept, leaning against him for several hours.

When we stopped for gas and a bargain motel near the Virginia state line, I gobbled down a fast food burger and slept restlessly, tossing and turning all night. The next morning, we hit a Waffle House and consulted a map as we lingered over our breakfast and a pot of coffee. We could push it and arrive in Nashville that night or divide up the trip and get there tomorrow. As we would have a free place to stay in Nashville for the duration and our cash supply was again in jeopardy, we decided to drive straight through. After James made a quick collect call to let Lenny know about our plans, we relaxed with one more cup of coffee.

"Our big adventure." I smiled at James.

"I love you, babe," he said with a grin.

"Love you more," I said, smiling back at him. And off we went.

## Chapter 18 - *Linger*

What can I say about our eight weeks in Nashville? Well, to start with, it was nothing like our first trip there just six months earlier. Honestly, it was like a whole different city. Gone were the large venue and the four-star accommodations, the top-notch caterers and the concierge service. In their place, we had a room in a row house downtown that Lenny had found for us. It didn't cost us anything, which was about the best thing you could say for it. With the shared bath down the hall and the lumpy double bed, it felt like the place where I had been living last year, before I went out on the road with Nomad. There wasn't even a hotplate, so we couldn't so much as boil water.

The work was good, however. The recording studio where Lenny worked featured state-of-the-art equipment, and the band that James was working with had topped the charts with their first release the year before, so the budget was big and the resources plentiful. Being rock and rollers, getting an early start meant it was midafternoon before things got started each day.

James and I generally slept in most mornings, and then we would roll out of bed (I mean that literally as the mattress sagged in the middle and we needed to perform some minor gymnastic moves in order to extricate ourselves from its clutches) and head out for a late breakfast, usually at the coffee shop across the way. Then we would return to our tiny room, take showers and throw on cleaner clothes. James would generally arrive at the studio right after Lenny and help his old friend get things set up before the other musicians arrived. I stopped going in with James as there was no room for me there, and there was nothing for me to do.

I started grabbing my journal and a cup of takeout coffee and spending a few hours in the park down the street or at the public library if it rained. Every few days, I bundled up all of our dirty clothes and dragged them down the street to a sketchy looking Laundromat. There was a takeout Chinese restaurant next door, so I munched on greasy eggrolls and drank hot, fragrant tea while our clothes tumbled round and round. I usually met back up with James around nine, and we would go for a bite to eat or join the rest of the band and studio guys at a nearby Mexican cantina that everyone seemed to like. A couple of times a week, we'd get comp tickets to a concert or a live taping (this was Nashville after all), so all in all, it was fun and very social, compared to our solitary summer on the island.

I was watching James carefully again as nothing says booze and drugs like a rock and roll band recording an album. He was getting high more than I had ever seen him do, but other than a beer or two, he didn't appear to be drinking much.

One night we were at Dirty Mary's with Lenny and a few of his guys enjoying Wet Wednesday's beer pitchers special, not to be confused with Thirsty Thursday's dollar shots night. I hopped up to clear the table in order for our overworked waitress to drop off a loaded platter of beef and bean enchiladas.

"Thanks," she told me gratefully. "You should work here. Are you looking for a job?"

*Was I?* "Sure," I told her. "I do need a job." I was getting really bored sitting around all the time. She sized me up and must have liked what she saw.

"C'mon with me," she said. "Let's go talk to Joe. He's kind of a prick, but not as bad as some of the guys I've worked with. At least he knows enough to keep his hands to himself. Oh, by the way, I'm Shelley."

"I'll be right back," I told James, who was deep in conversation with a couple of the guys, and followed after the fast-moving Shelley to meet Joe, who I apparently could count on to *not* be handsy. Minutes later, I had a job, or at least a trial job. I didn't *exactly* claim to have years of waitressing experience in so many words, but I didn't deny it either. I would work from 3-11, five days a week, with Sundays and Mondays off. I was given a couple of teeny tiny Dirty Mary T-shirts and an apron, but would need to wear my own jeans and shoes.

"Wear comfortable shoes," warned Shelley. "The guys won't be looking at your feet anyway," she added with a grin. "So, do you have a pushup bra?"

*Uh oh.* I promised to be back the next day for my first shift and rushed over to find James and the guys getting ready to leave. James and I were walking down the street to our room when I told him about my new job.

"I'm psyched," I gushed. "It's minimum wage, and they take out something called a tip credit, but Shelley says I should easily get $100 a night in tips. Can you imagine? $500 a week. We're rich."

James did not appear to be quite as thrilled.

"What's wrong? It's great, right?" Nothing. He appeared to be struggling to find the right words. "James, what?"

"Look, it's not what I would like to see my girlfriend doing, okay? Spending every night in a bar, with all those guys pawing at you? Hustling drinks for tips?" I remained silent, sensing there was more he wanted to say. "I just wish... I don't know, forget it! I don't have any right to.... Ah shit, whatever. Take the job, okay? It's not like I want you just waiting around for me every day. And we're only gonna be here for a few more weeks anyway."

Honestly? I was touched. I mean, I knew James loved me. He frequently told me that he did and generally treated me that way too. He was affectionate and sweet, and it was only natural that he would be protective of me.

"Don't worry about me, James," I told him. "I'll be fine. Anyway, Shelley will kick anyone's ass who tries to mess with me." I laughed. That was the end of that conversation, but the next night James showed up around nine and nursed a Coke at the bar until I finished my shift. And that became the new normal in our ever-changing relationship. He waited for me every night like that.

"Your boyfriend is hot. And sooo sweet. I can't imagine having someone care about me that much," Shelley told me, sounding wistful.

I agreed happily that James was just great. Dirty's was crazy busy most nights, but I always knew when James arrived. I would look over at the door, and seconds later he would walk in and amble over to the bar, guitar slung over his shoulder.

After making sure that I was present and accounted for, he took up his post and sat down to wait for me. He never acted jealous or anything and usually just ignored me as I raced around trying not to spill drinks and to remember everyone's orders. Most of our customers were regulars and word spread quickly that I wasn't 'available'. James was definitely staking his claim on me, and I was cool with that. Someone who had my back? That was new for me. I liked it.

Sunday was the only day we both had off, so we took to driving around and exploring Greater Nashville during the day. At night, we would often go to a movie or check out one of the restaurants that Lenny recommended. Every one of them featured live entertainment and great food. We were settling in nicely and started talking about our next move. The contract that James had signed would be up in less than a month, and we had no clue as to what we would do next. I was in favor of staying in town. I was bringing in enough money to support us until James lined up more studio gigs.

"Let's stay," I begged. "We love it here. We have friends and I make more money than I ever dreamed of. We could find a bigger place or maybe look for a better car? Huh? What do you think?"

The roadie wagon had been less than reliable and we'd had to have it towed back into town after it stalled out on us during one of our road trips. I knew that James had a sentimental attachment to the vehicle, as it was the last remaining link to his Nomad past. Well, that and his guitar. But James was noncommittal. Although he tended to speak about the future quite a bit, it was always 'some day,' not tomorrow. But I was enjoying the fact that we were both gainfully employed and vowed to make it last as long as I could.

One night, James showed up at Dirty's later than usual. He seemed preoccupied and didn't return my friendly wave. He was completely lost in thought, Coke untouched, when I finally made it over to where he sat.

"Hey you," I greeted him, leaning in for a quick kiss and taking the opportunity to sniff his breath at the same time. Nothing, no alcohol. Just a hint of tobacco. "You okay?" I asked him with a sigh of relief.

He was better than okay, he admitted, but declined to say why. "Later," he told me cryptically. It was weird, because James wasn't one to keep mum about how he felt, good or bad. Something was definitely up. The last hour of my shift really dragged, and finally during a lull, I got Shelley to agree to cover my tables and raced over to James.

"Let's go," I shouted and literally pulled him up out of his seat. "C'mon." Seconds later we were on the street.

But James stopped me. "Let's not go back there just yet, okay?"

I assumed he meant our shabby room, so I just nodded and we started walking in the opposite direction. Realizing he would tell me whatever he wanted to tell me when he was good and ready and not a second sooner, I kept quiet, and we strolled along holding hands for a few blocks.

Finally he turned to me. "I don't know how to say this Jilly," he began. "It's, wow, I don't know just what it is." He shook his head in wonder.

Suddenly I felt a chill. *Oh crap.* "Are you breaking up with me?" I asked with a tremor in my voice. "Did you meet someone else?"

James looked at me and burst out laughing. "Oh no, darlin'. It's not like that. It's good, for both of us. I promise." He held up his right hand. "Scout's honor," he added.

"You were never a scout." There was a park bench up ahead, and I steered him towards it. "Sit," I commanded. "Talk."

And so we sat and he talked and he kept on talking. It all came out in a rush. At first I couldn't understand what he was saying, but the more he told me, the clearer it became. He and Lenny had been fooling around in the studio for the past couple of weeks during breaks and before and after the band's recording sessions. James had confided that he had some 'new stuff', and Lenny was curious. James played him a couple of the songs we had written, and Lenny was really enthusiastic, so he convinced James to let him record them and now there were twelve rough tracks all ready to go.

"Ready for what?" I asked him with a lump in my throat. "What's going on?"

James hugged me and whispered in my ear. *"Guessing at Normal*, darlin'. My solo album."

I screamed loud enough for passersby to look at me in alarm. But they relaxed when they saw me jumping up and down and clapping my hands. Solo album? Yes! James just sat there on the bench, looking at me, with this huge shit-eating grin on his face. Suddenly I had questions.

"But wait, does Lenny think it's any good? I mean, I know it's good, hell, it's great, but does he think it's commercial enough? Will anyone buy it?" My random thoughts and musings, could they actually be anything anyone would want to listen to? Pay to listen to?

"Yeah, Jill," he told me, still grinning. "That's the best part. Lenny played the tape for the band and they loved it. Their

141

manager listened to it and he sent the tape over to their label and they went crazy. They want to sign me. I'm supposed to fly to New York on Friday for a meet and greet. Isn't that the best?"

That's when it finally hit me. It started to sink in. I collapsed on the bench next to James. The songs that we had made together, when no one wanted anything to do with either of us, were no longer something just between us. My poems and random phrases were going to be on James' solo album, and James would be signed to a recording contract with a label that most musicians salivated over. James was going to be big. I knew this to be true with all my heart. Deep down, I had always known it. I would have to let him go.

Tears steaming down my face, I looked up at the love of my life. "That's great, sweetheart," I told him. "I'm so proud of you," I added, trying to smile.

Ever perceptive, James held me at arm's length and spoke those three little words that I had been hoping to hear. "Proud of *us*," he told me. "We're a team, darlin', in case you hadn't noticed. Everyone knows that you wrote every word of those songs. You'll get full writing credit and your own contract, if you want. And we can talk all about it on *our* way to New York on Friday. And oh, yeah. You need to give your notice at the bar. You're not gonna need to wait tables anymore," he gloated. An album, a contract, New York? Everything was moving so fast, after being stuck in limbo for so long.

"Wait 'til I tell Teddy," I cried. "And Beth, and my mom! Wait, is it too late to call?"

"It's after midnight, babe," James told me. "Your calls are gonna have to wait 'til the morning."

"Okay," I consented. "But let's set the alarm. Oh wait, we don't have a clock. Is it too late to buy one? Oh never mind, I'm too excited. I probably won't sleep a wink all night."

But I did sleep that night, and the next day I called home and shared my good news with my mother and Ted. Then I called Beth, and she sounded pretty excited, despite the fact that Jesse had a serious ear infection again. I could hear him crying in the background.

"That's awesome, Jill," she told me. "Just the best. I always knew you... oh, who am I kidding?" She laughed. "I never saw this coming. Did you?"

I told her that I hadn't, and that I was just as surprised as anyone. I mean, maybe I always knew deep down that James would make it big somehow, but I sure never imagined that my songs would play such a role.

## Chapter 19 - *Crash Into Me*

Nothing in my twenty-two years prepared me for the six days we spent in New York. I had been there before, but only once. Beth and I had saved up and took a train to Times Square on New Year's Eve several years earlier. Just the two of us and 1.5 million of our closest friends waiting to watch the ball drop. We had hugged at midnight, and swore that we would return someday. And now, here I was! The record label reps were super. They had booked a junior suite for us facing Central Park, and told us repeatedly that if there was anything we needed, to just ask.

After a couple of days, I finally worked up the nerve to ask for what I really wanted—tickets to see the Rockettes at Radio City Music Hall. Corny, I know, but those girls just epitomized success and glamour to me, and I had always wanted to catch their show. That same afternoon, I got my wish. Marnie, one of the label's junior associates, and I watched spellbound from the third row.

"I'm sorry," I told her as we left the theater. "You must have pulled the short straw, huh? Having to babysit me?"

"No way," she insisted. "I'm getting paid and honestly, I've wanted to see this show myself. Besides," she added, "we would do anything to get your boyfriend to sign with us. He's gonna be big."

I repeated her words to James that evening, when we were relaxing in our spacious room prior to heading out to dinner with a few of the label execs.

"Big, huh?" James chuckled. "That'd be pretty cool, darlin'. Let's go see if we can make that happen." He stretched his arms and let out a long, satisfied yawn. Smiling, I climbed into his lap and we just chilled for a while longer, enjoying the amazing views and relaxing before making ourselves presentable for a night out. James looked amazing. Thanks to the label, James suddenly had a whole wardrobe of dress shirts, slacks, T-shirts and designer jeans.

I had confided to Marnie that I didn't know what to wear that afternoon as we walked back to the hotel. After placing a quick call to her boss, she took me to Macy's to pick up a couple of cocktail dresses and matching high-heeled pumps, as well as jeans and some pretty tops. On the way out, she must have seen me gaze longingly over at the lingerie department, and we popped in to scoop up some sexy new bras and bikini underwear.

"Of course, you don't really need a bra," she told me with a wicked grin. "And you could always go commando." At the sight of my horrified expression, she quickly added, "but let's not take any chances," and again pulled out her AMEX company card to pay for my selections. If this was what success was like, you could count me in, I decided.

When James and I walked into the restaurant a short while later, I was thrilled to see Ron had flown in to join us.

I ran into his arms and told him how much I had missed him. "But why are you here?" I asked him.

"I wouldn't miss this for the world," he told me. "When James told me he was going to sign, I knew I had to check things over first. I can't have my number one client sign a contract without me, can I?"

Wait, had James already told the label he would sign with them? What about me? Didn't I have a say? I tried to make eye contact with James, and somehow communicate that we needed to talk, but when he finally did look over at me, it was just to flash me a grin before he got pulled away to sit at the head of the large table with the big boys—and one big girl, I noted.

She was a tall, shapely blonde who made the power suit she was wearing look really sexy. I was relegated to one of the cheap seats, squeezed in between Marnie and a corporate bean counter from the label named Fred.

"Who's the blonde?" I asked Marnie, trying to sound casual.

"Oh, that's Sharon," she informed me. "She's my boss," she added, then promptly changed the subject.

Since I was not good at these types of affairs, I knew that there was only one way to make the evening more palatable. Cocktails. And keep 'em coming! An hour later, I was totally sloshed. Fred took off right after the main course, so it was just me and my girl Marnie holding down the fort at our end of the table. I lost count of the strawberry daiquiris we had consumed, but guessed at four apiece, when Ron slipped into Fred's empty seat a short while later.

"I dunno, Ronnie," I slurred. "Hmmm, four? Don't know. Don't care," I told him. I looked at Marnie, who was slumped over in her seat, looking sleepy and more than a little confused. "What do you think, Marnie, my dear?"

When she didn't answer, I told Ron quite seriously, "Maybe Fred coulda stuck around and counted for us. That's what he gets paid for, right?" I guess I had shouted out that last part, so I shouldn't have been surprised when Ron pulled me up out of my seat and dragged me out to the lobby with him. "Bye, James," I tried to call out as we left, but Ron shushed me and pulled harder.

"What the hell, Ronnie?" I hollered. "What's your problem anyway?" Ron pulled me over to a pair of chairs in the corner of the room and pushed me into one of them. "Christ, dude," I complained. "Lighten up."

Sitting in the chair facing me, Ron's firm hands on my shoulders kept me from slumping forward and his tone was stern as he warned me, "Don't screw this up, Jill. I mean it. James is about to sign a multi-million dollar recording deal tomorrow. This is huge. You can't blow it. I won't let you."

Millions of dollars? What the hell was he talking about? For my songs?

"Are you crazy?" I screamed back. "'We've only been here a few days. James can't possibly be ready to..."

"Oh, he's ready," Ron countered. "While you've been sightseeing and shopping, James has been hard at work fine-tuning his songs and..."

"My songs, Ron," I spit out. "They're mine. I wrote them. They're mine." I started to sob. It had been a long evening, and I was smashed.

Ron looked at me sadly and shook his head. "Well, tomorrow they'll belong to the label, so you had better pull yourself together if you want to be part of the deal," he advised me sharply. "Let's get you some coffee, sober you up, okay? Wait here and don't move. I mean it, Jill. I'll get you some coffee and we'll get you back to the hotel."

So I sat there like a good girl while Ron fetched me a cup of strong black coffee from the hostess. He sat patiently and watched me choke it down, and then minutes later, held my hair back as I puked the entire contents of all of the evening's excesses into one of the potted plants in the doorway.

"Christ, you're a mess," he muttered as he climbed into a cab after me, and we sped down Fifth Avenue back to the hotel. Feeling less drunk but totally exhausted, I allowed Ron to lead me into the room and I even lifted my arms up and watched as he slipped off my dress and stiletto heels and tucked me into bed. Before Ron left the room, I was out cold.

The next morning, my stomach roiled at the smell of the room service coffee, and I managed only to crunch on a piece of dry rye toast. I was embarrassed by last night's performance, and assumed James was a bit miffed at me, as he was really quiet and seemed to avoid making eye contact.

"What time did you get in last night James? I didn't hear you."

"Huh, what? I dunno. It was pretty late and I didn't want to wake you." He shoved a piece of toast in his mouth and wandered into the bathroom. *Hmmm. Why the silent treatment?* I followed him and watched as he shoved the shirt he had worn the night before into a dry cleaning bag.

"Hey wait. I have a few things to be cleaned too." I tried to take the bag from him, but he wrenched it away from me. "Christ, James. What the hell is your problem?"

In response, he stormed out of the room. "I'm dropping this off at the desk myself. Fucking hotel keeps losing my shit." The door slammed behind him and I sank down onto the cold marble floor. *What the hell just happened?* I caught a whiff of something musky. Perfume? Was James using new cologne? I was *not* a fan, but decided to hold off on making my opinion known. He came back to the room a few minutes later and found me looking out the window at the New York City skyline. He came up from behind me and pulled me into a hug.

"Sorry, Jilly," he whispered. "I'm kind of freaking out here. It's a big day for me. For us," he added when he caught sight of my crestfallen expression.

So after showers (separate), a handful of Excedrin and a silent cab ride over to the label's office, James Ryan Sheridan signed a four million dollar recording contract, promising full and total allegiance to the label, and Ron earned a six-figure commission from his favorite client, who he had never given up on.

"Congrats, Jamie. Welcome to the family," Sharon proclaimed, and everyone cheered.

"Jamie?" Where had that come from? James was *always* James, not Jim or Jimmy and certainly not Jamie. Even his mother called him James. But the man of the hour was decidedly casual as he explained to me that Sharon felt that 'Jamie' Sheridan was a better stage name for a solo artist.

"It makes me more approachable to my fans, Jill," he told me confidently. "It will resonate better with my target audience." *Sharon says so, huh? Sharon with the big boobs and the red lipstick? And the overpowering perfume that I recognized from earlier? Why was her stinky scent all over my boyfriend's shirt?* I was glad that we would be leaving in a few days. I'd had enough of that brassy bitch to last me a lifetime.

"Well, I'm sure Sharon knows what she is talking about, Jamie," I replied with a smirk, and watched as James went back to join the group for a celebratory lunch. I had decided to pass in favor of a nap, as I was certain that the smell of food would do me in. A couple of days later, we flew back to Nashville so that James could put the finishing touches on *Guessing at Normal,* calling in a host of fellow musicians to help out. He never said, but I knew he had left messages for Alex to join him in the studio, and held off as long as he could just in case his twin showed up. But Alex never called and never showed, so *Guessing* was produced and wrapped up that fall and at that point, there was nothing left for us to do but wait and see what would happen next.

*December 8, 1990*

*Dear Mom,*

*The meetings in New York went really well. James signed a huge recording deal with one of the very best labels. I can't tell you the exact amount cuz that would sound like bragging, but I can tell you there were an awful lot of '00000's !! Please let me know if Dad is still missing a lot of work, okay? I can send you some money, but I'm sure he won't want it, if it comes from his trampy daughter. Ted told me he called me that. It's okay, I don't care what he thinks of me anymore. So, tell him you won the lotto or something.*

*We are going to New Jersey for the holidays. I'm sorry to disappoint you cuz I had told you we might come there. But James wants to see his folks, so Beth will just have to take pictures of Jesse opening his gifts and send them to me. Honestly, you would think he was the only kid ever to believe in Santa. She keeps saying that it's the first Christmas that he really 'gets it', whatever that means.*

*So I'll see you in 1991, okay? Still no word from Susan, huh?*

*love you & Merry Christmas!*

*Jill*

## Chapter 20 - *Come As You Are*

So apparently, I *was* the type of girl you could bring home to Mother. Who knew? We had been staying with James' parents for a couple of weeks, and things were going really well. Mike and Kathy Sheridan were great, and I felt very welcome in their home. Mike was tall like his sons and with similar coloring, although he was mostly gray, and his skin was weathered from years spent working outside. It was easy to see where the twins got their good looks. He had a very easy way about him, and I immediately warmed up to him.

Kathy was a bit more reserved initially, but I soon felt very comfortable with the tiny auburn-haired woman who had given birth to the boys when she was roughly my age. She had stayed home with them until they went to high school and after that worked as a cashier at a local grocery store. Mike had been foreman of a factory in a nearby town for over 20 years, but had been downsized nearly five years before. Since then he'd worked at a big-box home improvement store, mostly outside in the landscaping department.

They were a really cute couple and still clearly in love after almost thirty years of marriage. Mike doted on his wife, and I noticed the two of them rarely missed an opportunity to touch each other in passing as they bustled about their Cape Cod style bungalow. I had asked them how long they had lived there.

"Almost thirty years, Jill. And if I have anything to say about it, we'll be here another thirty more. Can't you just see your mom, James? Pushing me around in a wheelchair, her in a walker?" Mike chuckled and hugged Kathy to him. She pushed him away and laughed, reminding him that he had better get started right away on a ramp for the front porch steps if it was going to be finished in time.

"Years ago," she told me with a twinkle in her eye, "this one was supposed to build me a hammock stand. He and the boys bought me a hammock from some mail order catalogue for Mother's Day. When I asked Mike what the heck I was supposed to do with it, he promised me that he would get started building a stand for me right away. That was twenty years ago and I'm still waiting, darlin'," she teased. Mike laughed along with her and swung her up in his arms and spun her around. "Put me down, you big dope," she protested as he kissed her cheeks and the top of her head.

James just grinned at their antics. "Well, you know what I have to say to the two of you, right?"

"Get a room," all three Sheridans shouted. I loved watching them. This was how James had been raised, I marveled. No wonder he was so loving and affectionate. I wondered what had happened in Alex's case? He was such a stiff! I couldn't imagine the type of girl who would put up with him.

We had driven to New Jersey after leaving Nashville. Once *Guessing at Normal* was a wrap, James had decided that waiting around for it to be released made no sense. He was antsy, and he felt that spending the holidays with his folks was a smart move for both of us. He had not seen them for over a year, but when he called from a pay phone, his mom was ecstatic about the visit that he proposed. Maybe home really was that place where they had to take you in after all.

When we showed up a couple of days later, neither of his folks seemed surprised that James and I were together. His mom let it slip that Alex had mentioned that I had joined James on tour last winter. If Kathy had made any type of advance judgment about me, she didn't let it show. I had not met a boyfriend's parents since high school, so I was a bit apprehensive. And it was pretty close quarters. The boys used to share the two tiny rooms upstairs, and James told me that they had always kept one room to sleep in and one to 'play' in.

"We just never wanted to be apart," he confided with a grin on his face and a distant look in his eyes. "Even to sleep. Alex was the first person I wanted to see in the morning, and the very last person I wanted to talk to at night. Until you came along, Jill."

So maybe I had been right all along, I realized. Alex was jealous of me; he saw me as a threat. I mean, don't get me wrong, I was not the first woman that James had fallen for. A long line of mostly tall, blond beauties had preceded me, but apparently I was the first one to join Nomad on the road. *Maybe I was different*, I thought as I surveyed the twin bed we would be sleeping in. We ended up shoving two mattresses together on the floor of one room and using the other as a little sitting area when we needed some time away from his parents. Originally erector sets and model trains had filled the space, to be replaced over the years with a well-worn sofa, a TV and a stereo. Remnants of those earlier days remained, with music posters still gracing the walls of both rooms, and discarded guitars and a banjo jammed into the closet.

Fortunately Mike had recently transformed the other closet into a tiny half-bath using his employee discount at the store. This convenience provided us with some much-needed privacy, although we still had to shower in the bathroom on the first floor. I loved prowling around the rooms, looking for clues to my boyfriend's past.

"Alice Cooper, huh," I laughed gazing upon the tattered poster that had been tacked up probably fifteen years ago. "Seriously, James? The Godfather of Shock Rock?"

"Hey, Alice was way ahead of his time, okay? Who were you listening to when you were twelve? Donny Osmond?"

I lunged at him. "Take that back," I warned him. "I never listened to him. Not ever." We wrestled playfully 'til things got kind of steamy. "Sshhh. Your parents will hear us," I warned. James jumped up and turned the radio on. The sounds of Top 40 rock filled the room. He came back to me with a sexy grin and joined me on the bed.

"Can I help it if you get so hot and bothered?" Then he started up in a whispered falsetto. "Oh Donny! Oh yeah, baby. Just like that. Oh yessssssss!"

"I don't sound like that," I protested. "You wish I sounded like that." I pulled his T-shirt over his head and grabbed at his belt buckle. He offered no resistance.

"Let's just see what you sound like now, darlin'," he chuckled and within seconds, our clothes lay discarded and for a while we forgot all about his parents and Guessing and Alex's ghost. It was just the two of us in that little room that afternoon.

I was really enjoying our time in New Jersey. Alex had chosen to spend the holidays catching up with an 'old friend' in the city. He had promised his mom that he would take the train down from New York and come for dinner and an overnight visit, but we had not seen him. It was just as well. I knew James was pretty nervous about what was happening to his album, and it was a lot easier for me to give him the support he needed without my nemesis around.

James had been abstaining from alcohol during our visit, and although I saw a few bottles of beer in the fridge, none was offered or consumed, at least not in my presence. One night James convinced his folks that we would take them out for dinner to repay them for all their hospitality. They protested, insisting that they were happy to stay in, but we ended up driving to the shore for fresh seafood at a restaurant overlooking the ocean.

After we were seated, James asked for a beer from the waitress. I saw his parents exchange a look, kind of a 'what are we going to do now?' look. Kathy asked for a Virgin Mary, and Mike and I opted for ice water. James raised his beer in a toast to all of us finally getting together, and to the future success of *Guessing*.

We clicked our glasses, with me and his folks holding our breath. There was a collective sigh of relief when James turned down the waitress's offer of a second beer, and instead switched to ice water. *He doesn't have a problem... he's in control*, I told myself.

After a delicious meal of shrimp cocktail and grilled swordfish, Kathy leaned over and gave me a hug. "You're so good for him," she whispered in my ear, and I knew she was crediting me with his apparent ability to control his drinking. I wondered just how many nights his folks had dealt with the drunken, belligerent James that I had witnessed for the first time eight months earlier in Dallas.

I hugged her back and although I wanted to reassure her that her boy was doing great, I didn't want to give her false hope either. "I'm so glad we came," I told her, and that would have to be enough.

During our visit, James and I had a chance to flex our domestic muscles a bit. James mowed the lawn and removed leaves from the hedges. He helped his dad repair their ancient snow blower and then spent hours cleaning the sidewalks and driveways of every house in the neighborhood after the first snowfall. I helped Kathy decorate the house inside and out for Christmas. The tree was beautiful and real! So much nicer than the fake plastic one my family had been putting up for as long as I could remember. One day I walked over to the grocery store where Kathy worked. I returned home with the ingredients to make beef stew for dinner and a sour cream coffee cake. I had shocked my mother when I'd called her to ask for the recipes.

"But Jilly, are you sure? How about making a cake from a mix? It would be simpler and you wouldn't…"

I cut her off. "Screw it up? Gee thanks, Mom. Glad you have so much faith in me."

"You know that's not what I meant. I just don't want to see you disappointed if it doesn't come out right."

"I know, Mom. Don't worry, okay? It'll be fine." *Geez. It's just a cake.* Before I hung up I promised that we would visit again soon. And I told her I loved her.

The cake stuck a little in the pan but it tasted pretty good, and the stew was a big hit. I told the hard-working couple that James and I would take over dinner preparations for the rest of our visit. Other than a couple of pizza and Chinese food runs, we did pretty well working side-by-side in the tiny kitchen. I spent a lot of my time reading the stack of women's magazines that Kathy had been stockpiling, searching for recipes that everyone would enjoy. I was learning that family mealtime was something to actually look forward to when it didn't include yelling, swearing and crying.

The more James kept saying how great it was to be home and what a welcome change it was from the constant travel, the more I could tell that he missed being on the road and that he was getting a little restless. But he was sober, and generally his mood was quite good. Most nights after dinner, the four of us played cards or board games, drinking a pot of coffee and eating the baked goods that I had prepared that day.

One night, Brian and a couple of James' pals from high school showed up and the four of them went out to the garage. I hugged Brian warmly and joined them briefly, but went back in the house as the musical instruments came out and a joint was passed around. They got pretty loud, and I could see his folks were nervous about the neighbors and their reactions to the music. I sat in bed and read for a while and finally fell asleep to the steady thumping of a bass guitar.

We all went to midnight mass on Christmas Eve and awoke the next day to a bright blue sky and more fresh snow. It was our first Christmas together, and I was grateful that we could afford to contribute to the pile of presents under the tree. James bought a state-of-the-art CD player for his folks and a large collection of CDs to replace the vinyl records they enjoyed. Mostly country and Southern rock for Mike and Broadway show tunes for Kathy.

"As soon as *Guessing*'s released, I'll send you a dozen copies," he promised. Kathy got all choked up at that, and Mike spoke for both of them when he told James how proud they were of him.

I had wanted to get something special for the Sheridans, and had been going crazy trying to figure out just the right gift. I ended up painstakingly copying all of Kathy's tattered recipes, including a few from my mom, and had assembled a snazzy-looking family cookbook complete with illustrations. Kathy was thrilled. I wasn't as creative when it came to a gift for Mike, but he seemed very happy with the leather work gloves that I splurged on after seeing him frequently wearing a ragged pair for the past weeks as he worked outside.

James and I had sent Teddy a check earlier in the month, with instructions to purchase something special for my folks, and to put the balance towards a more reliable set of wheels. I had shipped gifts for Beth and Jesse the week before, and she had already called me, sounding thrilled with the complete set of Disney movies on VHS and the assortment of designer jeans and tops I had chosen for her. I had guessed on the sizes after seeing her the last time, and it sounded like I did a pretty good job. She had finally lost the last of the baby weight, and was excited to have a new wardrobe to show off her slim figure.

When it came to shopping for my boyfriend, however, I was stumped. A few shirts and a pair of Doc Martens seemed so inconsequential compared to this whole new life James had given me. So with Kathy's help, I ordered passports for both of us, and they arrived just in time on Christmas Eve. It was my way of letting James know that I believed in him and that international success was in his future. I packed mine away, but

I tucked James' into a leather holder and wrapped it up. In hindsight, I wondered if quality leather items were really required to have *Genuine Leather* stamped in big gold letters, but it looked nice, and it was the thought that counted, right? I had no idea what James might buy for me and despite my continued snooping, I hadn't found a single thing. On Christmas morning, I unwrapped a warm cozy sweater from his folks and delighted in the volume of individually wrapped gifts that filled my stocking; useful things like lip gloss and gel pens. I saw James watching me as I finally got to the last of my stocking stuffers.

"Open it," he said with a grin. "That one's from me."

As I tore the paper from the tiny package, James came over and knelt down beside me. I looked up in surprise when I found a lovely engagement ring with a slim gold band and a beautifully cut oval shaped diamond. I don't know anything about carats or clarity, but it was the most beautiful thing I had ever seen. Tears streamed down my face as James slipped it on my finger, murmuring, "Marry me, Jill. Make me the happiest man on earth."

In response, I hugged him tightly and whispered, "Yes, James. I'll marry you. I love you so much." We hugged, kneeling on the floor, rocking back and forth. Kathy clapped her hands in excitement, and she and Mike came over and hugged me close.

"Welcome to the family," Mike told me. "This calls for a toast." I was relieved when I saw the bottle of sparkling cider that he was waving around. James had told his parents about his plan a couple weeks back, and Kathy had helped him pick out my ring.

I was stunned and happy and a little nervous, but I got caught up in the holiday spirit as a handful of James' relatives were due for dinner later that day. I peeled potatoes and chopped up celery and onions for the stuffing and even basted the turkey. The rest of the day passed quickly, but I managed to find the time to call my mom and then Beth, to share my exciting news. My mom sounded surprised, but she rebounded fairly quickly as the discussion progressed to the ceremony itself and the location for the reception.

"We'll try to help you out some," she confided. "I've been saving a little here and there."

I assured her that no monetary assistance would be necessary. After all, the second payment of James' advance would be coming soon and besides, we didn't really want anything all that elaborate. Beth was over the moon. It was easy to imagine her jumping up and down, as her breath was coming in quick gasps when she congratulated me.

"And don't even tell me that anyone besides me will be your maid of honor," she threatened.

I promised her there was no one else I could even imagine standing up for me and since I hadn't seen my sister Susan in over a year, I figured that was a safe bet.

"You could be a June bride," Beth told me. "We need to go dress shopping. When are you coming home?" Home? Where *was* that anyway? In New Jersey with the Sheridans? At Ron's house on the island? Back on Jericho Road? I shuddered.

"I'll have to get back to you on that, my friend," I told her. "I need to talk to James first."

At the sound of my fiancé's name, Beth's tone became low, conspiratorial. "Is he, you know? James, I mean..." she whispered.

"What?" I teased. "A Republican? No, I don't think he's ever even voted."

"Jilllllllll!! I hate when you do that. You know what I mean. Is he drinking or what?" she cried in exasperation.

"No worries," I assured her. "He's fine. We're fine. We're getting married!!" After promising to at least consider her toddler Jesse for the role of ring bearer, I hung up and turned to James. He was deep in conversation with his dad and Uncle Richard, but he grinned and gave me a big thumbs up. Vowing to pin him down on some wedding details after the holidays, I joined Kathy and her sister, James' Aunt Donna, in the kitchen. We worked together on the finishing touches for what turned out to be a great meal. I was turning into a regular Suzy Homemaker.

**1991**

## Chapter 21 - *(Everything I Do) I Do it for You*

Turns out that not much discussion was required re: the Griffin/Sheridan nuptials after all. Two days after Christmas, Sharon called from the label. They needed James out on the West Coast right away for some meetings and post-production stuff and told him that he should plan to be there for a couple months at the very least. James got it into his head that we should be married before we went. It was apparently a big deal to him.

We had been living together for nearly a year at this point, so I reckoned that a wedding ring couldn't change very much. On the spur of the moment, we drove to Atlantic City with Kathy and Mike, found one of those all-night wedding chapels and tied the knot on New Year's Eve. Kathy was initially not in favor of the plan, and wanted us to hold out for a spring wedding with both families present, but James was adamant, so she and Mike walked me up to the altar where James was waiting for me.

I wore one of the dresses from the New York trip and carried a bouquet of pink roses with baby's breath. James sported a white dress shirt with a skinny black tie and jeans. I had cut his hair right before the holidays, and I managed to squeeze in a haircut and manicure that morning myself. We repeated the words that the chapel director recited by rote and seconds later, we were husband and wife!

James swept me up in his arms and carried me back down the aisle since we didn't have a threshold to call our own. The 'Loving Arms' staff had a tiny white cake and a bottle of lukewarm champagne waiting for us, so we cut the cake and took a swig of the horrible bubbly drink. James didn't even touch the glass to his lips, a fact that his parents and I noted happily. In the one Polaroid photo that the chapel took of us that evening, I look kind of dazed, but the camera always loved James. He had that sexy grin that always did me in, and his eyes were so blue.

I wished that we had a real wedding album and a few more guests, but what can you do? Alex had called the night before, and I answered the phone. He was drunk and was rambling incoherently about marriage and what a big step we were about to take. I think he said, "I love you, Jill," just before I handed the phone over to James. My mind was racing as I watched James listening to his twin. *Did Alex really love me?* Was that why he was always so awkward around me? I remembered our kiss in Dallas and shivered. I had probably let it last just a teensy bit too long, I realized. When James finally hung up, he told me that Alex was going to try to join us the next day. But he was a no-show, and that didn't surprise me in the least.

So it was just the four of us on our special day. We left the chapel and found a steakhouse that looked promising. We made it an early night and went back to our hotel where we had booked a couple of rooms. Although James and I joked about the fact that it was indeed our wedding night, we fell asleep quickly and didn't actually consummate our marriage until early the next morning. Lying in James' arms felt wonderful, and I was feeling pretty jazzed about our upcoming trip to LA.

"Promise me," I murmured softly. When James didn't answer right away, I thought he might have fallen asleep.

But then he stirred and asked a bit cautiously, "What, Jill?"

"Promise me, that we'll always make time for this, for us," I responded, sweeping my hand around to indicate our rumpled bed and our semi-naked bodies.

I felt him relax. With a chuckle, he assured me, "Oh, we'll *always* have time for *this*, darlin'."

After a quick shower, we met up with my in-laws for a lavish New Year's Day brunch, and then drove home to pack for the trip to LA. I called my mom to tell her that her daughter was now a married lady and promised her that we would renew our vows and have some sort of celebration that spring back home.

She took the news better than Beth did. After my best friend finally realized that I was not kidding and that I had indeed gone and gotten married without her and that I wasn't even pregnant, she told me that I was the most selfish person that she had ever met. She went on to say that James had changed me (not for the better) and that she didn't want to talk to me ever again. I hung up the phone in tears, but James took action when he saw how upset I was. A short while later, he got Beth on the phone and begged her not to blame me, that it was all on him. He also promised to arrange airfare for her and Jesse to come out and visit us later in the month, and she said she would 'think about it' and to put me on the phone.

"Beth," I began tentatively. "I'm sorry. I mean, I understand that you wanted to be there for me and I really appreciate that, you know? It would have been great to have you there, to stand up for me like you always have. Everything just happened so fast. I'll make it up to you, I swear. But please, be happy for me, okay?"

I held my breath, waiting for her to respond and finally, she did. "I *am* happy for you, Jilly. More than I can say. I just, I don't know. I wanted one of us to have it, you know? The big wedding, the white dress, champagne and chocolate covered strawberries? It sure won't be me, but I wanted it for you. I love you."

I could hear her starting to sob. I joined in and we shared a good long distance cry that turned to semi-hysterical laughter when I repeated 'chocolate covered strawberries' in a goofy voice. I promised Beth that I would see her next month and hung up feeling relieved. I saw James watching me from across the room.

"You okay, darlin'?"

"I'm great," I assured him. "Never better."

So we packed up our things once again, realizing that we would need to buy new clothes once we got out there. Mike and Kathy drove us to the airport, and after many hugs and kisses and promises to write, we boarded our flight for our next big adventure. Nothing would ever be the same again.

## Chapter 22 - *Californication*

The label had arranged a small, furnished house for us in a quiet suburb less than a half hour from their LA offices. Most days, a car would be dispatched for James mid-morning, and he took to spending hours with the execs, talking launch strategy and marketing plans. With no car and nothing to do within walking distance, I was spending most of my time tanning on a chaise lounge in the back yard, or zonked out in front of the TV. After a couple of weeks, I was lonely and getting really pissed off.

"What do you do all day?" I greeted him one night rather peevishly, as he came rushing in. "Hard day at the office, dear?"

"It *is* hard work, Jill," he responded crossly. "What do you think? You cut an album and just put it out there?"

*Yeah, that* is *what I thought*. Screw him.

"Well then, *Jamie*, why don't you educate me on just what it takes?" I challenged him.

He crossed the living room and disappeared down the hall towards our bedroom, muttering something about not having time for this shit.

"Hey, what the hell?" I took off after him. "Where are you going? I was talking to you," I added as I noticed him rustling through his closet. I sank down on the edge of the unmade bed. Was he heading out again? "You just got home."

James was being rather evasive, I thought, as he turned to answer without actually looking at me. "It's a business thing,

Jill," he told me. "I know you've been alone all day and I promise I'll make it up to you."

"When? Make it up to me when?"

"Soon, okay? I promise. But right now, I've got to get moving. I have to..." He stopped when he heard a car pull in the driveway and give three loud toots of the horn.

I crossed over to the window and looked out at the driveway. A flashy looking red sports car was idling, and the driver was Sharon, all blond hair, big boobs and collagen-plumped lips. Marnie had told me that she was divorced and in her mid-thirties. As one of the few women on the label's executive roster, I foolishly had thought we could be friends, do girl things, you know? But she had rebuffed my overtures and seemed to focus all of her attentions on her male colleagues and, of course, James.

"Her lipstick matches her car," I noted drily.

"What?" James looked up in alarm as he tucked a fresh shirt into his jeans and found a belt. "What about lipstick?" he asked.

"Never mind," I told him. "Hey, have a ball and be sure to tell Sharon I said hi."

Not picking up on the sarcasm dripping in my words, he raced by me, giving the top of my head a quick peck in passing. "You're great," he told me over his shoulder. "Think of something you want to do this weekend, okay?"

Murdering Sharon and smacking the crap out of James were about the only things that I really wanted to do at the moment, but I don't think that's what he had in mind. Without even waiting for my reply, he was out the door, slamming it behind him. I went back over to the window to watch him jump in beside Sharon, and I continued to watch until the little car roared away and out of sight, because when you want to pour salt on your wounds, you want to be sure to empty the whole shaker.

"Asshole," I fumed. "Bastard." I collapsed on the bed. I was lonely and bored to tears. The only guest we'd had since moving in nearly two months before was Beth. She came out on James' dime and stayed for four wonderful days. Her mom had graciously offered to keep Jesse and allow Beth a little 'me' time. We had so much fun! The label pulled out all the stops for us. They provided us with a driver, tickets for a few TV show tapings including Beth's fave, *Rosie*, dinner reservations each night at all the top-rated restaurants and even a day at Disneyland. James was able to join us for dinner twice, but got called away on Beth's last night, just as we were being seated. I followed him out to the sidewalk, leaving poor Beth all alone.

"Why do you need to go?" I asked him heatedly. "This is bullshit. My friend came all this way and..."

"Yeah, she's *your* friend. *I* have to work. Someone has to."

"Screw you, James Sheridan," I hollered after him. "I work. I wrote all those songs, in case you forgot."

"As if you would ever let me forget," he returned with a smirk. *Oh. Hell. No.* Holding his hand up, he hailed a cab. "I'll leave you the car," he told me. "Just tell Carl and he'll take you anywhere you want to go."

As the cab pulled up to the curb, I turned to go back in the restaurant. I hated to face Beth after what she had seen. I stopped when James called my name. Maybe…? Rolling down his window, he yelled out to me, "Order whatever you want, okay? And get some dessert. You're getting too skinny." And with a wave, he was gone.

I dragged myself back inside and like a true friend, Beth didn't say a word about his leaving. We ordered a round of drinks and then another and hours later, staggered out to the car.

"So thoughtful, huh, Beth? That husband of mine. Leaving us the car *and* Carl. What a thoughtful sweetheart he is, don't you think?" I was slurring my words but managed to inject just the right amount of sarcasm—or so I thought. Beth was out cold, I realized when I turned to my friend.

"Home, Carl," I called out, then started giggling after adding, "Home, James." Beth came to just long enough for me to help her into the house and down the hall to her room. I moved the wastebasket over to the side of her bed, knowing my bestie's penchant for early morning vomiting after a night of heavy drinking, then got myself into my own room. I popped a couple of Extra Strength Excedrin and brushed my teeth, but skipped removing my makeup. Who would notice if I had pores the size of craters? I thought morosely. *I bet Sharon has teeny tiny little pores. I know she has a fat ass.* She was easily two of me. Screw her and screw James, too. *I just hope they aren't screwing each other* was the last thought I had before I passed out.

In the days after Beth left, James was more attentive to me. He still spent countless hours with Sharon and the crew, but he was home most evenings and joined me in ordering takeout from a different restaurant every night. But that night, he went out with the lovely Sharon again. I had started thinking of her that way. Not just Sharon, but *the lovely Sharon*. I didn't feel like being alone, so I jumped up and grabbed the phone off the nightstand. *Two can play this game*, I reasoned. But I stopped when it hit me, not for the first time, that I didn't know a soul in this time zone. Except for the label folks I had met (and they were all on James' side anyway, I knew) there was not a single solitary person who would want to hang out with me. I shuffled into the kitchen and grabbed the folder of take-out menus. *Thai*, I thought. *Tonight is Thai.*

"No, just one. Just for me," I told the young girl who took my order. I decided to change into comfy PJs while I waited for my dinner. Maybe tonight I would figure out how to work that big, complicated TV and the satellite dish too. Usually I just punched buttons on the huge remote until I found something to watch. But tonight, maybe I could find a movie on pay-per-view. So I settled in for another night alone and was sound asleep on the overstuffed sectional sofa when James came tiptoeing in just as the sun was starting to come up.

*March 11, 1991*

*Dear Beth,*

*I am glad you got to come to visit us in Southern California! I love it out here sooooo much!! James feels really bad that he wasn't able to spend much time with us while you were here, but I told him you understand. It's not always like that you know? Sometimes, he's around so much I get sick of him. Just kidding. I guess that's what married couples do, you know?*

*Hey guess what? I finally figured out how to work the TV and the satellite dish, so we are watching all kinds of brand new movies at home. No one in LA goes to the actual movies anymore. That's what the tourists do!*

*Did that guy Tony ever call you for a second date? I'm sure you're right about Jesse not being a real plus when you're in the dating world, but any guy who doesn't love your kid is not the guy for you anyway. Hell with 'em, that's what I say.*

*Tell your mom and dad that Jill says hey and kiss Jesse for me.*

*Love,*

*Jill*


*P.S. Don't feel bad about calling me collect next time, okay? Just do it. James doesn't mind, believe me, I know money is tight for you.*

## Chapter 23 - *Losing My Religion*

The phone woke me from a deep sleep. James pulled a pillow over his head to drown out the noise as I dug around to find it and put an end to that infernal ringing. It had been several weeks since our big blowout argument and things had gotten better. The album had finally been released, and I hoped I would be seeing more of my husband. The weekend before we'd rented our own car, a convertible, and drove up the Pacific Coast Highway. The top was down, but I kept *my* top up until we pulled off the road onto a deserted side street in order to allow my husband to ravish me. Back on the road and with the wind blowing through our hair, James took the hairpin turns like a champ. We teased each other and laughed, and James sang to me as he drove, his right arm holding me close to him. But now it was 8 a.m. on a weekday, and neither of us was laughing or singing. We were sleeping—or trying to.

"Hello," I croaked into the phone.

"Put Jamie on," was the lovely Sharon's greeting. Too exhausted to be annoyed, I called out to James that his better half was on the line. I could hear her chuckle as he grabbed the phone from me.

"You're hilarious," he told me and then gave his full attention to the call. From my vantage point at the other side of the bed, all I heard was his end of the conversation. It sounded like, "Wait, what?" "No way," "Are you kidding me, Shar?" "Honest?" "Yeah, that's terrific." "You're blowin' my mind," and finally "'Okay, see you in a few."

Hanging up the phone, he turned to me with this big goofy grin on his face. "You're not gonna believe this, Jill."

Okay, he had my attention. "What's up?" I asked, rolling over to face him.

"*Guessing*," he responded. "*Guessing at Normal* is the fastest selling album in the whole country according to Billboard magazine—and *Jericho Road*? It broke into the top 20 on the rock charts." He lay back on the bed, fist pumping the ceiling. "It's happening, it's really happening," he repeated half to himself.

I couldn't speak. I could barely breathe. I had written most of the songs on the fastest selling album in the country. I had written a Top 20 song. And my husband could sing the crap out of everything I wrote, even without his brother's help. With a whoosh, I could breathe again. I jumped up. I felt like dancing.

"Dance with me, James," I implored. I pulled him up and started twirling us around. "C'mon, don't poop out on me!"

James allowed me to swing him around the room for a few moments before we collapsed on the bed. *Man, I need to get in better shape*, I realized as I lay on the bed huffing and puffing like a two-pack-a-day smoker. I was down to less than a pack, most days. Hey, don't judge. I'd been under a lot of stress. Beth had already given me a hard time during her visit and that had not proven effective, so save your breath. Ha Ha! See what I did there? I turned my attention back to my husband, who was making his way towards the bathroom, stripping off a pair of baggy gym shorts as he went.

"Hey, where're you goin'?" I called out. "Why don't you come back here and show me what makes you #1?" I teased. We had just heard 'change of life' type news. A celebration was in order and at this time of day, sex was about the only thing I could think of. Or pancakes.

"I gotta hit the shower," James informed me, sticking his head out long enough to smile gently at me. "The label is putting together a little something, and..."

"I wanna come," I whined. "No fair." Yes, I *was* six years old. But seriously, why wasn't I invited? James came over and sat down on the edge of the bed.

"I just didn't think you would want to. I mean, this is only the beginning. There'll be lots of other parties. It's a marathon, not a sprint, darlin'."

*Fuck this*. I was going to go with him. "I'm going. They're my songs. I have every right to be there," I told James frostily, and disappeared into the bathroom before he could answer back with some lame-o excuse.

Twenty minutes later, we were speeding towards the office in the lovely Sharon's two-seater. Other than exchanging a quick look—her raised eyebrow probably communicating 'What the hell, Jamie? What's she doing here?' and his shoulder shrug telling her 'I have no idea. Just go with it, Shar', there was no further discussion as we took off down the road towards the freeway. I was jammed in between them with the emergency break handle wedged up my butt and my feet resting in James' lap. The wind took a toll on my hair, which just minutes before had actually behaved for once. I was riding up higher than my husband and his um, colleague, so I was a prime target for bugs and other flying debris. Ugh. I was really glad when we finally pulled up in front of the office.

"Let's make sure Carl can take us home later, dear," I said to James, as I flashed a big fake smile in the lovely's direction. Possessively, I took my husband's arm and swept into the lobby towards the elevator, leaving Shar to deal with the valet attendant. She was walking towards us when I basically pushed my husband into one of the waiting elevators.

"Hold the door," James commanded but, whoops!

"Oh my," I sighed good-naturedly as the elevator door closed on her fat, smug face. I let out a little giggle. "I can never remember which button closes and which one opens the doors. Silly me!"

James just shook his head and looked up at the ceiling as if he was searching for a way to escape. We exited on the 17th floor and strode towards the reception desk. I knew that Shar would be right behind us, so I wanted to keep moving. The less I saw of her, the better, especially on our big day.

I looked around for Marnie or some other familiar face, when suddenly, I saw the display. *Guessing* LPs were arranged for maximum exposure on the eight-foot table in the center of the conference room. Dozens of images of James with his guitar. I had seen copies of the album art before, but this was the first time I got to actually hold one in my hands. I let go of James' arm, ignoring the crowd of people who had suddenly appeared and, turning down offers of crab puffs and those little spinach pastries that James loves, I approached the table and grabbed one of the records.

"C'mere, you," I cooed, and almost reverently started turning it around and around in my hands. I had helped with the liner notes inside, but I had never seen the list of songs in order like on the backside of the LP. *I know these songs*, I thought with a smile. *I wrote them.*

And yes, there it was in black script next to every single song. Lyrics by J. Sheridan, Music by J. Sheridan. *What the fuck?* My heart started pounding, and I knew that despite the fact I had yet to eat anything that day, I was going to be sick. I pushed past the crowd of people who had entered the room behind me.

"Excuse me. Please. MOVE!!" I finally shouted and raced towards the restroom. Out of the corner of my eye, I saw James and Sharon standing side-by-side, deep in conversation over in the corner. That situation, whatever it was, would just have to wait. I had a toilet with my name on it waiting down the hall. I managed to get inside the stall just as I started to gag and throw up, but I missed and drenched my shoes. Cute woven wedges too! I threw up again, and this time I was on point. Kudos to me. I can aim my vomit, and I can write a hit song. Too bad I just couldn't get recognized for it. *J. Sheridan!* I had never actually changed my name from Griffin, but maybe it happens automatically when you exchange vows? But J? Really, J? Everyone in his right mind would assume that it stood for James, not dumb-ass Jill. Did James know? Was it part of some big conspiracy to push him to the top alone? Jamie Sheridan, singer/songwriter? Was that why he didn't want me to join him today? He certainly knew me well enough to know I would freak out. Was he just trying to postpone the inevitable?

I sank down onto the floor of the stall and removed my shoes. I was sitting on a puddle of my own vomit. Barefoot. My hair was a windblown mess from the convertible. My stomach felt rumbly and my throat was raw from retching. It couldn't get any worse.

It got worse. First a gentle little knock on the door. Then the sound of the door opening. And a worried blonde's face appearing anxiously around the door. Crap. From my vantage point on the floor, I was pretty sure that she couldn't see me, but I could certainly see her.

"Jill? Are you okay?" she called out, her voice high and breathy.

I debated not responding. Maybe she would give up and leave me the hell alone. But she called my name again, a bit more forcefully this time. "Jill?"

"I'm just peachy, Shar," I responded. "I'll be out in a jiffy."

"James and I were worried. He sent me in to check on you," she added. James and I? There was no James and I, only James and me. I crawled out of the stall, not caring that Sharon could see me in all my glory.

"Shar," I began innocently. "Can you do me a biiiiig favor?" Her blue eyes widened as she crossed the room towards me.

"Of course, Jill," she assured me. "What do you need?"

"I need you to stop fucking my husband, okay? Is that clear enough for you? I sure wouldn't want to give the wrong impression," I continued, delighting in her look of surprise. "Wrong impressions, you know? Nasty things, don't you think? Like the impression someone might have if they read, for example, that the words and music off a hit album were both written by, I don't know, let's just for the sake of argument, say J. Sheridan. Or if a slutty blond with a fat ass was hanging all over someone's husband? What kind of impression could you draw? Is it still a *wrong* impression if you draw a *correct* impression, but the behavior is *wrong*? What do you think?" I pulled myself up into a standing position on shaky legs and walked right up to her.

She had the height advantage by almost a foot, especially since I was barefoot and she had on four-inch heels. But I was the injured party here. I had been royally screwed by this woman, professionally as well as personally. I also had the element of surprise going for me. She was expecting me to be a good little wifey, hiding behind my charming husband. The little woman. Not going to happen. I was about to play dirty. *Game on, bitch!*

"Barefoot," I told her, wiggling a toe in her direction. "Barefoot and pregnant, what a cliché I am," I giggled. My, oh my, was that another look of surprise cast in my direction? "What, you didn't know?" I simpered. "Oooh, my bad. Yeah," I added with a grin, patting my flat stomach, "it's a blessing. We're just thrilled. Okay, this is where you're supposed to say 'congratulations.' Why do you look so surprised? Wait, did he tell you that we weren't sleeping together anymore?"

Sharon should never play poker, I decided. I could tell from her shocked expression that it was exactly what she had been led to believe. "Well, you know James. You can't believe a word out of that man's mouth, especially when's he's fucking you. But worth it, huh? I mean, like wow, am I right?" I finished triumphantly. Poor Sharon. I was as disheveled a mess as anyone who had ever graced the label's sacred halls, and I had been sitting in my own vomit. But she had been served!

"Jill, it's not what you think," she began nervously. "James and I, we..."

"Stop right there, you husband-stealing bitch," I warned her. "You don't get it. There is no James and you. He's a married man and a client. What do you think Ed and the boys upstairs would think if they found out how you manipulated my poor naïve husband? Plying him with liquor when you know he has a drinking problem? Keeping him out until all hours when his poor pregnant bride sits home alone? Shame on you." I threw that last line over my shoulder as I pushed my way out of the bathroom, yanking the silk scarf she had been wearing around her neck off of her as I passed. It was starting to smell in there and I had said all I needed to say to the lovely Sharon. Besides, this scarf would be perfect to wrap around my waist to hide the vomit stains on my ass.

I made my way down the hall into the reception area, now teaming with label execs and staff workers. James was standing by the door, waiting for me or maybe for Sharon. I guess he was waiting for whoever emerged from the ladies' room first. I was glad it was me. Was he? He looked a bit surprised and more than a little nervous. Maybe he recognized the scarf?

"Jill," he began. "Wait. It's not what you think."

I turned on him and kept my voice low. "It's not what I think? Really James, is that the *best* you can do? I mean, everyone knows you can't write a fucking song, but I figured you could at least come up with a better defense than that." He reached out to grab my arm, but I pulled away from him. Furious now, I wanted to scratch his eyes out. After I blackened them, that is. "Don't you talk to me," I threatened. "I hate you. You promised to honor me. Right in front of your parents. You were the one who wanted to get married. Why? So you could drag me out here and humiliate me like this? Steal my songs from me. Take credit for..."

Wait a minute. An idea so horrible, so underhanded was starting to take form. No, it couldn't be. I was not thinking clearly from all of this stress. But I had to know. "Why did you rush to get married before we came out here, James? So that I would take your last name and everyone would think you wrote all those songs?"

The look of shock on James' face was so authentic, I wanted to believe him when he denied it. "Oh God, Jill. No, never. I would never try to steal your songs. I love you and I'm so proud of you, darlin'. You're my wife. I'll get the label to reprint the covers. I didn't even notice it myself at first. We'll make this right, I promise."

"Your promises don't amount to jack-shit," I told him. Okay, maybe it was an honest mistake, but that didn't excuse the fact that he was obviously sleeping with the lovely Sharon. "You bastard. You cheating bastard." I pushed him out of my way and started to head towards the elevators. "Get your things by the end of the day," I warned him. "Or I'll throw them out. On the street. But don't worry. I'll be out of your hair soon enough. As soon as I work out a few legal issues, I'll get on the first plane so you and your little whore can play house together. Got it?" I turned and walked away before he could even respond. But I had one more thing to add. "Hey, James?" I called, turning to face him.

"Yeah, Jill?" he said hopefully. *Awww.*

"I'm taking the car. Sharon can bring you anywhere you want. And hey, have a few of those spinach things. You're getting too skinny." And I left.

I walked out into the bright sunlight and marched right up to Carl, who had been leaning against the town car, smoking a cigarette.

"Take me home, okay? I just want to go home." *Home? Yeah, right.*

"Are you all right, Jill?" he asked, taking in my wrinkled dress, messy hair, bare feet and raccoon ringed eyes. Then he got a whiff of me, and his eyes widened in alarm. Ever the professional, he took my arm and got me settled in the back seat without saying a word.

We drove home in silence. I mean, what was there to say, you know? I had been conned, cheated on, lied to. I was such a cliché! The unsuspecting wife, the dumb-ass high school graduate who had probably signed away any legal rights to what might end up being a fortune. God, I was an idiot. I pounded my fists on the leather seat. I'd trusted James, I'd trusted Ron, and I'd trusted Sharon and her whole team of cutthroat slime balls.

I had never expected to be rich and successful, you know? This whole fame thing had come out of nowhere. I could live without it and all the trappings. I missed my little room and my crappy car. I missed whiny Fran and the housekeeping crew and the sleazy motel guests. Most of all, I missed Teddy, Beth, my mom. What would I say to them? How could I go back there with my tail between my legs? And what about Mike and Kathy? Would I ever see them again? Ever sit in their tiny kitchen, drinking coffee and playing cards? I let the tears flow as we made our way back to the little house in the hills. Carl pulled into the driveway and hopped out to help me. Like I was an invalid or something, he led me up the walkway and, taking my house keys from me, unlocked the front door.

"You gonna be okay, Jill?" he asked, concern for me written all over his face. I assured him that I would be, and he left me alone. "Call me if you need anything," he called out as he closed the door behind him.

I sank down on the couch and sat there for hours, alternately thinking and trying *not* to think. I could hear the phone ringing in our bedroom, but I ignored it. It was probably James or someone from the label or some random telemarketer. I didn't want to talk to anyone. My husband had been cheating on me, and I had failed to protect myself, emotionally or financially.

Growing up, all I remember from my parents' fights was my dad threatening my mom that she would end up in a cold water flat if she ever left him. Where would I end up? For the first time in my adult life, I had let someone in, allowed myself to be vulnerable. And how did that work out? I didn't care about the money so much, but I knew I was going to have a fight on my hands in order to be recognized for my contributions to *Guessing*. Despite James' protests, I just couldn't separate the fact that we had gotten married within months of the album being released. Was it just a coincidence?

My head throbbed and my heart was pounding as I thought about calling a lawyer. But for once in my life, I was going to ask for help. I would need someone to fight for me. My future depended on it. I tried to think about all of the gossip magazines I had been reading. Stories about celebrity divorces filled their pages. Was California a joint property state and what did that even mean anyway? But we'd gotten married in Jersey. Would that have an impact on any settlement I might hope for? Was that part of James' master plan to cheat me out of what was rightfully mine? But then why marry me in the first place? Oh yeah, the last name thing. I wanted to talk to someone, but I wasn't ready to open up to Beth or my mom.

I thought about calling Marnie, but quickly dismissed that idea. Taking me shopping, making dinner reservations, scheduling haircuts and manicures? Yeah, that was all part of her job description. She had come out to California from New York as part of the team that the label had put in place for the launch. But holding my hand? Tea and sympathy? No, that was more than I could reasonably expect from her. I thought about calling Ron as the sun was going down, and I finally got up to switch on a few lamps. But Ron was James' manager, and James was the enemy, right? Of course right. Ron was out. Screw him too! I never wanted to see him again for as long as I lived.

All I had ever wanted was to be safe and happy. That's not too much to ask for, is it? I deserved it, right? I'm a pretty nice person, or at least I try to be. I don't litter, and I pay my taxes, or at least I used to. Why did this happen to me?

Deep down, the whole James and Sharon thing? Maybe I had suspected something was up. I mean, she was a beautiful woman, even if she was old enough to be James' much older sister. And James? He had that sex appeal that attracted women to him like crazy. And he was an amazing lover, always up for a romp in the bedroom or on the couch or floor or backseat of the car.

I shuddered as I looked around the small house we had been living in for the past few months. There was hardly a surface that we hadn't made love on. So why cheat on me? I was sexy. I mean, not right at the moment, but generally. I never rejected his advances and frequently made some of my own. I was good in bed, wasn't I? Adventurous. Up for anything, more or less. I was blushing, thinking about some of our past sexcapades. So if he had strayed... It wasn't my fault!

Sharon must have talked him into it, I reasoned. When had their affair begun? Last week? Last year? Back in New York? My head was swimming with X-rated visions of my husband and that blond slut whore. This wasn't getting me anywhere, I decided.

I wandered into the kitchen and checked out the contents of the fridge, but nothing looked appealing. Vowing to clear out all of the takeout containers and the half empty juice bottles in the morning (James had thought that a juice fast would give him more energy so he had been starting his day with a different type of juice, usually abandoning them in favor of a croissant or bagel by lunchtime), I decided to order a pizza, but hung up the phone when I realized it was 3 a.m. Not even in LA, I thought, so I grabbed a handful of sunflower seed rye crisp crackers (so gross, but free of artificial colors or preservatives) and trundled off to bed. I threw my pukey dress and Shar's disgusting silk scarf in the trash and slipped between the sheets of the unmade bed that, until that morning, I had been sharing with my husband. Once again, I let the tears flow and cried myself into a fitful sleep.

## Chapter 25 - *Something to Talk About*

*'Singer/songwriter Jamie Sheridan is the best new artist in a decade.'*

*'If I had to guess, Sheridan's life will be anything but normal for a long, long time!'*

*'Guessing solo artist Jamie Sheridan is glad he grew up on Jericho Road!'*

The next few days were so fraught with drama, tears, phone calls, visits and apologies out the wazoo that I could barely keep them straight. But to summarize, the critics had nothing but the highest praise for *Guessing*, I *was* planning on letting James move back in on a trial basis, I was rich and getting richer, and Teddy came to visit.

Okay, here's the full story. Sales of *Guessing* were beating everyone's expectations. The music writers that wouldn't even return phone calls a year before were lining up to interview James. He was going to be on the cover of *The Rolling Stone*! It doesn't get any better than that for a recording artist. I was so proud of him, even though I still wanted to kill him. We had been talking on the phone every day but I just wasn't ready to see him yet. The label put him up in a hotel downtown, and despite all the temptations, he seemed sober whenever we spoke. He also sounded miserable, and he said he wanted to come home. I told him that he would have to sleep in the guest room at first and agree to zero contact with the lovely Sharon and oh, btw, that's the *unemployed* lovely Sharon. I was right about CEO Ed and his minions frowning upon their top execs mixing it up with the talent, especially a hot new talent like 'Jamie', who was taking over the airwaves. Sharon was called on the carpet and fired the day after she paid me a visit in the ladies' room. Marnie called to tell me all the details, then brought over Chinese food that night to celebrate. Turns out that Sharon wasn't such a lovely boss and Jamie wasn't her first dip into the label's talent pool. Some financial auditor went over the last two years of her expense accounts with a fine-toothed comb and it looked like our girl was playing fast and loose with the company credit card.

They were even talking criminal charges for a while there. And who knew Marnie was such a riot? After a few beers and a little coaxing, she did a spot-on imitation of Sharon groveling for her job that had me laughing so hard, I actually peed my pants. I hoped that with Sharon out of the picture on a day-to-day basis, I could count on my husband to lose her number and not take any of her calls. He swore that, although inappropriate by just about anyone's standards, his relationship with her was mostly flirtatious and that he never actually 'slept' with her. I wasn't sure if I believed him or not, but that's hardly the point anyway. He confided in her. He chose her over me time after time, and I swear I could forgive a quick roll in the hay, but this was way more intimate.

I needed time to heal, but how could we work on saving our marriage if we were separated? James also promised that we would look for a house of our own, and get a car for me so I was not so isolated. I hoped that I could trust him again.

On the financial front, Ron assured me that I would be credited with writing all of the songs on *Guessing*, except for *Dance with Me*. Also compensated. Me personally, not *the wife of Jamie*

*Sheridan*. As a show of good faith, a bank account in the name of Jill Griffin Sheridan was opened with an initial deposit of $100,000. It was thrilling and scary to have that much money in the bank after a lifetime of living hand to mouth. I wasn't sure exactly how the industry worked with record sales and royalties and all, but trust me, I was going to learn.

I had a meeting set up with a lawyer that Marnie found for me. I had already talked with her on the phone and she sounded savvy and specialized in entertainment law. I swore that I would never again let myself get pushed around. James could break my heart, but I would have a huge monetary cushion to land on either way. I hope that didn't sound cold. I wanted to save my marriage, but I wasn't going to be old dumb-bunny Jill anymore.

It turned out that my lawyer was a real go-getter. At our first meeting, she pored over all of the journals and notepads I had been writing in for years. She sneered when I assured her that I had already been paid a lot of money and that the label had promised to take care of me. "We'll get it in writing," she assured me. Next, she paid a visit to the label and negotiated a super deal for me. *Guessing* would be re-released and *Jill Sheridan* would receive writing credit for all but one of the songs. The contract we signed spelled out exactly how my share of record sales and recording rights would be calculated. The first thing I did with all of that money? With Teddy's snooping, I was able to track down the loan documents for my folks' house on Jericho Road and I paid off the mortgage. Every penny! My mom cried over the phone when she found out and tried to convince me that my father was 'touched' by the gesture.

"It's okay, Mom. I did it for you. It's all for you." I was starting to tear up too.

"Be sure to thank James for me, okay? Are you sure he can't come to the phone?"

"Next time," I assured her. Was it even worth trying to remind her that the songs were mine? Maybe next time.

Most of the members of the executive board at the label reached out to me with notes, flowers and calls. No one actually said, "I'm sorry we let an unbalanced psycho shitcan your marriage and feed demon rum to your husband," but I got the message loud and clear that everything would be done to protect James *and* me, and that they were committed to helping us to manage our careers in a professional manner.

Huge floral arrangements and baskets of muffins had been arriving just about every day. One of the cards congratulated me on my 'good news', a veiled reference, I imagined, to the pregnancy that I'd lied about to Sharon. She must have reported it to someone, but that's as far as that rumor went.

I called to start a subscription to *Variety*, the entertainment Bible out here, and I pored over the articles relating to the music industry every day. *Jericho Road* broke into the Top Ten as a single and *Guessing* was the fastest selling LP in the country for several weeks in a row. The video was in constant rotation on MTV and it was cool to watch live shots of my husband singing intermixed with black and white images of what was supposed to represent his years growing up. The launch was all planned and strategized and actually felt kind of manipulative, but what did I know, huh? But I was learning and light years away from that naïve girl who, up until recently, thought that when an album was released the fans actually had something to say about which songs were played and when. *Silly me.*

I had decided not to tell my mom about our separation, and I avoided the situation with Kathy and Mike too. But how many times could they call right when James was hopping in the shower or right after he walked out the door? Finally, I'd had it. I called James in his hotel room and hissed at him. "Call your mom, you self-centered jerk. She's worried about you, and she needs to hear your voice. You know what she's thinking, don't you?" *That you are drunk and lying in a ditch, of course.* "Talk to you later. Bye, bye," I ended sweetly.

I also chose not to mention anything to Beth during our bi-weekly phone calls. She could definitely relate to being cheated on, but I was married and my situation was way out of her league.

But I had to talk to someone, so I chose Teddy. Poor kid! A freshman in college and busy studying for finals but he's my brother, and he loves me, so as soon as he finished his last exam, he drove himself to the airport, left my old car in the long-term lot and caught a flight, courtesy of the label. I still had a corporate credit card stashed away for 'emergencies', and I figured this qualified. It was the first time he had ever flown, and I think he loved the whole experience, especially when Carl and I met him at LAX with his name on a big sign. He rushed right over to me and swept me up in a hug and told me that everything was gonna be all right.

I had a whole itinerary planned for his first trip to the west coast, and we got started right away. Carl abandoned his post guarding the car after the first few stops and joined us as we played tourist. We stopped for an elegant lunch at the Ivy on Sunset Strip and I watched my 19-year-old brother order a beer. The waiter asked for our drink orders and although Carl and I were abstaining, we encouraged Teddy to order whatever he wanted.

"Won't they card me?" he whispered. I assured him that he looked of legal age and that he would be fine, and he was. The waiter winced visibly when my brother asked for a Budweiser, but served it to him with a flourish just a few minutes later. If Ted was intimidated by the service, the beautiful people milling around or the astronomical prices, he didn't show it and after lunch, we continued our sightseeing.

I had considered putting my brother up in a hotel for a few days, since I knew James was due to move back in—to the guest room. But I decided that now that I had my little brother close to me, I was going to keep it that way. Besides, the hotels were all the way downtown, and we would spend too much precious time in transit. The first morning, I came into the kitchen to find Ted trying to figure out the high-tech coffee maker. I took over and directed him where to find cups and the coffeecake I had purchased. We set up our breakfast on the counter island that dominated the space and pulled up a couple of stools.

"So when did you start drinking coffee, little brother?" I teased as the dark roast aroma started to fill the air.

"I drink lots of things now, sis," he assured me with a grin. "A lot has changed since you left."

I took a deep breath and decided to postpone a lecture about the perils of drinking to excess for the moment. But if I noticed any signs of a problem, I would be all over him. "Quite the big man, huh?" I continued. "All grown up, are you?"

"Oh yeah, I've even gotten laid," he told me with a gleam in his eye. *Wow*, I thought. *Look at us Griffin siblings getting all up close and personal.*

"Who's the lucky girl?" I asked lightly. I assumed it would have been a girl, but you never know for sure, do you?

"Girls, plural," Teddy bragged. "And I'm a gentleman. I don't kiss and tell."

Yikes. Teddy, a ladies' man? Well, why not? At nineteen, he was tall with a husky build and wavy brown hair. *He was a hottie with a body*, I realized. Where had my nerdy little brother who used to follow me everywhere gone? I made a mental note to ask Carl to be sure that Ted knew how important it was to practice safe sex and use condoms. Because it was easier to talk about such things with a relative stranger rather than a relative, right?

"So talking about kissing and telling," my brother continued smoothly, "Where's your jackoff husband? Am I going to get to see him during this visit or what?"

Oh yeah, that. I had only told Ted that James and I were having problems and that he was not staying at the house right now. I had not wanted to get into all the details about Sharon and the writing credits and the money. But I guessed I had to speak up. Time to come clean. I waited until my brother had a mouthful of cinnamon swirl cake before I did. When I told him that James might or might not have been sleeping with Sharon, his eyes just about bugged out of his head.

"That asshole," he roared, jumping out of his seat. "Where is he? I'm gonna kill him."

"Calm down, tiger," I warned him as I pulled him back to his seat. "There's more, and you have to let me get through this, okay? I've got it all under control." So I filled him in on all that had been going on since we had arrived on the West Coast five months ago. A couple of times he clenched his fists, and once he smacked his hand hard on the marble counter, but other than that, he let me tell my story without interrupting. When I ended with the part about the money that was now in my name, I stopped and waited for his reaction. He stayed silent, but I could tell his huge brain was working overtime to try to process everything.

"Well, what do you think?" I asked him nervously. "I know it's a lot, but Ted? C'mon. Talk to me." While I waited, I took a sip of my now tepid coffee. Yuck. I grabbed our cups and poured what was left in them down the drain, then refilled them and returned to my brother.

"So, what you're telling me is James is a lying cheat who sleeps around, steals your songs and is now offering to pay you a fraction of what they're worth. And you're letting this asshole move back in, huh? Is that what you're telling me, Jill?" Teddy's tone was cold and I could see he was trying to control his temper by speaking softly and carefully measuring his words.

Well, yeah. I guess that's what I was saying. But I leapt to James' defense anyway. "James didn't know about the songs, Ted," I assured him. "He would never steal my songs on purpose. It was just a slip up, but the label's gonna make it right. They promised."

"But he left you here night after night. That bastard cheated... on you," he said, seeming amazed at the very thought.

I interrupted him. "Hold on, Ted. He's still my husband."

Teddy looked at me in mock surprise. "Wow, a good little wife defending her drunken bum of a husband," he said with a sneer. "Hmmm, who does that sound like? Anyone we know? Huh, Jill?"

Wow, that was a low blow. I felt like I had been punched in the gut. I looked at my brother sadly. "I'm not Mom, Ted. And James isn't Dad," I added defensively.

"Yeah, you're right, Jill." Ted nodded. "You don't have three kids to raise and only one paycheck coming in. And besides, we have no proof that Dad ever cheated on Mom, so yeah, your situation is totally different. Wow. Great coffee cake, sis. Can I cut you another slice?" He reached over and helped himself to the cake. "Or do you want to stab me with this knife?" he added with a grin.

Teddy was right. I had been played. Big time. I hunched over the counter and choked back a sob.

He looked at me sadly and took one of my hands in his much larger ones. "Sorry Jill, but if you brought me out here to blow sunshine up your ass, that's just not going to happen. You need to protect yourself and see what's really going on. I've got your back, but you have to face reality. I love you."

That did it. I finally broke down and cried. I had thought that I had no tears left after that horrible week, but I did. Lots of them.

"I want this to work Teddy," I sobbed. "I still love James, and I want to write more songs, and I like living out here. I can't go back there." At the very thought of leaving James and going back east alone, I began to cry even harder. My little brother, who I used to protect and comfort during our dad's drunken rages, had switched roles with me. He was here to look out for me, and I was so grateful for that. We sat there for a while longer, my head resting on the counter and Teddy awkwardly patting me on the back and murmuring reassurances.

"We'll figure this out, Jill," he told me. "I promise." And we did.

## Chapter 26 - *One Week*

A few days after that, James moved back in. Not in my bed or even in the guest room, but on the couch in the living room. He always bragged he could sleep anywhere, so there you have it. I didn't think my brother should be inconvenienced for the rest of his stay and I certainly wasn't going to let James anywhere near me. I was still so mad that I could hardly look at him, but I tried to be civil for the sake of the children. In our case, 'the children' was my visiting brother.

Teddy was wary at first, and James was still on shaky ground, but one night the three of us ordered pizza and watched The Rolling Stones in concert on pay-per-view. For a while, everything felt great. But then we all said good night and retired to our respective beds. James knows that watching Mick Jagger gets me all hot and bothered so I'm sure he had expected me to take his hand and lead him back to the promised land, and I almost did. But I wasn't ready to be intimate with him and wasn't even sure if I ever would be. I thought about making him get tested first. That skanky Sharon was probably crawling with STDs.

What I really wanted was a home (in both our names) and a car only in mine. The latter was easy. I had always dreamed of owning a baby blue Mustang convertible, so I literally drove the first one I tested right off the lot. Papers signed, I sped off towards home, leaving James and Teddy following behind me in the rental car. As soon as we arrived back home, I ran in and grabbed the camera and tossed it to my husband.

"Take a picture of us," I commanded and posed with my brother for a number of photos featuring my new set of wheels. "I'm sending some to Mom and one to Beth too." I completely ignored James, who stood by and watched us.

*What an odd experience for him*, I thought dispassionately. *He's always been the center of attention wherever he goes*. I decided to throw him a bone, as it were. "You can maybe drive it sometime," I assured him and walked back into the house. I ignored him all afternoon until that night when we drove the Sunset Strip with the top down, and I even let him ride shotgun.

The house hunt was much more difficult. When I found out what our price range was, I was floored. So much money! But that was before I found out what homes in the pricey LA market cost. We could get a pool *or* a view, not both, and there were so many different neighborhoods to consider. Our agent, a middle-aged woman named Ruth, tried to include the good school system as a selling point for one area, but I assured her that we could care less about the schools.

"Oh, never say never," she said with a twinkle in her eye and then exchanged a wink with my husband. Yeah, no.

Teddy came with us during those first all-day excursions, but it was getting close to the end of his visit, so we decided to take a day off and spend it at the beach. I was psyched that Marnie wanted to join us, so the four of us hopped into my car and drove west to the coast. I hadn't had sand in my toes since we'd left the island almost a year before, and I was immediately hooked. The beach, the surf, even the seagulls drew me in. We spread out blankets and folding chairs, played in the surf and baked in the hot sun.

"What do you think?" James asked me mischievously, indicating Marnie and Teddy, who were darting in and out the waves. Marnie was squealing, and I could hear Teddy laughing as well. I rolled over and faced my husband.

"Not everything is about sex, James," I answered him crossly. "They're just having fun. And besides, he's way too young for her." I figured Marnie to be maybe five years older than my teenage brother.

"I'm six years older than you," my husband reminded me with a chuckle.

"Yeah, and look how well that's turned out," I chided him. "And besides, it's different." I rolled back over onto my stomach and stayed that way long enough to get such severe sunburn that hours later I experienced chills, fever and nausea. That night, I lay in a fetal position on the bathroom floor moaning in pain for hours, alternately asking James to put more ice on the towel he had placed on my back and minutes later, to remove it in order to wrap another blanket around me.

"Just kill me," I begged through chattering teeth, but my doting husband assured me that he could never do that. Marnie and Teddy finally left to grab a late dinner after James convinced them that he had everything under control, so it was just the two of us for the first time in weeks. I hadn't ever seen James in the role of caregiver since I was rarely sick, and it might have been pretty cool if I hadn't felt so horrible. After I let James lead me to bed sometime after midnight, I was grateful for the cool lotion that he spread gingerly on my lobster red shoulders.

"Mmmm, that feels good," I told him, and it did. When, a short while later, he slipped silently into bed beside me, it felt like the most natural thing in the world. Early that morning, I rolled over to find him sprawled out and snoring ever so lightly. Seeing him there was worth feeling the pain that shot through me as my blistering back came in contact with the mattress, so I rolled back over with a smile on my face. If we were going to get through this rough patch, we would need to be close again, I reasoned. Otherwise what was the point?

# Jill's Journal

Maybe I should walk away
Why should I stay?
You tore out my heart
On that horrible day
I can't see 'me before you' any more
Were we ever 'us'?
If there's no 'me' after you're gone
What the hell am I fighting for?

## Chapter 27 - *Un-Break My Heart*

So at least one good thing *did* happen as a result of our day at the beach. Besides getting back together with James, that is. I found our house! But then I lost it. I had seen an amazing house for sale when we got lost on our way to the beach a few days earlier and had a general sense of the neighborhood, but I couldn't remember exactly where it was. We drove around for an hour trying to find it.

"It was grey, I think," I told James as we drove slowly through the maze of side streets. He was patient as I repeatedly told him that there was just *something* about that house, and that I had to see it again. I had gotten us lost before, so I guess a residential street "near the beach" could have been in several different directions. I let James drive so that I could keep watch. "Turn down this street," I would direct him and then minutes later, "Okay, head back to the main road."

I was just about to concede defeat when I had a flash of recognition. I remembered the house we were passing, and I knew where we were. "Bear left down there—" I pointed. "— and it should be right about... oh, there it is," I cried triumphantly. It was indeed grey, fairly large for the neighborhood and totally modern in design. The lot was kind of small, but I could imagine the view from the back of the house would be spectacular as it faced toward the mountain range bordering LA County. Best of all, there was a big 'For Sale' sign prominently displayed. I shivered with excitement. "Let's write down the phone number, okay? What do you think? Do you love it? I love it," I told him. This was the house for us. I just felt it. James let out a low chuckle.

"If you love it, darlin', then so do I," he assured me. "Happy wife, happy..."

I cut him off. "C'mon, maybe they'll let us take a look inside." I jumped out of the car and ran up the walk. There was no one at home, I realized after repeatedly ringing the doorbell and knocking on the door. So we drove home, called our agent and then waited for a couple of days while she set up an appointment for a viewing. Apparently the divorcing couple who owned the home were at odds with each other on just about everything, including when a good time for a showing should be scheduled as they would both need to make themselves scarce. But finally, the day arrived, and Ruth sounded confident as she pulled into the driveway in her minivan.

"It's only been on the market for a week or so," she informed us. "But it's priced to sell." I raced up the walk for the second time that week and then waited impatiently for James and Ruth to join me. She unlocked the door with her special realtor's key, and we were finally inside. I took a deep breath and didn't detect any animal smells, so they probably didn't own any pets. The last place we had gone to was ripe with odors from a trio of indoor cats who trailed along behind us for the whole tour. Ruth had not been in the least bit deterred and took it in stride.

"A coat of paint and some open windows, it'll be good as new," she said matter-of-factly. *And new carpets*, I thought. *And you don't have to live here, Ruth.* But this house? No smell at all, except for a subtle scent of lemony furniture polish. A large open foyer led into a huge space that was meant to encompass both the living and dining areas. With hardwood floors and a cathedral ceiling, it seemed enormous, especially since there were only a few pieces of furniture and no window treatments. I had finally stopped referring to anything used to dress up a window as curtains, after listening to Ruth. I also started using the term *spaces* rather than *rooms* and I knew that sightlines were critical. I was learning real estate speak, I guess. The view from the picture window was everything I had hoped for. A modern kitchen, a small room that I imagined could be a den, and a powder room made up the other half of the main floor. I giggled as James gave me a smirky look when Ruth mentioned how 'well-equipped' the kitchen was. He was so *not* a grown-up.

'You're bad," I whispered. "Behave."

I gave my attention back to Ruth. "Perfect for entertaining," she declared as we swept back through the living space. Yeah, definitely.

"Next up, the bedrooms," James whispered in my ear as we made our way up a half flight of stairs. There were two good-sized bedrooms with a shared Jack & Jill bathroom and a small linen closet. The master bedroom was huge, with room enough for a king-sized bed and a large sitting area.

"You could put a TV over here," suggested Ruth, pointing to the corner where two chairs were facing each other.

"We don't believe that TV sets belong in the bedroom, now do we, Mrs. Sheridan?" James teased. I just shook my head at my husband and turned to Ruth, who was blushing furiously.

"You'll have to excuse my husband, Ruth," I told her. "He has a one-track mind ever since he got out of *prison*." James took that opportunity to pounce, and he picked me up and swung me around the spacious room. I laughed and begged to be put down, but James wouldn't let me go until I declared out loud that I loved his one-track mind and everything else about him, too.

By that point, our agent had left the room and was carefully inspecting the linen closet when we joined her in the hall after checking out the adjoining bath and walk-in closet. Guess she wasn't used to such playful clients, but she recovered enough to show us the back yard that featured a stone patio and a small garden.

"There's enough room for a pool," Ruth announced, "but that wasn't on your must-have list anyway. Maybe a hot tub?" she ventured.

*Oh yeah*. Steam, bubbles, me and James naked. I shivered, and a quick glance at my husband confirmed that he was thinking the same thing I was. So while Ruth was typing up the offer for the price we agreed upon during the drive home and negotiating on our behalf, James and I were coming to terms on our own and believe me when I tell you, both parties were completely satisfied with the outcome. Oh, and our offer was accepted. We were homeowners!

Rock 'n roll wives all fall into one of the following categories: Rock and rollers in their own right (a la Patti Scialfa Springsteen), super models (Paulina, Christie) or the childhood sweetheart who stays in the background tending the home fires. (Mrs. Bono, Mrs. Bon Jovi) I am N/A, none of the above. I have zero musical talent (as anyone who has heard me sing in the shower can testify to) I lack the height and looks to model anything and my domestic aptitude...well, let's just put it up there with the zero musical talent and call it a day. I don't have an issue with self-esteem, really I don't. For someone who has accomplished remarkably little with her life, I am probably a bit too confident, maybe even cocky. I try to be open to new things, new experiences and vow to never sit it out when I can dance. Metaphorically, that is. I can't dance either.

"Hey, Yoko. Sorry, did I wake you?" Christ, it was Alex, the only person ever to refer to me as Yoko. Big surprise, he still blamed me for breaking up the band.

"Hey, Alex. What do you need?" I managed. I would try to be nice, try to be patient. Poor Alex. He never got over his brush with minor success, brief as it was. The guy peaked in his mid-20s, and I think deep down, he was waiting to catch that brass ring again.

The other band members had moved on, but not Alex. James had the looks, the personality, and the talent, and Alex, born just a few minutes after James, had been trying to catch up ever since. I mean, he was nice looking and all, had an okay voice and played a decent lead guitar. But he was never a star. It just wasn't in the cards, not for Alex. I knew James missed him like crazy and tried to find a place for him while recording *Guessing*. But Alex wouldn't hear of it. He had only returned one phone call from James during the whole time we were in Nashville. He told James that he was a sellout and a whore. He called me a bitch and worse.

"I don't need your charity. The two of you can go fuck yourselves," he had sworn, right before James hung up the phone, shaking and pale.

I went to comfort him, but he held up a hand to stop me. "I need some air," he told me and took off in the direction of the recording studio. He walked back in to our little room hours later sober as a judge and admitted to bribing the janitor to let him in so that he could listen to his tapes over and over.

"I'm not a sellout. Those songs? They're good. I'm proud of them," he added somewhat defiantly. "Alex doesn't know what the fuck he's talking about."

I was so glad to see him alive and sober that I didn't take his head off for causing me to lose a night of sleep. I had called Dirty's hours ago and asked Shelley to call me if he came in. She hadn't called, so I knew he hadn't been there. But there were so many other bars on our street, and I had feared the worst.

"Of course you're not," I told him. "C'mon. Come to bed. We can still get a few hours in before you need to go back to the studio." And that was the last we had heard from Alex for months, except for his drunken ramblings the night before we got married. Did Alex really love me? *No way*, I decided.

But he had started calling regularly a few weeks before, shortly after we closed on the new house and moved in. I knew James treasured those calls, and of course their parents were over the moon that the boys were talking again. I got that. I mean, I hadn't spoken to my older sister Susan in a couple of years, and if my folks weren't so dysfunctional and caught up in their own crap, they probably would have felt bad about that, too.

But Alex seemed to call frequently when James wasn't at home. He never kept me on the line or anything, he'd just say 'tell him I called, Yoko.' It's not like James had anything close to a normal routine here in LA, so maybe it was just my imagination that I was always the only one home whenever Alex called. I'd never had a close relationship with Alex anyway. But that morning, I tried to be friendly.

"So what's up, Alex? How's it going?" I asked with all the interest I could muster.

"Everything's great, er Jill. Thanks for asking," he replied with a sarcastic edge probably only detectable to me. Like those whistles that only dogs could hear? Well, I'm the dog in this scenario. "And how are you?" he continued. "When are you going to make my brother a daddy?" AAARRRGGGHHH!

"I know you didn't call at 7 a.m. to ask me that, Alex. What do you want?" I was quickly losing patience with him, this thorn in my side, this pain in my ass. *I'm only 23 years old! My biological clock hasn't even started ticking yet.*

"Relax, Yoko. I wanted to talk about something with my brother. Put him on, would you?" As if I would have stayed on the phone this long if I had been able to pass it off to James.

"He's not here, Alex. He must have gotten up early again to go for a jog," I told him. "Sometimes, he..."

"Sounds like my brother's lost that lovin' feeling, Yoko. What *will* you do? Have you identified your next victim yet? Any more bands to break up?"

"Listen, asshole. I don't have to justify myself to you, and if you think I owe you an apology, well, you can just...."

Just then James came striding in to our bedroom, asking, "Who's on the phone? Is it Alex?" I was glad to see him and happy to pass him the phone. He was always so eager to talk to his brother. "Hey bud, what's happening? Are you giving my wife a hard time again?" Whatever Alex said in response must have been simply hilarious as James let loose with a belly laugh. *Thank you, sweetheart, for defending me. Way to choose sides!*

Alex had his total attention and he was listening intently, nodding and saying encouraging things like "Yeah," and "Sounds good, bro."

I'd had enough of the brotherly love fest. I found my terrycloth robe and, wrapping it around myself, flounced downstairs in search of some peace and quiet. I wandered into the kitchen, found a bottle of juice in the fridge and opened the sliding glass door to the patio. It was already hot out and the temperature would continue to climb all day, I assumed. Early morning was the best time to sit out here, or late at night. I made a mental note to talk to James about selecting a hot tub. He had taken to joking that his honey-do list seemed to double with each passing week, but he actually seemed to enjoy completing a lot of the projects that needed his attention.

I plopped down on one of the chaise lounges and chugged a good portion of the bottle of juice. I was thirsty and still fuming over Alex's call and the fact that my husband never called his brother out on my behalf. Ever. I was contemplating lighting a cigarette from the crumpled pack in the pocket of my robe. I was down to only a few a day at that point. I know, why not just quit, right? James had quit a few weeks back, and I knew he really hated to see me light up. He was adamant that I not smoke in the house so I rarely did. Nothing like a former smoker acting all high and mighty with the rest of us mere mortals! He wasn't drinking either. He had been transformed with a single-minded focus. He wanted his upcoming tour to kick ass, and he repeatedly told me how important it was that he be in the best shape possible.

"It's not like with Nomad, Jill," he lectured, ignoring my smirk. "Those guys had my back." *Yeah, the same guys who fired you from your own band*, I thought wryly. *With friends like that, who needs...* well, you know. "Out there on the road, it's just me," he continued, gesturing as if to include all the wide-open spaces beyond our little cul de sac.

Yeah, just you and a 12-piece band that the label had assembled for the *Guessing* tour, plus three backup singers. But in his defense, final practice sessions were about to begin, and I knew he was a little shaky. It had been over a year since his disastrous last live performance. So I had been tolerating his lectures and trying to ignore his judgmental tone on what I ate or chose to smoke.

His schedule had always been erratic, but since we had moved into our new home, it was even worse. If he wasn't out jogging or doing pushups in the front yard (shirtless to boot, what *would* the neighbors think?), he was at the studio working on being the best rock star *ever*. I get very sarcastic when I'm tired. But to be honest, he had another goal in mind that summer. To knock me up. He was convinced that it was the right time for a baby. I was not on board with the idea.

"C'mon, Jilly. It'll be great," he would plead. "Can you imagine? A little cutie-pie running around here? What a great life we'd have." Other arguments weren't quite so sweet. And you wouldn't be alone so much. And you could put some meat on those bones. And then you'd have to quit smoking. And popping those pills that I know you've hidden all around the house.

Busted! I had been stashing pills for the past few months, even before the lovely Sharon and I went toe to toe in the ladies' room. I was a fan of AA: Adderall and Ativan were my drugs of choice. The Adderall left me jittery with no appetite, and the Ativan allowed me to get a few hours of uninterrupted sleep at night. I had been feeling self-conscious about my weight, for the first time in my life. A friend of a friend had apparently seen me out one night and ventured a guess that I might be pregnant. In my defense, it was a typical food baby. Just a little bloated tummy that would be gone the next day.

But the rumor spread like wildfire. Who knew that the state of my womb was of such interest to anyone other than me, James and the gynecologist that I swore I would set up an appointment with and soon? I think that's why 'you know who' probably believed my claim of being barefoot and pregnant that day. She had probably heard the rumor herself. So I asked around and presto, a couple of little pill bottles had appeared as if by magic. It was only until I dropped a few pounds, I told myself. That was ten or twelve pounds ago.

So there I was, chilling on the patio, catching some early morning rays and enjoying my pink grapefruit juice when James came sauntering out to join me.

"Hey you." I used my hand to shield my eyes from the bright sun. "What's up with Alex?" I asked in as conversational a tone as I could manage this early in the morning. "What's so important that he had to call..."

But James interrupted me. "Alex wants to tour with me," he said with a huge grin. "The Sheridan brothers together again," he concluded almost reverently. "Can you imagine?" Oh, shit. Yes, yes I certainly could.

Jill's Journal

I'm shopping at Barney's these days instead of Target, but I'm still the same bargain hunter I always was. Whoever said 'money changes everything' didn't know me, I guess. Old habits die hard! I still check the price tags and I go right to the sales racks. Yeah, I now spend more on a single pair of jeans than I used to spend on a whole year's worth of clothing, but they make my butt look amazing and I bought them on sale, so there's that.

Find out where everyone gets their dresses for award shows!

Call tanning salon and book a package.

Make hair appointment!! Jose?

Call Marnie- spa day?? What's a Brazilian??

## Chapter 29 - *Runaway Train*

The transformation was now complete, I realized as I watched my husband prance around our living room. Okay, he wasn't really prancing, but I was kind of in a crappy mood, so it sure *felt* like he was prancing. For weeks, James had been getting ready to go on the solo *Guessing* tour. I thought that the pushups, the jogging and a squeaky clean lifestyle were all that "getting ready" would entail. But I underestimated the extent to which the label was willing to go to "package" him and I sure never pictured James actually going along with some of the changes that had already occurred. They were counting on 'Jamie Sheridan' to sell out the concert halls being booked around the country, and so far, it looked like their wishes were coming true.

So how do I describe my new, but not necessarily improved husband? Well, starting from the top, his hair. He had worn it long for years, but had let me trim a hunk of it off the summer before on the island and again during the holidays with his folks. But now after a day at the spa, it was really short, combed back with way too much product (I was betting on mousse) and then tweaked a bit on top to give him a kind of messy, just-rolled-out-of-bed look. I could smell the hair spray from where I sat on the couch. Yuck. His facial hair was completely gone, and I saw for the first time that he had a cleft in his chin and realized what amazing cheekbones and facial structure he had. I couldn't get over the difference, as his entire adult life he had sported a mustache with and without a beard or at least some scruff. His chin and the space between his nose and his upper lip (there's a name for it but I can't for the life of me remember what it is) were so pale. I wasn't going to say anything to spoil his exuberant mood, but he brought it up.

"Alan says that a little foundation will even out my skin tone for now." He rubbed his chin thoughtfully with his neatly manicured hand. "And they're scheduling another facial for later this week to slough off any more dead skin cells. I may even need a dermabrasion treatment," he added somewhat hopefully. I didn't know what I hated more—the fact that he was getting these high-end services or that he was actually looking forward to them. *Okay, what have you done with my husband, you metrosexual poser?*

And his clothing? All new and designer. I managed to rescue a particularly ratty pair of gym shorts and a black wife-beater from the pile going into the trash, but I wasn't quick enough to grab a pair of his tattered jeans. Someday he's going to realize that he misses these things and won't have a thing to wear, I reasoned. For lounging around, he had actually started wearing one of his two new tracksuits. One was navy velour, and the other was charcoal grey and made of some type of polyester. So gross. It wasn't that long ago that we used to make fun of people who wore outfits like those. I mean, not to their faces or anything, just usually the mall walkers who were older than our folks.

He was going to join me for a quick trip to the grocery store one day, and I cringed when he came out dressed in the grey outfit. At least for jogging, he wore normal shorts and tees, and that was about the only time his array of tattoos was visible. But nothing was faded or ripped, and everything featured that friggin' swoosh design. When we went out, he generally wore a pair of creased and cuffed slacks and an open collar dress shirt and he bought a pair of loafers, which he wore without socks. He looked okay, but I liked the old James better, if you want my opinion. But of course, no one did. Not even James.

I'm sure it sounds like I was jealous or something, but I wasn't. I could book spa treatments and go on shopping trips too. And it's not like I was some old stick-in-the-mud who resists change. I wouldn't say I actually embraced it, but I was usually open to change if it was for the better. But I'm a firm believer in the old adage "If it ain't broke, don't fix it." And my husband wasn't broken, damn it. I *was* a fan of the healthy, substance avoiding James, but wished he would stop the constant talk about good carbs and bad carbs and crap like that. He was beginning to sound like a real tool.

We were kept in the dark as to what James would be wearing on stage. I prayed it wasn't something shiny or stretchy or anything too buttoned down, reminiscent of early Robert Palmer. It was fine to dance around in a music video wearing a suit, but not for a live concert. I could still recall the long-haired rocker who prowled the stage like a sexy jungle cat wearing nothing but a pair of ripped and faded jeans that rode really low around his skinny hips.

He had a great ass, I remembered fondly. He still did, but nothing he wore showcased it as well as those old jeans. *I miss that guy*, I thought sadly. *I married that guy, not this one.* I knew that everyone changes, grows, matures. That's part of life. But in just a few weeks Jamie Sheridan had become someone the guy I married would have hated and maybe even wanted to beat the crap out of. I smiled, thinking how that would look: the old James and the new Jamie standing side by side. I knew which one I would choose.

"What do you think?" he asked me. What did *I* think? Wow. Well...

"You look amazing, James," I told him, and he beamed at me. Same sexy grin, same glittery blue eyes, I noted with relief. And just seconds later, I got my wish to see the before and after versions because longhaired Alex came strolling in, looking more like James used to than ever. The long hair, the scruffy face, the faded jeans. Even the same grin, as he walked towards his brother and locked him a bear hug. It was the first time they had laid eyes on each other in almost a year and a half.

"Christ, James. You really should lock that door. Anyone can just walk right in here and steal all your nice stuff," he warned, watching me the whole time. Alex was looking really good. Maybe he could get James to roughen up his slick exterior a tad. If anyone could, it would be him.

"Hey, Alex," I greeted him warmly. "How was the trip?"

It felt really good to keep busy, I decided. Those last few weeks before the tour started, I was on a mission. When my journal ramblings became the songs on my husband's best-selling LP, thousands of fans wrote to him. "You get me," they told him. "Finally someone understands."

But he didn't, not really. James grew up in a solid blue-collar family. Minimal dysfunction, with loving parents who doted on their talented twin boys. So he knew next to nothing about domestic abuse or zero self-worth. Or what it feels like to grow up in a barren household where the only emotion regularly expressed was anger. But he listened to me, often asked me to explain a phrase or emotion, and he tried to understand.

And to his credit, he breathed real life into every one those songs. Another artist could have turned the lyrics into a bunch of sappy sad songs, but not James. *Guessing* was hopeful, optimistic and feel-good music, but not bubble gum. There was a fine line between heartfelt and maudlin, and James managed to toe that line perfectly. I had started to read every fan letter that came in and actually tried to send a personal response to each one, until the numbers reached well into the thousands, and I had to concede defeat.

Now a staff of three was responsible for James' fan mail. I only read bits and pieces, but I made sure that his accountant wrote some large checks to Teen Suicide hotlines and other organizations for runaways and domestic abuse prevention. It was the very least we could do.

James had been extremely attentive to me, especially that last week before the tour began. He made sure to be home each night to have dinner with me, even if it meant Chinese takeout or a pizza delivery. Alex joined us only on occasion, and even though he was staying with us for now, I rarely saw him. So I was kind of surprised when the night before they were due to leave, Alex was waiting for us in our living room. James and I were returning from an early dinner at this little Italian place that we both loved. I halfheartedly offered Alex the doggie bag of chicken parm that I had hoped to save for my next day's lunch, but he turned it down.

"Thanks Jill, but I'm good," he assured me. *Wow, did he just call me Jill?* "C'mon, Jamie my boy, we have a tradition to uphold. Time to boogie." James groaned and held up his hands in protest.

"No, Alex, we're too old for this shit," he protested.

*Wait, what shit?* "What's going on, guys?" I asked, trying in vain to keep the panic I was starting to feel out of my voice. "What tradition?"

James just shook his head while Alex explained. "Every time Nomad went on the road," he told me, "we always went out the night before to celebrate. It's bad karma if we don't. We gotta do it. C'mon, James. Lose those friggin' slacks of yours and let's go." I could see James' resolve fading and seconds later, he was walking down the hall to change his clothes.

I used it as an opportunity to threaten Alex. "Why are you doing this, Alex?" I kept my voice low, but I wanted him to know just how serious I was.

"It's tradition, like I told you, er Jill." He laughed. "Stop worrying. I know how to handle James," he said confidently. 'Better than you do' was implied.

"You don't believe in karma, you big poser. And if anything happens, I will personally kick your ass," I threatened. I stepped back as James joined us wearing a pair of designer jeans that I had never seen before and a dress shirt that he left half-buttoned, untucked with rolled up sleeves. His hair was tousled and he looked better than I had seen him look in weeks. More normal, like his old self. He walked over to me and gave me a hug.

"Love you, darlin'. Gotta go," he whispered as he turned to follow Alex, who was already out the door. I followed him and stood in the doorway watching them drive away. Alex had purchased a sporty little car to drive out here in, and I smiled at the sight of the two tall guys twisting like pretzels in order to climb in. I bit my tongue to keep from calling out a warning to be careful and instead just waved as they drove away.

I actually enjoyed the solitude that evening, even though I knew it would be the first of many nights alone. Weeks before, I had decided that I wouldn't go on the first leg of the tour, but would meet up with James and his band in a few weeks, and I was still feeling good about my decision. I wanted some time alone to write, and I was planning a trip up north to the wine country with Marnie.

I had eaten a big dinner and was getting sleepy and still feeling full when the late night talk shows came on. I decided to turn in early, and I must have fallen asleep right away. I figured Alex would look out for James, right? I mean, who in their right mind would want to start a big tour with a hangover? I was sound asleep early the next morning when I heard a loud crash from the living room, and I sat up. *Crap.* James was not beside me in bed. Could he have gone for an early morning jog? I should probably investigate. As I tiptoed down the hall, the sound of voices grew louder. I assumed it was James and Alex, but peeked around the corner just to be sure. *OH. HELL. NO.*

Swaying in a corner of the room, the brothers were hugging and swearing to never let anything or anyone come between them again, including the lamp formerly on the end table. James was particularly emotional on the subject. Seconds later, he tripped over an ottoman and crashed onto the sofa. I watched in amazement as his long frame adjusted itself to the contours, and he passed out. I raced over to Alex in a fury.

"What did you do? Alex? What happened?" I cried. This was just the worst thing ever.

"Just like old times, hey, Yoko?" Alex was slurring his words.

"Nice going, asshole," I whispered furiously. "He's been sober for months. Thanks a lot."

"He's a big boy, Yoko. Why don't you get off his back? And mine too, while you're at it."

"That's easy for you to say, you jerk. He's back on stage tomorrow night. He can't afford this kind of a setback."

"Chill out, sweetheart. Your meal ticket can handle it. Why don't you go back to bed?" Alex's tone was dismissive, and he didn't sound all that drunk any more.

"Why don't you go fuck yourself, Alex?" I yelled as I pushed past him. I didn't want to take his advice but as it was 5 a.m. and I was only wearing a thin T-shirt and a thong, I really had no choice but to head back to the bedroom.

"Hey, Jill?" Alex called out to me. "Looking good."

He smirked, and I realized just how much of me he had seen during our brief encounter. With what little dignity I could muster, I flipped him off and, after stomping down the hall, slammed the door. *Take that, you big jerk!* I stayed in there for a few hours, forcing myself to stay away from James. I really wanted to go out there and slap him silly, right after I beat the crap out of his dumb-ass brother. But I figured there was already enough crazy going on. So the hours dragged, and by the time I emerged, a young assistant from the label was barking orders into the phone, Carl was packing the car to take the guys to the airport, Alex was running around looking like he'd had a solid eight hours of sleep, and James was sitting on an armchair in the corner of the room, his head propped up on one hand as he silently surveyed the goings on. He looked like hell. I walked over to him slowly.

"You're all packed, right?" I asked with what I hoped was wifely concern. I saw him nod slowly, but he wouldn't make eye contact with me. "James," I continued, "you should probably eat something."

He shuddered slightly, and the hand that had been holding his head up moved to massage his forehead. His chin dipped to his chest and he slumped forward. Speaking in a flat monotone, he told me sadly, "I never meant for this to happen, Jilly. I swear it."

*Oh, James.* My heart was breaking for this sweet man, so tortured by his demons. I pulled him in and held him close to me. "I know that, sweetheart. I know," I murmured. "It's okay. Everything is gonna be okay." I kept repeating it, and we sat like that for a while, slowly rocking back and forth. The flurry of activity continued around us, all to guarantee that Jamie Sheridan and company would be ready to begin a grueling six-month tour later that morning.

I blinked, and they were all gone. The house was once again quiet, and I was alone.

## Chapter 31 - *More Than Words*

"Just don't freak out on me, okay, Jill?" If Marnie's words weren't enough to set off alarms in my brain, the tone of her voice was. I was immediately on high alert.

"What are you saying exactly?" I asked my friend. It was a couple of weeks since James left to begin the tour, and everything seemed to be going well for him on the road. I talked with him just about every day, but it was hard because of the time changes and the fact that he was always surrounded by so many other people; everyone seemed to want a piece of Jamie Sheridan these days. I was planning on meeting up with the tour in a week or so.

"It's probably nothing, Jill," she continued hesitantly. "It's just, well, I don't know... but if it were me, I would want to know."

I was starting to get really worried. "Know what? Tell me, Marnie."

I heard her take a deep breath and I could just picture her sitting at her desk, which would be piled high with contracts and forms and other correspondence. I imagined she was chewing on a pencil as well, as she was having a hard time since she'd quit smoking cigarettes the month before. Then I heard the unmistakable clicking sound that a disposable lighter makes, followed by a sharp intake of breath. Marnie was smoking! This could not be good. Another deep breath and finally she started talking. I fumbled around to find a cigarette of my own from the crumpled pack in the pocket of my robe. I lit up and waited.

"It's James, Jill. There've been reports that he's, well..."

*Oh, crap.* "He's drinking? Is that what they're saying, Marnie? Well, don't believe it. I've been talking to James every day, and he sounds good. I mean, I would know, right?" I felt a sense of relief. James was flying high, selling out night after night. What an easy target he made for the rumor mill!

"Well, no, Jill. It's not the drinking," Marnie said slowly. "It's, um, Amber."

What? Amber Leigh, the young blond pop singer and James' opening act? "What about Amber?" I asked, already knowing what Marnie would say next.

"Oh Jill, it's probably nothing, but I guess someone saw her leaving his hotel room the other morning, and there's a photo in *THE STAR* of them, well, hugging." My heart started pounding and I bit down hard on my lower lip. I started to whimper, and I couldn't stop myself.

"Noooo. It can't be true. James promised me." My voice trailed off, and I sat there staring at the phone in my hand. Son of a bitch! What a fool I was to believe anything that he told me.

"Listen to me." Marnie's voice was stern. "We'll figure this out, okay? Please don't panic. I would've come over there myself, but Ed's called a meeting to discuss well, damage control, so I can't get out of here right now. One story claims that she's only seventeen, but we're pretty sure that she's really nineteen, so that can't come back and bite us. But later today, I'll be there for sure. I'll bring lunch over, okay? What sounds good? Deli? I'll stop by Jason's, huh? You love their pastrami. Jill? C'mon, don't shut down on me. It'll work out, I promise."

"Sure, deli. Yeah, sounds good," I told her woodenly. "See you after a bit then." I hung up the phone and lay back down on the chaise lounge. From my vantage point on the deck overlooking the lap pool we had recently installed, I had a beautiful view of the canyon and beyond that, the mountain range in the distance. I flicked my cigarette into the pool and watched it slowly float away from me. I had to do something, but what? Should I just ignore the whole thing and hope it went away? Call James and demand the truth? Contact a lawyer and serve my asshole husband with divorce papers? Try to get hold of Alex and get his side of the story? Fly out and catch my cheating husband in the act? It all seemed like way too much effort, I decided. I lit another cigarette and stretched out on the chaise. I would figure something out after a little time in the sun. I was exhausted, so I stubbed out my cigarette and closed my eyes.

After a couple of hours in the sun, I felt like I was ready to take charge. I had a printout of the tour schedule, so I checked it out and found that my lying cheating, bastard of a husband would be in Atlanta for the next three nights, staying at the Marriott adjacent to the Coliseum. So I booked a flight to Atlanta using the label's platinum American Express card. I decided not to tell anyone what my plans were, not even Marnie. Without the element of surprise, I was unlikely to find out just what the hell was going on.

The whole time I was making my travel arrangements and packing, thoughts of my sexy husband and a busty, blond teenager rolling around in bed kept circulating. I wanted my marriage to work, didn't I? Would I fight for James? An idea came to me, right then, and not a very original one I'm afraid. In fact, if you believe what you see on daytime TV, it's actually quite common. I slipped into the bathroom and while the limo driver was idling in my driveway, I was reaching up and yanking out my diaphragm. If we ended up together, maybe it was the right time to give James what he had been pestering me about for the last several months. If he left me, I sure wouldn't need to worry much about birth control, now would I? The whole way to the airport, I closed my eyes and tried to relax, but the images kept coming. I knew that if this continued, I was in for a long and restless flight to the East Coast. As soon as I got through security at LAX, I bought a large bottle of water and used it to wash down a couple of the Ativan I had thought to bring with me. By the time I boarded the First Class cabin a half hour later, I was starting to get really wobbly. I was sound asleep within minutes, and I slept soundly for the entire six-hour flight.

## Chapter 32 - *You Oughta Know*

Arriving in Atlanta, I stopped at the first place I could to get a large cup of black coffee. The pills hadn't worn off yet, and I would be damned if I was going to sleepwalk my way through the next few hours. I would have to be at my sharpest when the time came to confront my husband and his skanky whore girlfriend. I know, tell me how you really feel, right? I hadn't factored in the time change, however, so by the time I got to the hotel, James was already at the venue. I decided to get a room of my own so that I could shower and do something to my hair. I wasn't ready to enter my husband's empty room and find all sorts of evidence that he hadn't spent the night alone. I was quickly losing my confidence and was starting to second-guess my whole plan. But I had gotten myself all the way there, so I could hardly chicken out at that point.

The next few hours were worse than I had even imagined. And let me tell you, I have a pretty vivid imagination. When I left the hotel, I walked over to the concert hall and located the back door. It has been my experience that these doors are rarely locked and that was the case here in Atlanta as well. I made my way through the maze of darkly lit hallways towards what I imagined would be the stage. The music got louder as I slipped through the final doorway and found myself backstage. I could see Alex in a corner with his guitar, several other musicians that I had never met milling about and the trio of young African-American women who were the back-up singers sharing a can of Coke. No sign of James. But I heard him before I saw him. He was on stage with Amber Leigh, his opening act, and the two of them were singing a lovey-dovey duet. I crept out of my hiding place in the shadows and walked towards Alex and the rest of the band. The only person who would have recognized me was Alex, and he was busy tuning up, so I actually got pretty close to the stage before I was spotted. Some official-looking young guy with a clipboard and a walkie-talkie approached me first.

"Excuse me, miss. You're not allowed back here," he advised me rather brusquely. I ignored him and kept walking toward the stage. I figured as pissed off as I was, I could probably take him in a fair fight. But Alex looked up and when he spotted me, hurried over.

"Back off," he warned Mr. Clipboard. "She's with me." He approached me warily, as if he wasn't sure what I would do next. Well, join the club! I had no freakin' idea myself.

"Jill," he said softly. "When did you get in?" I pointed at the stage where the lovebirds were still singing.

"How long?" I asked. "How long has this been going on?" Alex shrugged in response, and I lunged at him. I pounded my fists on his chest and struggled when he tried to subdue me. He finally got me in a hold of sorts, which kept me from whaling away at him, and then he dragged me out the side door. He tried to get me to calm down, or at least to shut up, and I finally did both. I sagged against him in defeat. To his credit, he didn't try to deny anything or even defend his brother. Miss Thing had made clear her intentions to seduce my husband right from the start, he informed me. She bragged to the back-up singers that she would be sleeping with James by the third night of the tour and it looked like she'd gotten her wish. James was clearly eating up the attention and, as big a flirt as I knew him to be, I figured he gave as good as he got. I didn't ask Alex if he had tried to stop James, to talk some sense into him. I didn't ask if he had planned to reach out to let me know what was going on with my wayward husband. What would it really matter anyway?

"What do you want to do, Jill?" Alex asked me with concern in his voice. "Do you want to stay here, or go back to the hotel or go straight to the airport? What do you want?"

What did I want? Hell, I had no idea, but going back to the hotel seemed like the easiest thing to do. I would wait for James in my room and when I saw him? Well, I didn't really know what I would do then exactly. So I let Alex lead me out front so I could catch a cab. He closed the car door after me, and then stuck his head into the open window. He kissed me lightly on the cheek and told me sadly, "I'm so sorry, darlin'."

*Wow. This must be some serious shit if Alex is going all warm and fuzzy on me.* "Thank you, Alex. Tell James I need to see him," I added. Talk about an understatement! Alex waved in response and hightailed it backstage. I made it back to the hotel and let myself into my room, where I sat in the dark and began the wait for my husband to come and find me.

## Chapter 33 - *The Boy is Mine*

I must have fallen asleep, because when I jerked awake suddenly, James was sitting beside me on the couch. He gave me a tentative grin and whispered, "I love watching you sleep, Jilly."

I struggled to sit upright. "How long?" I asked through clenched teeth.

He shrugged. "Just a few minutes, I guess."

"How long with *her*, James?" I demanded.

He gave me a long, hard look and appeared to be running through a variety of different responses in his mind. Finally, another shrug, and "Not long, darlin'. It just..." He shook his head sadly. He hadn't even tried to deny it. I pushed him away as he started to move in closer to me. I had to know.

"Why, James? I don't get it. Aren't I enough for you? When have I ever turned you down? What is it, huh? Were you drunk? High? Just looking to get laid and I was 3000 miles away? Trolling for jailbait? Was she just too good to resist? Why?" I leaned back and closed my eyes. Looking at his sad, guilty face just made me want to punch him. But his continued silence caused me to sit back up and face him squarely. "Do you love her?" I asked weakly. Finally I got a reaction.

"No. God no, Jill. It's not like that at all," he insisted. "I just fucked up. I'm so sorry."

"Just fucked up, huh?" I sneered at him. "No, James, that would be like forgetting my birthday or not calling to say you'll be late for dinner. Sleeping with a teenager? That's a whole other category, you asshole." I couldn't be around him anymore, so I jumped up and pointed to the door. "Get out. This is my room. I hate you. Get the fuck out of here."

But James stayed seated, just looking at me with those goddamned glittery blue eyes.

"Fine," I decided, "you stay and I'll leave. You make me sick," I called over my shoulder and stormed out of the room. I half-hoped he would come after me, but he didn't. So I walked through the lobby and crossed the street to another hotel. If he came looking for me, he would probably think I would be down in the coffee shop, I reasoned as I found a seat by the window in the large lobby. Screw him!

I finally gave up at around 5 a.m. The sun was coming up, and the fact that I had only slept for a few hours in the last 48 was finally catching up to me. I crossed the street and let myself back into my room, certain that James would have given up by now. But he hadn't left.

He was sprawled out on the coach sleeping soundly, so I sat next to him and pinched his arm until he woke up. We cried, and we hugged, and he made all kinds of promises and he told me how much he loved me. He led me to bed and made love to me like it was the first time for us, and afterwards, he held me in his arms and we slept that way for hours.

I stayed in Atlanta for a few more days and James introduced me to the entourage of musicians and roadies and assistants he had been traveling with. They were all super nice and very friendly. I was made to feel very welcome by everyone. Alex kept his distance, but I would catch him staring at me from across the room whenever our paths crossed. What was he feeling for me? Pity? Love? I had no clue.

And poor Amber Leigh? It was tragic, really. Out of the blue, she was diagnosed with laryngitis and extreme exhaustion, so she had to leave the tour and go home to Podunk, Kansas or wherever the hell she was from. Her replacement as an opening act was a simply delightful young man named Chris Lewis from Maine. He was a really good fit with James' style of music, and the audiences really seemed to like him. Of course there were no more heartfelt duets any more, but what can you do? That's show business.

*October 8, 1991*

*Dear Beth,*

*I was really surprised to get that package from you in the mail today. Everything in those trashy rags is a lie!!!! I mean, you know that, right? Next thing you'll read is that James and Sir Elton John were in a three way with Madonna, for God's sake. You can't take those stupid headlines seriously. They are just trying to sell more papers with their ridiculous made up stories.*

*There was absolutely no need for you to mail me copies of those stupid tabloid covers. They sell them here in California too!! I have seen them myself and believe me, they are FAKE!!! Those liars can take a picture of James and a picture of Amber Leigh or any other slutty blonde and make it look like they were together. If you look closely, you can tell that the arm that's wrapped around Amber in that picture of her wearing that trashy red dress is not even James' arm. It's all a big lie and I can't believe that you and your mom fell for it.*

*So stop reading this garbage okay? There is nothing to worry about. Give Jesse a kiss from his Aunty Jill and tell your folks I said hi. I think I'll be back east soon and maybe we can actually get together this time. I know I still have stuff stored in your basement, but I'm pretty sure that I don't need any of it so feel free to trash it, okay?*

*Lots of love,*

*Jill*

# Jill's Journal

I am starting to believe my own story.

The one where no one really understands
how hard it is to love the larger than life rock
star

that I helped to create.

The story where I lie to friends and family and
myself
I don't know if they believe me but I think I do!

He lies, he drinks, he cheats. James is not perfect

But neither am I.

I lie and pop pills and tho I haven't strayed
It's only because I don't want anyone else

Not in my bed and not in my heart

If I left him, what would my life be like?

I'm not staying for the money, I've got my own

I don't have to stay. I have options

I choose to stay. This is where I want to be.

Most of the time.

## Chapter 34 - *I Try*

I flew back home when the tour was leaving Atlanta and heading for Charlotte, NC. I hadn't been on the road for a while and had forgotten just how exhausting it could be. Glad to be back home, I mostly kept to myself in my dream house in the hills outside of LA. Marnie came by a few times and I talked on the phone a lot with my mom, Teddy and Beth, but was quite content to sit in the sun and write in my journal or read a book. I never told a soul about what had transpired in Atlanta.

Soon there were more exciting things to talk about anyway. Grammy nominations had come out and *Guessing* had been nominated for album of the year and *Jericho Road* for song of the year as well as record of the year. James was up for the record nod and I was named as songwriter. I was a Grammy nominated songwriter!

I ended up hiring an agent because the constant stream of phone calls was overwhelming, and requests for my services were coming in fast and furious. It had never occurred to me that I could write more songs, especially for anyone but James, but the demand was there, so I started to sort through the offers with Ari and her staff at the agency. Even my mom got involved.

"How about Tom Jones?" she asked me. "Have his people contacted you yet?"

I tried to let her down gently by disclosing the names of some of the artists that *had* called, but she wasn't convinced. "You should call him," she told me firmly. "You could write Tom a big hit."

I agreed that it would be a real thrill to work with him and that I would see what I could do to make that happen. I was speaking with James every other day or so, but our conversations were mostly limited to all of the exciting Grammy news and my sudden rise in popularity as a songwriter.

He ended each call with, "I love you, Jilly," to which I usually responded, "I know you do," or if I was feeling especially charitable, "Yeah, me too." I did love my husband, but I decided to sit this one out for a bit. No more rumors made their way to the West Coast but I steeled myself, knowing that as a Grammy nominated artist, his higher profile would warrant more dirt. But all of the news about him was good and photos of him jogging shirtless in the park or leaving the gym with a couple of the guys were popping up everywhere. But the lull wouldn't last for much longer.

One day, my agent called me. "Anything you want to tell me, girlfriend?" Ari began in a conversational tone.

"Um, no, why?" I asked her. *What now?*

"Well, it's just that some paparazzi snapped a photo of you yesterday leaving your *doctor's* office, and it looks to me like you're, what, maybe four months along? It's running in *People* and *Us* and *The Star* and *Access Hollywood* called and they want an exclusive. So, anything you want to tell me?" she repeated. Oh yeah, that.

I struggled for a moment before I answered her. "Yeah, well, I should probably tell James first, you know?"

## Chapter 35 - *Give Me One Reason*

"I just can't believe this." James was in shock. "I thought we were being so careful."

"I can't believe *you*," I cried. "For months you've been nagging me to get pregnant and now I am and you can't believe it?" I wanted to reach through the phone and choke him with my bare hands.

"Well, it might have been nice to hear it directly from *you* instead of some reporter," he complained. "How could you keep this from me? And besides, we haven't been together in months, so just how..." he trailed off. Either he was accusing me of cheating, or he just realized that this pregnancy was the result of the makeup sex we had in Atlanta. Bingo!!

"Don't even go there, James. It's yours and you know it. I don't sleep around, unlike some..."

"Christ, I was wondering when you were going to bring that up again," he snapped. "I mean, we've been talking for almost five minutes, so you're overdue."

"The only thing overdue is my period, you jerk. So when are you coming home?"

I gave him a couple of moments to ponder my last question. It was late night on the East Coast, and I had been trying to reach him all day. This was not the type of news you want to leave in a message. But a reporter had caught him off guard. I could picture James, exhausted but elated after another sold-out show, getting a microphone shoved in his face and being hounded for a comment by some smug hack. I suddenly missed my husband very much and wanted the Cold War I had been fighting with him to end.

"James," I started. "It's going to be great. You'll see. I've already been to the doctor and she thinks that I'm off to a good start. The next visit, they'll even be able to tell us the sex." Silence on the other end. "I'm not sure," I continued. "It might be fun to know, so you can start planning. But on the other hand, it would be such a fun surprise. I don't know. What do you think?" I wanted him to talk to me. *Say something, anything*, I begged silently.

James sounded aloof and resigned when he finally spoke. "Whatever, Jill. Whatever you want, okay? I'll talk to Ron tomorrow and see if I can swing it to stop by in the next few weeks. I'll let you know. Good night."

*Okay*, I thought sadly. *Say anything but that.*

*February 2, 1992*

*Dear Beth,*

*Of course I am thrilled to be pregnant and James is too. He has always placed me up on a pedestal, you know? Only now, he's even more loving and thoughtful than ever. He cried when I told him. Tears of joy! We have been planning this pregnancy for ages but I waited to break the news til I was past the first three months. I guess I'm just superstitious. I knew if I told James, he would want to cancel the tour and come home and spoil me rotten and that's just not fair to all the fans and all of the musicians he employs. They have families to support after all! And now, we'll be our own little family. And baby makes three!! I'm not sure if I can squeeze in a trip back east in the near future and I don't want to risk anything by flying around in my last few months. But I will call you soon, okay? I want to hear all about Jesse's third birthday party. Tell him his Aunt Jill sends a big hug!*

*Lots of love,*

*Jill*

*P.S. If you are ever in the neighborhood, could you swing by and say hi to my mom? Whenever I talk to her, she sounds so stressed, even more than usual. Teddy swears everything is still shitty and status quo, but I think she's really worried about my dad's health. I guess she doesn't want to burden me with everything I've got on my plate. Thanks!*

## James' Defense

*The timing sucks, okay? I've got all I can do with this tour and all the press and now my wife is pregnant? I can't even remember the last time we had sex, for God's sake. I know I had been pressuring her last year to make a baby, but between the little pills she had stashed everywhere and her making sure to stay on birth control, getting pregnant just wasn't in the cards. But things have changed. The Guessing tour is important to me. I've been working my whole life for this and I can't blow it. Night after night, sold out venues so huge I can't even see a single fan's face. And the lights? It's just a big fuzzy blur out there. I need to focus and I can't do that if my wife is calling me every night begging me to come home and paint the nursery. Okay, to be fair, Jill hasn't done that, but she might. I just want to relax after the show and have a few drinks, maybe smoke a joint with my brother. Is that too much to ask? The whole mess with Amber was a big mistake. I don't know what I was thinking. I've never been able to be with just one woman, but I know Jill is too good to risk losing. So I sleep alone every night on the road these days. I'd be glad to go home to my wife whenever I can, but I just don't see how bringing a baby into all of this is a good idea. If Jill had asked me, I would have told her that. But she went ahead and did it without me. I'm really pissed at her right now.*

It would be an understatement to say that things were complicated back then. On the plus side, *Guessing* continued to be the top-selling album in the country for seventeen weeks in a row. No other LP even came close, and people in the know were predicting that it would win a Grammy for best rock album. *Jericho Road* was the #1 song on America's Top 40 for seventeen weeks, and it was also up for a couple of Grammys. It would have been amazing to win best record (James) and best song (me), but there were other songs in each category considered to be top contenders and it was an honor just to be nominated, right?

*Dance with Me,* James' sweet ballad that he wrote for me was rumored to be the #1 theme song for high school proms as well as the #1 requested song played at weddings. It almost hadn't made it on the album, since it didn't really fit with the other more angsty rock songs. But I loved it, and I had talked James into convincing the label to include it. The *Guessing* tour continued to earn rave reviews and sell out huge venues, and everyone at the label was happy about that. Tours were frequently looked at as break-even, a necessary marketing tool to help sell more albums. But Marnie had heard Ed from the label tell Ron that the *Guessing* Tour was the most profitable that the label had ever sponsored and that at the rate it was going, it would be among the top five highest grossing tours of the decade. So when I tell you that the business end of the Griffin/Sheridan collaboration was going gangbusters, I really mean it.

The personal side, however? Not so much! I had only seen James a handful of times since our baby-making rendezvous in Atlanta nearly six months before. Although I teased him that I couldn't get any more pregnant than I already was, he rejected all of my advances in that department, and I couldn't see the wall he put up crumbling any time soon. I was pretty certain that it wasn't my big protruding belly and ginormous breasts causing his lack of desire. If I had to guess, it was because he felt like I tricked him somehow. And I guess I did. Probably not a very nice thing to do to the man you love, but cheating on your wife with both a fat-assed label exec and a slutty teen pop star in a single year isn't exactly kosher either.

I only knew that I wanted this baby very much and that I loved being pregnant. I would have loved it even more if the father of my baby-to-be would get on board. When I had missed my first period, I didn't give it much thought. I have never been very regular and ever since I had lost most of my body fat with my AA regimen, it was even less predictable. But by the second month, I pretty much knew. I had quit cigarettes, as well as the prescription drugs I had been abusing, as soon as I got home from Atlanta. I was regularly eating healthy food for the first time ever and taking my prenatal vitamins and walking around my neighborhood for a half hour or so each day. When I wasn't getting ready for the baby to arrive, I scribbled in my journal and even wrote a new song for a certain top female country singer who was about my age. We met face to face a couple of times, and I was thrilled to find she was nothing like the airhead bimbo who couldn't seem to keep a man for more than a month that the media made her out to be. One night at my house, we talked for hours, made brownies and ate the whole pan (someone has a sweet tooth!!), and she ended up sleeping in the guestroom that night. I almost called Beth to say, "You'll never believe who is sleeping over," but I decided not to. Everyone has a right to some privacy. Even famous people.

Marnie and I had painted the nursery a pale green color, and I decided to forego a specific theme. I mean, why go with an outer space motif if the kid ends up liking dinosaurs or soccer? I felt fairly certain that I was going to have a boy. I'd been referring to him as Junior, because I hated to get too set on a name if James didn't end up liking it. We weren't really together as a couple, but I wanted him with me, and if he wasn't here now, at least I could hold the door open for tomorrow.

At least Junior had three very enthusiastic grandparents on board. My mom swore she would fly out when the baby was born, and she told my dad that if he didn't like it, he could lump it. Kathy and I spent a lot of time talking about the baby during our weekly phone conversations, and she and Mike planned to visit us as well. *Now if I could just get your dad on our side, Junior!*

## Chapter 37 - *Daughter*

The last couple of months of my pregnancy got pretty complicated. Although I had sailed through without even a touch of morning sickness up until that point, my ankles started to swell up and my doctor put me on bed rest for the duration. Preeclampsia was the official diagnosis, and although I fussed and moaned about it, I was actually relieved. I had been putting on the bravest face possible for months, and this whole charade of acting like I was doing just fine on my own was exhausting. I was actually quite grateful for a medical excuse to rest up before the big event.

Marnie and Ari took turns spending a fair portion of each day with me, usually spent on the phone, as they both still had full-time jobs. I would generally recline on a chaise by the pool or on the sofa in the living room watching TV or reading. I didn't feel the need to follow orders to rest *in* bed literally, but I was off my feet for most of the day. Marnie had to go to New York for a couple of weeks during the last month, so she and Ari convinced me to hire a nurse to live in.

I resisted at first, but finally consented and, to be honest, having Tiki come and live with me was an absolute godsend! She was highly recommended by the visiting nurse agency she worked for, and I took to her immediately. Tall and big-boned, Tiki was strong, efficient and very kind. Although I tried to get her to call me Jill, her Jamaican upbringing prevailed, and the first thing I began to hear each morning was her lilting voice telling "Miss Jill" that it was time for breakfast. She would come in bearing a tray of fragrant herbal tea, fresh juice and a square of some light and flaky pastry that she always managed to have on hand.

Sometimes she and I would watch TV together or listen to music on the surround sound stereo system that we had installed right after we moved in. She favored reggae music from her own country but came to enjoy some of the power ballads and commercial pop songs that I preferred. Right after she listened to the entire *Guessing* LP for the first time, she turned to me in amazement. She actually had tears in her eyes as she leaned over and hugged me.

"So much pain in this little body," she murmured softly, and I broke down for the first time in weeks and sobbed. I admitted just how much I missed my husband, and how difficult the last year had been. We stayed that way for quite a while and after that day, Tiki became my most trusted ally. She would end up living with us for years, but at the time, it just felt good to know that someone had my back. Especially someone who had never even met James. She was all mine. I could really open up to Tiki about all of my fears: building a life without James, raising a child on my own, the guilt I felt about not being there for Beth and my mom, all of it. I was still protecting my missing husband, and though he had betrayed me, I couldn't admit it to my mother or my best friend. I didn't have to appear to be strong for Tiki. I could just be me.

My due date was quickly approaching by the time James came home to stay. He had been telling me that he would be there with me when I gave birth, but I had come to believe very little of his promises. If I expected next to nothing from my husband, then how could he disappoint me, right? I knew he was still upset with me, and I was quite anxious by the day he was supposed to show up. I had been expecting him and asked Tiki to help get me ready. I never exactly got that pregnancy glow you always hear about, but my hair was freshly washed and pinned up, as it had gotten very long and it was thick and glossy from all the vitamins and good food I had been consuming. Tiki helped me apply some makeup and got me into a brightly colored maternity romper that Ari had bought me. I had never bothered with maternity clothes all this time, as I rarely went anywhere except to the doctor's. I had taken to wearing James' T-shirts and a raggedy pair of his gym shorts, so it was a shock to see myself in anything bright and colorful. Tiki painted my nails a hot pink and was just about to start on my toes when we heard the front door open and close, and we looked up in time to see James come striding in. I held my breath as I waited to see his reaction. There I was, sprawled on the couch with forty pounds of baby weight, a new hairdo and a large Jamaican woman with my foot in her hands.

"James," I cried. "You're here!"

His eyes got misty, and his voice was hoarse as he crossed the room and told me, "I'm here, Jilly. I won't leave you again, darlin'." Tiki could be pretty quick for a woman of her size, and she moved away discreetly as James knelt in front of me. He took my hands in his much larger ones and gazed at me in wonder.

"You're so beautiful," he told me in a whisper. "You're amazing, Jilly. How could I have missed all this?" he asked sadly as he took me in: large belly, huge boobs, swollen ankles and all. He pulled himself up and sat beside me as put his arms around me, stroking my hair and my back.

"Can I?" he asked shyly as his hand came in contact with my huge stomach.

I pulled both of his hands to rest on me as I told him that I had been waiting to share this with him. His glittery blue eyes filled with tears as he explored what was once a very familiar body.

"Enjoy it while you can," I teased. "In a couple of weeks, I'll be your scrawny wife again." He responded by kissing me, and we moved around cautiously to adjust to my increased proportions. Finally, we got it right, and we lay together for the first time in ages. I finally introduced him to Tiki, who wisely left us alone to brew some tea. By the time she returned, balancing a large tray heaped with goodies, we were both sound asleep in each other's arms. We slept away the afternoon and ended up eating Tiki's jerk chicken and fried plantains out on the patio hours later.

When I awoke near dawn the next morning, I thought it was heartburn from all the spicy food, and I lay back for a moment, happy to be in James' arms. But another sharp pain hit, and I realized it was show time. James and I rushed to the hospital, and our daughter Carly Griffin Sheridan was born eight hours later. She weighed in at a dainty 6 lbs., 9 oz. and measured 20 inches long. She had her father's dark hair, but her eyes wouldn't reach the same shade of blue for several more weeks. Mother and baby were doing fine, James was happy to report to our family, friends and, of course, the media.

Maybe it was the fact that we were now a family of three, or maybe it was Tiki's steadying influence or possibly it was due to James' first break from touring in a year. Whatever it was, I can honestly say that the next several years were the happiest in our marriage and, hands down, the best ones of my life. Carly was an easy baby and a very happy one. She nursed contentedly for the first several months, but we switched her over to a bottle when it became evident that our voracious daughter needed more nourishment than I could provide. She was sleeping through the night at three months old, and she was equally at ease in anyone's arms—mine, James', Tiki's or any of the houseguests we had during that time. The place next door came on the market, so we bought it and turned it into a guesthouse and recording studio. It seemed easier than moving, at least at first, until the renovations really began in earnest. Between my mom, Kathy and Mike, Beth and Jesse and Teddy, it seemed like there was always someone joining us at the breakfast table.

Since Tiki was now living with us, and Alex, Marnie and Ari were always stopping by, it just made sense to expand our living space. We hired a part-time housekeeper to cook and clean and kept Tiki on as Carly's nanny and my 'assistant.' She enjoyed taking care of all of the details that made up our busy lives, and it was always entertaining to listen to her arguing on the phone.

"No way, mon," she would say forcefully. "Miss Jill not gonna wait for dat delivery at no end of the week. You suppose to deliver today, huh? C'mon now, you can do it, yes?" She would hang up the phone and wink at me, and the rocking chair for the nursery or the crate of Maine lobsters packed in dry ice would magically appear later that day.

James was busy supervising the renovations, especially the first floor recording studio, and he could frequently be seen wearing a hard hat as he walked over to the busy construction zone to consult with one of the architects. He and Alex spent a lot of time poring over the blueprints, and by the time they finished tweaking everything, a million dollar studio was built next door. Whenever my in-laws came out from New Jersey, Mike spent his days working on the residential side of the guesthouse, and Kathy and I enjoyed our time shopping and looking over catalogs to find furnishings and accessories. In the end, two large guest suites, each with their own bath, a good-sized living area and a small galley kitchen afforded our overnight guests comfort and gave us some privacy as well. Tiki installed a huge whiteboard in our kitchen to keep track of the incoming and departing flights of our guests and their preferred sleeping accommodations. She was thrilled when we bought her a brand new Jeep to shuttle everyone around in.

James and I had happily resumed our own schedule of regular sex, two weeks before my doctor suggested it was feasible, and we enjoyed spending hours in bed together, rebuilding the intimacy that had always been such an important part of our relationship. I still got weak in the knees when he walked into a room, even if he had only left for a short while, especially if he was only wearing a towel and that sexy grin of his. He seemed content puttering around the house and carried Carly just about everywhere. There was no talk yet of a follow-up tour and *Guessing* was still a top selling LP, especially with the boost it got from a Grammy win for best album. *Jericho Road* held on to the number one slot for almost half a year, despite the fact that it didn't pick up a single award.

I had viewed the ceremony months earlier on TV with Marnie and Ari by my very pregnant side. We watched silently as two label execs accepted *Guessing's* award on James' behalf at the end of the night. James and I had been living apart for months, and at the time, I figured that James had stayed away from the ceremonies because he didn't want me to attend with him. He later admitted that it was nerves that kept him away. My cocky, self-confident husband had his own doubts to deal with at times.

In other family news, Teddy graduated with honors from the state university and after he decided to go to law school, James convinced him that only a top school would do and to let us foot the bill. So my little brother came out to California, is studying at Stanford and loving life. He wants to work in entertainment law, a decision I'm sure that all of the Sheridan legal hijinks inspired. I was just so glad to have him on the same coast, a sentiment apparently shared by his girlfriend Marnie.

Cupid struck again last year when Alex decided to make it legal with a pretty massage therapist named Melissa. They had been living together for a couple of years when she gave him an ultimatum: marry me or get the hell out. Kathy and Mike flew out for the simple ceremony and we all watched in awe as a radiant, eight months pregnant barefoot woman in a flowing white dress officially joined the Sheridan clan. James was the best man, and the bride's sister served as maid of honor.

The outdoor reception featured mainly vegan fare, so after the new bride's water broke during their first dance as a married couple, and an ambulance took the newlyweds to the hospital, we stopped at In 'n Out Burger for a quick meal before heading there ourselves. Just a few hours later, Ryder James Sheridan joined the family, weighing in at a robust 9 pounds. Four-year-old Carly was thrilled to meet her first cousin, even though she confided to James that the only boy she really liked was her daddy and that all boys were icky and had a penis.

But I can't lie and say that absolutely everything was great. We hit a few bumps in the road during those happy years. Amber Leigh, James' opening act for the first few weeks of the *Guessing* tour, hired an attorney who filed a lawsuit on her behalf. James was accused of sexual harassment and creating a work environment that was 'uncomfortable' for the young artist. The label was charged with her wrongful termination, and everyone involved wanted to make the whole mess go away.

I don't know just how much money she ultimately received to settle and I don't really want to. That was definitely a period of time that I never again wanted to revisit.

When Carly was just a few weeks old, my dad died very suddenly of a heart attack at the age of 53. Since I had not been cleared by my doctor for travel, I had to skip the funeral, which Teddy told me was a very quiet affair. Tiki arranged for a large floral arrangement to be delivered to the funeral home. I convinced my mom to pay us a visit a few months later to meet her granddaughter, so she flew for the first time and stayed for a couple of weeks. I swear she looked ten years younger and really seemed to enjoy our new baby girl, the warm weather and meeting all of our friends. We had a few preliminary conversations about moving her out here, but I think she was still hoping that Susan would be looking for her someday. I got that. I mean, if Carly and I were ever separated, well, I would try to be where she could find me. Even Jericho Road.

So we had our ups and downs just like everyone else, but something happened that almost caused our marriage to implode. It occurred just before Carly's first birthday. James had been finishing up a round of talk shows and press engagements to promote his Grammy-winning LP and was being interviewed by some blond airhead on one of those Entertainment Tonight clone TV shows. Not having done her homework, she asked James what it felt like to write all those amazing songs. James later swore that he must have misunderstood the question and claimed that the question he heard was about how it felt to *sing* all those amazing songs. In any event, he answered with his trademark grin and a rote response.

"I'm very proud of the album and I love performing it live for my fans. I'm just so pleased that the music resonates with so many people."

I was hyperventilating by that point, as I watched from my living room. "Tell her I wrote the fucking songs, James," I screamed until Carly started to cry and Tiki had to take her to her room.

The reporters' follow up question was about me. "I understand you're married, James," she said with a twinkle. "How does your wife feel about all your success?"

I waited for him to say that we were partners, and were both successful and that I wrote all those songs. But instead, he grinned again and told her, "Jill is my biggest fan. She always believed in me, even when we could barely pay the rent. She's my muse and the mother of our baby girl." Then he started to wave at the camera. "Hi, honey. Hi, Carly. Daddy loves you."

The reporter ended the segment with some lame verbiage about just how many *Guessing* LPs had been sold, blah, blah, blah. I clicked off the TV set and threw the remote control across the room. *Muse? I'm his fucking muse?* The phone started ringing, and the calls didn't stop for hours. Everyone I knew had seen James on TV and wanted to chat. 'Didn't he look great?' and 'Wasn't that so cute how he waved to Carly on national TV?'

The only person who figured out why I was not at all pleased and sounding so hostile was my friend Beth. She and I had our differences over the years, and we were no longer as close as we had been as teens, but she knew me better than just about anyone. "He called you his muse, Jill. What a totally dick move. You wrote those freakin' songs. Maybe he was your muse, huh?"

*Thank you, Beth!* I unplugged the phone after that, and I found my old pal Ativan a short while later and washed a couple down with a bottle of beer from the back of the fridge. Even carrying my extra post-baby weight, those suckers always knocked me on my ass, so I never even stirred when James climbed into bed with me.

The next day, I was still mad as hell, and I screamed and yelled and threatened legal action if James didn't issue some sort of retraction. Three days later, a full-page ad in Variety featured a loving letter from James to me, giving me full credit for writing all those songs and thanking me for inspiring him to perform them. The phone started ringing again, and my agent Ari became convinced that my song-writing career had just begun.

## Chapter 39 - *Ray of Light*

So I guess my relationship with Alex finally came full circle. After his son was born and Melissa and the baby were asleep in the hospital room, Alex came to find me. He told me he needed to talk to me, so James went home to be with Carly. I said that I would follow him home in just a bit. I honestly couldn't remember the last time I had been alone with Alex and was a bit apprehensive as we helped ourselves to coffee and found a seat in the nearly deserted hospital cafeteria.

That's when he told me... everything. Apparently, he had been attracted to me back in the early days, but kept his feelings to himself once it was clear that James and I were actually going to be a couple. He apologized for coming across as downright hostile to me. He admitted to being really uncomfortable seeing me and James together. Soon after, his feelings of jealousy were replaced with a genuine concern for me. He saw me as extremely vulnerable and ill prepared for the rigors of a relationship with a hotheaded and flirtatious rock star with an alcohol problem.

"James was like a tidal wave," he remembered sadly. "I hated to see the damage that he could do to someone like you."

I reached over and grabbed his hands in mine. "I'm stronger than I look, Alex. I tried to tell you that," I reminded him.

He chuckled and grinned at me. "You surprised me, Jill. I always underestimated you." He shrugged and added, "I couldn't have ever imagined the success you'd have with your writing and how famous you two would be. I'm a fan, you know. Probably your biggest one. And all this," he gestured around the cafeteria. "This is all on you."

"Say what? What's on me, Alex?"

"I watched you. Loving James and supporting him. Sticking with him through everything."

"What a treat that must have been." I rolled my eyes and chuckled. "Not exactly the poster children for a happy marriage, huh?"

"Jill, I'm serious. You guys are tight. Maybe a relationship doesn't require two perfect people in order to work."

"Yeah, we're both far from perfect, Alex."

"But you're happy, darlin'. And so is my brother. And you've got a kid."

"And so do you. Speaking of which, you should get back." We got up to leave and Alex pulled me in for a hug. I stiffened up, before I realized it was just a friendly sort of hug. The only other time we had been this close was that awful night in Dallas. But that was two weddings and two kids ago. I relaxed against him for just a moment before I pulled away. "Enjoy this special time, Dad. And don't count on getting any sleep for at least the next two years."

"G'night, Jill. Drive safe, okay? And hey, thanks for everything." He waved and strode purposefully towards the door.

"Goodnight Alex," I called to him. I watched him head towards his family, then drove home to my own.

Jill's Journal

I'm taking something back I never should
have lost

I'm moving ahead but I'm taking my time

I'm finding my voice and it's sounding fine

I've paid the ransom

I'm a hostage no more

## Chapter 40 - *I Believe I Can Fly*

I will never forget the first time I heard "Hostage" being played on the radio. I was at the mall, trying on bathing suits with Marnie. We were sharing a large dressing room, and we kept tripping over four-year-old Carly, who was sprawled on the floor coloring. She was using a white crayon, and she kept looking at the image that only she could see on the white paper. She kept chuckling and shaking her head. She slays me, I swear. I always tell her, "You're the best time I've ever had, Carly bear." And it's true.

So we're laughing and pulling on dozens of suits in search of the perfect one when I heard it. It was my song, playing on the in-store sound system. I shrieked and begged the girls to listen with me. Marnie started jumping around, and Carly decided to join in the fun.

"It's Mommy, it's Mommy," she sang and twirled around 'til she got dizzy and landed in a heap of discarded Lycra and Spandex. It wasn't actually me, of course. I couldn't hold a tune to save my life. *Hostage* is a song that I wrote about how I got rid of the negative emotions that were holding me back. Finding a good therapist that I could trust and giving up the pills were not easy. I had let shame and fear and insecurity rule my life for too long and I finally decided that enough was enough. The big break for me was letting go of the responsibility I felt towards James. Don't get me wrong! I loved the guy and couldn't imagine my life without him. But I had a daughter to raise. If James wanted to get drunk or high, that was on him. If he went on a bender and I didn't hear from him for an entire lost weekend, it wasn't my fault. If he wanted to get help, I would support him.

"Detach with love" was what my therapist Laraine told me. I finally found my voice and figured out that I had something to say. *Hostage* was honest and raw and the young woman who recorded it was singing the hell out of it. It was the first single from her best-selling album, and I knew it would get a lot of radio airplay. But the first time you hear your song, your story? It's like magic, like nothing you can imagine.

It was different with the songs on *Guessing*. It was only five years since it was released, but I had changed so much since then. Listening to James sing our songs was amazing, but for someone new to choose me and love what I had to say? Thrilling! So I sat on the pile of swimsuits with my darling daughter and my dear friend, and we sang the words I knew so well. It was a very good day!

**1998**

### Chapter 41 - *What's Up?*

Things were really quiet after the renovations were done, and the construction workers all moved on to other jobs. Our steady stream of guests from out of town was more of a trickle, and Carly was starting first grade. There was a school bus that serviced our neighborhood, and it even stopped in our little cul de sac, but as a stay-at-home mom, I decided I could shuttle my precious baby back and forth each day.

I had given up my beloved Mustang a couple of years before in order to drive a more practical mini-van. Every mom I knew had one. I fit right in! Carly had always had lots of play dates and had even attended half-day kindergarten. She was more than ready to make the leap to big-girl school, as she called it. Me? Not so much. The first day was impossibly hard and the second, simply miserable, but by the end of the first week, I was able to walk away from the school and not dissolve into tears on the drive home. During the second week, I decided that I needed some socialization myself, so I dressed for yoga, figuring I could take in a class after I did the drop-off. I was not expecting the crowd of paparazzi who surrounded me on my way out of the school, and I freaked when microphones were shoved in my face and the shouts to "Look this way, Jill," and "Over here, Jill," started up. I hightailed it to the car and was about to issue a curt, "No comment" when I realized that I had no idea what I was *not* commenting about. I finally turned to one of the less aggressive guys and asked him directly what was going on. He looked at me curiously and smiled as if I had said something funny. His forehead wrinkled in concentration as it dawned on him that I really had no idea what was going on.

"Ask your husband," he advised. "Ask him about Leah Donovan."

Leah Donovan? I knew that name. She had been James' girlfriend before me. They had been together, on and off, for a couple of years, I recollected. I didn't think James had seen her in at least eight years, but when it came to my husband, I had learned to not be surprised about anything. I decided to forego yoga in favor of heading home to take the reporter's advice. I had to talk to James.

"What's this about Leah, James?" I called out as I stormed in through the back door. I flung my keys down and took off through the house. No sign of him, so I raced next door to the recording studio where he spent a good portion of his time. Heart pounding, I flung open the door and spotted James sitting in the far corner of the large space with his back to me. I crossed the room, trying to keep from getting hysterical. What fresh hell was this?

"James," I hollered, and he jumped at the sound of my voice. He pointed to the phone he was holding and gave me the classic, 'just a minute, this is an important call' gesture so I held back and tried to listen. From what I could tell, the other party was doing most of the talking, leaving James to nod and say things like "Okay, I get that," and "Yeah, you're probably right."

When he hung up the phone, it was a moment or two before he finally looked at me. I could tell this was pretty serious and I figured it had something to do with Leah. I hoped like crazy that she wasn't claiming to have a child of his that he knew nothing about. Plenty of stars get hit with paternity suits, and so far James had dodged that bullet. Until now? He seemed sad and a bit on edge as he looked at me and slowly shook his head.

"James, what's going on?" I demanded. "What's this about Leah?"

At the sound of her name, James closed his eyes and moaned. "Oh Christ, Jill," he mumbled. "This is seriously fucked."

It took a while, but I was soon able to patch together the whole story. According to the plagiarism lawsuit Leah was filing against my husband, she claimed to have written Nomad's only hit song *Over You* nearly ten years before. It hadn't bothered her when Nomad was enjoying their modest success, but now that Jamie Sheridan had hit the big time, the ante had been upped. She saw her ex boyfriend as a cash cow, and she was ready for her payday!

The worst part about the whole thing was that although the song in question was not on the *Guessing* LP, James had always made it part of his regular set list in concert because his fans always requested it. Just how much of the highest grossing rock tour in music history's success could be attributed to that one song? Well, that's what Leah's lawyers wanted to know. According to the lawsuit, they would settle for ten percent of the gross to date, or if that offer wasn't acceptable, they would let a jury decide.

I have never been a math whiz, but even I knew just what that could mean. Probably $10 million dollars, maybe more. The tour had been so successful that I was pretty certain that some bean counter was still tallying the totals, and here was Leah with her hand out. For several days, I heard snippets of the talks between James, Ron, the label's in-house legal department and the team of copyright sharks that had been hired. Every conversation focused on the financial implications and the damage that something like this could do to the moneymaking machine that was Jamie Sheridan. I tried to shelter Carly from all of it and was grateful for Tiki and Marnie, who took turns driving our daughter to and from school, as I was still getting followed everywhere I went by the press. The house phone never stopped ringing, and I had finally unplugged it. I really had nothing to say on the subject, at least not at first.

The third night of *LeahGate*, I went to bed early, but was still awake hours later when James crawled in beside me. I turned to face him and suddenly I had to know. Everyone had been assuming that Leah was just trying to cash in, and no one seemed to believe her claims of authorship. But this wasn't my first time at the rodeo. I knew better than anyone just how easily things could go from black and white to a very muddy shade of gray, especially when millions of dollars were at stake.

"James?"

"Yeah, darlin'?"

"She wrote it, didn't she?" I knew I was right.

"Yeah, I guess so. I mean, we were pretty wasted most of the time back then. But, yeah..."

"You have to pay her, James. It's only fair. Make her an offer, huh? Make this go away, please." I watched as my husband's glittery blue eyes closed and he let out a deep sigh. "It's the right thing to do, James," I persisted.

"I know you're right, darlin'. I'll talk to them tomorrow. We'll make it right."

And the next day, James convinced everyone that a cash settlement was the best move. No one wanted a lengthy court battle, except maybe the lawyers, so it was done. Even though the terms of the agreement were supposed to be kept confidential, the media reported that Leah had accepted a lump sum payment of $7 million in exchange for the exclusive rights to her song and had agreed that she would not pursue any future claims. The label execs were understandably upset, as was Ron, since much of the settlement came out of their pockets and with legal expenses, the whole debacle had cost nearly $10 million. I have no idea how much Leah actually received after legal expenses, but I hoped it was more than enough for her to live on comfortably. I was relieved to put the whole thing behind us and get back to our lives, raising Carly and making more music.

I had been writing songs with some new recording artists, and James spent much of his time in the recording studio next door. He had handpicked a select group of musicians to collaborate with on his follow-up LP and had found a new producer, an industry veteran, who claimed to want to unveil the 'real' Jamie Sheridan. I had already started working on some songs for him, but one day James told me not to bother, that he was going in a different direction with this one.

I was hurt at first, but decided to continue to peddle my songs elsewhere. One of the musicians working on the new record was Alex, and since he was now living a couple hours north of the city, he and Melissa and Ryder took up semi-permanent residence in the guesthouse. It was nice getting to know my sister-in-law better, and she and I spent hours each afternoon playing with the kids as soon as Carly got out of school. James and I were getting along better than ever, and we enjoyed having more family around. I grew to love entertaining and Sunday night dinners at our house became a tradition. Teddy and Marnie were regulars and Ari and her on-again, off-again boyfriend Joe frequently showed up. Several of our neighbors dropped by and brought wine or elegant desserts. I kept the menu simple but there was always plenty to eat and no one left without a doggy bag. We played music and watched the kids race around. Life was good and I was happy.

**2000**

## Chapter 42 - *Lose Yourself*

"I just need a couple more days. How about by the end of the week?" I was anxious, but trying not to sound it. I really wanted this job. It was a great opportunity to break into the pop charts with an up-and-coming young artist who was going solo, leaving the boy band he used to front. My songwriting career had had its share of chart toppers, beginning with the *Guessing* songs from nearly 10 years ago. But other than James, all of my songs had been recorded by young women and I really wanted to prove that I was an equal opportunity songwriter.

Corey Brennan, this kid from Seattle, could be just the break I needed, but I had been unable to meet the deadline his label had set. I had screwed up royally, and called his manager to ask for an extension. I didn't want to play the 'mom card' so I hinted that I had been trying to finish up work for another artist in order to focus on this excellent opportunity to work with young Corey.

"We could do lunch on Friday. Does that work? I'll have everything you need by then." We made plans to meet and I hung up the phone, relieved for an extension. Now I needed to get going and write some hit songs. Piece of cake, right?

I padded down the hall to our bedroom and surveyed my walk-in closet. I was searching for my trusty 'yoga' pants, the ones that had never experienced a downward dog during all the years I had worn them, and my lucky tank top. The pants were in a heap on the floor right next to the hamper where I had left them the night before, but the top was nowhere to be found.

I had been wearing it when I finished writing *Hostage*, my biggest non-*Guessing* hit almost 5 years earlier. I had set it aside so that I would only wear it for songwriting, but it had been awhile and I couldn't find it anywhere. I grabbed a hot pink tank and vowed that it would be my *new* lucky top, slipped into a pair of flip-flops and I was ready to get started. I had been up for hours, already showered, poured cereal and juice for Carly and driven her to school, wearing my bathrobe. Came home, groveled on the phone and now it was time to settle down and start writing.

But first I needed to straighten up my very lived-in kitchen. I loaded the dishwasher, wiped down the countertops and sorted through the stack of mail from the last couple of days. There was no shortage of mindless jobs to be done keeping our lives organized, and never more so than during one of Tiki's vacation breaks. We had been giving her four weeks off each year, so every few months we would go through the withdrawal pains of trying to manage without her for a week or so.

I didn't begrudge her the time, not at all. If anyone deserved some time away, it was Tiki. I always expected James to step up during those times, to be just a bit more present, you know? The first couple of times, I had assumed that as the large calendar was clearly marked as such, James would recognize that he should plan around her time off. But he went on, blissfully unaware that I might expect him to pick up some of the slack. I finally decided to be more direct with him.

"James, you know that Tiki is taking a week off at the end of the month, right?"

"Huh? Yeah, I guess so. Well, good for her. She deserves to get away." He went back to his eggs and his Blackberry.

"But James, it gets pretty crazy around here when she's gone. I need to know that I can count on you," I pleaded. He looked at me blankly for a moment, then nodded.

"Sure, darlin'. Whatever you need. Just let me know."

And that was the end of that conversation. But other than driving Tiki to the airport ten days later, James went on about his days as if nothing was different. If he noticed that we were eating takeout nearly every night or that the laundry was starting to pile up, he never said. I chauffeured Carly around and volunteered in her classroom two mornings a week, made her lunches and kept the house in some semblance of order. I spent the little time leftover on the phone drumming up business and tried to devote at least an hour a day to writing.

It was an ongoing challenge. It's not like you can say, 'Okay, I have 45 minutes. Now sit down and write something good.' The creative process doesn't work that way, at least not for me. I need inspiration and trust me, it's hard to write love songs when you're feeling stressed and a whole lot less than loving. I tried to understand what it must be like to be James, really I did. I sometimes would imagine life married to a teacher or a plumber. Someone with a less erratic schedule and a greater sense of responsibility. I mean, he loved us, James did. But spending time with us wasn't really a priority for him. There was always something... an important lunch date, a trip he needed to take, an appointment in New York that he just couldn't postpone.

He had been under a great deal of pressure to finish *Jamie, Live* and the delays and cost overruns were starting to become a real problem. I asked repeatedly if I could do something to help out, but James had been adamant and wouldn't accept any help, not from me. *Guessing* had been our project, but *Jamie, Live* was all on him. So I tried to stay out of his way and kept mum when his time at home was nearly non-existent and I didn't tell him that Carly had asked, "Does Daddy still live here?" one morning at breakfast. It would have broken his heart to hear that, but of course, he would actually had to have been there in order to hear it.

"Of course he does, Carly bear," I responded. I tried to keep my tone light. "Where else would he live, silly?"

She just shrugged and continued blowing bubbles into her chocolate milk. That night when James came home hours after Carly had gone to bed, I pressed him. "Go kiss her goodnight, James," I told him. "She misses her dad." I wanted our darling girl to know just how much both of us loved her.

I had commitments to keep as well and I was getting sick and tired of always playing second fiddle to my husband. One night as he was packing his bags, I told him. "I'm tired of playing second fiddle, James. Just once, maybe you could put my needs first, you know?"

James looked at me and just shook his head. "I'm too tired to fight with you, Jill. I have to catch the redeye in order to be in the studio first thing in the morning. I told you that the other day."

"I don't want to fight either. But James, we miss you. Carly needs you and so do I," I ended in a whisper.

He looked up from his packing long enough to pick up on the fact that I was sad, not mad. He put down the shirt he was attempting to fold and walked over to me. When I didn't move over to give him room next to me on the loveseat, he scooped me up and sat down with me on his lap. He pulled me close and stroked my hair gently.

"Oh darlin'," he began. "I hate this, I really do. I just have to get this sucker wrapped up and ready to release. The label is breathing down my neck, and if there are any more delays, I don't know what they'll do. It's just a little while longer, okay? Can you be patient just a while longer?"

What could I say? I looked into his glittery blue eyes and smiled at him. He looked exhausted, like he hadn't slept in a week. "I know, sweetheart," I reassured him. "But this weekend? Let's spend a day at the beach, okay? Just the three of us. We can pack a lunch and just have a lazy day together. Have some fun. What do you say?"

I held my breath until he nodded. "Sounds great, darlin'. It's on. And you know, Carl won't be picking me up for another hour," he added in a conspiratorial tone. "So if you can help me finish packing, maybe we could have a little fun ourselves, just you and me. What do *you* say?"

*Hell, yeah!* I hugged him to me and whispered in his ear, "Screw packing, Jamie Sheridan. You can buy whatever you need in Nashville tomorrow, you big superstar. Screw me instead." So he did and we managed to have our fun, pull together most of the essentials he needed and only kept poor Carl waiting for 20 minutes in the process.

Inspired, I threw myself into writing that night and kept at it all week long. James was true to his word, and was home in time to spend Saturday at the beach with me and Carly. We had lots to celebrate that day since less than 24 hours earlier, Corey Brennan and his manager had signed me to write three songs on his debut album. They loved what I had written.

"Where did you come up with this one?" young Corey had asked me over hazelnut cappuccinos. He was referring to the lyrics from "Even If I Wanted To," detailing a lover's quarrel centered around the difficulties of finding time for romance, and having to settle for quickie sex instead.

"I have a very vivid imagination," I assured him.

**2004**

## Chapter 43 - *End of the Road*

*'It's like he was sleepwalking the whole way through.'*

*'This was an okay record, but nothing like his first time up at bat. Sheridan strikes out.'*

*'Looks like Jamie was 'Guessing' he could make a better album. Guess again, music fans.'*

*'Check for a pulse. Is Jamie really live?'*

James' second solo album, *Jamie, Live*, was a total commercial failure and was panned by almost all of the music critics whose opinions still mattered. The tour that had been planned to support its release sputtered and died somewhere in the Midwest, and James was back home with me and Carly months before we had expected.

I was sorry for him, because I knew how hard he had worked and was surprised at how poorly *Live* was received. It had been more than five years in the making, costs had soared, and the label almost pulled the plug on at least two separate occasions. I had expected that it would have been fairly successful, especially with the contributions from all of the musicians he had managed to include on the LP's 11 tracks. The label was fairly complacent about the less-than-stellar response and seemed to take the losses in stride, but no one was talking about James making another album either.

I for one was glad to have my husband home again. Carly was almost thirteen and getting to be quite a handful. She had a real mouth on her, and screaming "I hate you" and slamming doors had become her standard response to just about anything I said, especially when it was just the two of us. For a short while, James served as a buffer for us both. "Tell your daughter she's not going out of the house dressed like that, James," would be countered with, "Tell *her* that everyone dresses like this and to get a life, Dad."

James took the whole thing in stride, but I knew it bothered him to see his two favorite girls at odds with each other. "Don't let her push your buttons, Jilly. Pick your battles," he would advise me. "You should listen to your mom, Carly. She knows what's best," was how he usually responded to Carly's complaints. Despite the friction, it was good to be together again as a family and at the last minute, we decided to book a tropical getaway over the holidays. It was paradise and would become a new family tradition, I decided shortly after we arrived. We slept late, played in the surf, and got burned to a crisp one afternoon. We spent the next day lazing around the suite, watching movies and picking at room service trays. My fondest memory was of hugging my daughter close to me on Christmas Eve, after she joked about how hard it would be for 'Santa' to find us. She had her dad's height and already stood half a head taller than me.

"I love you, Carly bear," I snuffled into her shoulder as I held her tight. She relaxed long enough to tell me that she loved me too. James was videotaping the whole thing, but put down the camcorder long enough to wrap us both up in his arms and for a short while, we three were the only people on earth. The next morning, we watched as Carly unwrapped the few gifts we had managed to bring with us and were delighted at her reaction when she discovered that the MP3 player she had been hinting about was among them. She and James had found me a lovely pair of earrings at one of the resort's gift shops, but I had nothing for James that year. He always was hard to buy for, and I had run out of time getting us ready for the trip.

"I already have everything I need, darlin'," he murmured in my ear, causing Carly to suggest that we "get a room." We all laughed and went out to brunch, then spent the rest of the day on the beach. It was the happiest day of my life, and I wanted us to stay on that island forever, safe and happy and together. But before I knew it, it was time to head home.

We were still doing well financially, so it wasn't like James had to go find a real job or anything. In hindsight, maybe it would have been easier if he had. He frequently got up to have breakfast with Carly, something that I had given up on awhile before. I never knew who would be sitting across the table with me any more: the crunchy granola vegan who sneered at my offer to make her bacon and eggs? The drama queen who complained about the unjust policies of a school system who actually thought that anyone could learn at this freakishly early hour? The sweet girl who would hop up to refill my coffee cup and offer to split her blueberry muffin? No, I was glad to relinquish that responsibility to James and spend an extra hour alone in bed.

After dropping Carly and her best friend Lily off at school, James would slip back into bed with me and some mornings, it was almost like our early years when we were young and couldn't keep our hands off each other. But those lovely moments were frequently cut short due to an appointment or a work deadline. Usually mine, as I was getting more work than I could handle, and if James seemed a little lost those days, as I rushed off to take care of business, well, what could I do? I was the new "It" girl when it came to songwriting, and I wanted to make the most of it.

Once in a while, Alex would come by the house and he and James would hang out by the pool and smoke a joint or have a couple of beers. I figured that he would get back to doing something more productive soon, and that if anyone deserved a break, it was James. Before I knew it, he shed that lethargy and started to seem more energetic. He would bop around the kitchen as I pulled together our evening meal and sneak tastes from whatever I was preparing, usually heated-up dishes that Tiki would leave for us. We never replaced the cook when she resigned, and Tiki had happily resumed the responsibility of meal prep for our household. She had moved into her own place recently in order to spend more time with her new boyfriend, but showed up most days to cook, straighten up and hang out with me and Carly. She was always so mellow and relaxed, a polar opposite of my frenetic husband who talked a mile a minute.

James started spending more time in the studio, and since it was so well soundproofed, I couldn't hear any of the music he was creating over there. More and more guys were coming by at all hours, and if he didn't always introduce me to them, well, that was okay. Whenever I asked how it was going, he would just grin and tell me that it was going just great. We both had a lot on our plates, and if he seemed a little edgy at times, I just chalked it up to the fact that he was still going through a big adjustment. A couple of times, he was really short with me and once he screamed at Carly for leaving the lights on when she left the room. She ran off to her room in tears.

"Pick your battles, James," I reminded him. I was completely dumbfounded when he responded, "Fuck off, Jill. I wasn't talking to you."

I stomped off to the bedroom, and finally resigned myself to sleeping alone when it became evident that he was not going to be joining me that night. I could see the lights on next door, so I assumed he was working on something. The next morning he apologized to both of us.

"I'm so sorry, my loves. I'm just in a bit of a bad patch right now," he admitted, before kissing us both. I tried to put it all behind me as well. But things continued to get worse. Anything could cause James to flip out, and I found myself able to breathe normally only when he was out of the house. Poor Carly and I were walking on eggshells and trying to shelter James from just about everything. He was so moody and easily provoked.

"What's wrong with Dad?" Carly would ask me, her bright blue eyes filled with tears. "It's like he hates us or something."

I would tell her that 'No, of course he loves us, sweetheart,' but I found his erratic behavior increasingly hard to defend, and I was in the dark as to what was going on, since James was shutting me out more and more.

When Alex found James unconscious on the bathroom floor in the guesthouse late one morning, and he was rushed off to the hospital in an ambulance, I had a hard time believing what the medics were telling me. A cocaine overdose was the last thing I expected.

Jill's Journal

I guess I could have stayed in LA when the decision was made for James to move to New York. I would have needed to shuttle Carly back and forth cuz keeping her from her dad would never work and splitting up would never work either. Not for a young girl who worships her daddy and cried herself to sleep every night he was in rehab. Not for a recovering addict who has to believe in something beyond a bottle or a line of coke. And not for a wife and mom who would trade everything for her family to be together and happy. So I'm going to give living back east a try. Maybe I can reconnect with my mom and with Beth. I have been lying to them both for so long, I honestly don't even know where to start. And I can work anywhere. I just need my journal and some gel pens, maybe my computer and a fax line. I want a normal life with James and Carly. I want us to be happy.

We came so close to losing you

I realize that now

I need you here. I love you so

Living without you? I wouldn't know how.

May 5, 2005

Dear Beth,

We are delighted to be back on the East Coast, and I am loving life in New York City! Kathy and Mike are over the moon that their granddaughter is living so close by. All the best schools are here anyway, so it all worked out timing wise. The co-op we bought on the Upper East Side was recently renovated so it was pretty much move-in ready. I don't blame Tiki for deciding to stay put, but I hope that she'll be able to visit soon. I hope Jesse got the check we sent him. He must be so happy to have graduated high school. What are his plans? Are you looking at any colleges?

I really hope that you are not reading any of that nonsense about James and his supposed stint in rehab. It was a ridiculously mean spirited attempt on the part of those hacks at The Star. That photo of him lying on that hospital gurney after he OD'd? It was totally fake and whatever 'hospital spokesperson' they quoted must have been high themselves. James was treated for exhaustion a few months back, and he really did need a couple months of R & R, but who wouldn't right? I mean, sign me up, right? But we are all settling in beautifully, and life is good. I hope that you can come to the city really soon. I'm in the middle of redecorating the guest suite so maybe you could stay in a hotel nearby? My treat of course! I know Carly would love to see her 'Aunt Beth'.

Miss you loads. Lots of love,

Jill

## Chapter 44- *Closing Time*

James was doing so much better! Everyone said so. Some announced it out loud and wanted to share their thoughts with everyone within hearing distance. James' dad Mike, for instance. He would greet James with that iron grip handshake of his and boom out just how great his boy was looking. Others wouldn't say anything directly to James, preferring to pull me aside and offer me their views on just how fit or rested or relaxed or happy or well my husband looked to them. The folks from the label who still came around on occasion tended to fall in that last group. My close friends, the ones who really know just how difficult that last year had been for us, tended to focus more on me. They wanted to know how I was and how it felt to have James home with Carly and me again.

To be honest? I was a wreck, thank you very much. I missed James like crazy when he was in rehab. He seemed to be doing reasonably well for an alcoholic/ drug addict in recovery but it felt weird to be living under the same roof with him again. My husband, my partner, the love of my life for almost half of my life. I loved him, but I couldn't trust him. I craved him, but I was afraid to open up. I wanted him to be close to our daughter, but if he broke her heart again? Well, I couldn't let that happen, now could I?

James' psychiatrist was the one who had suggested we break ties with LA and move back east. Too many temptations, too many bad habits that would have been hard for James to break. Just about all of my friends, my agent, Teddy and Marnie, Alex and his family and all of my clients were left behind too, but is any price too great to get your husband sober, huh? Of course not! And James would have done the same for me if the situation had been reversed.

So there we were, in the city that reportedly never sleeps, in a huge pre-war co-op with a doorman and a Starbucks on every street corner. It was a whole new start for us, a fresh one. Carly was pretty good about having to move. She was a tough kid and more than anything, she wanted James to be okay. We got her into a great school geared for creative kids like her, and she was thriving.

We settled into a comfortable routine. James got up early each day to have breakfast with Carly before she went to school. Then he and I drank coffee together or went for a walk around the neighborhood. He usually left the house mid-morning for his daily session with his therapist. At noon, he attended one of the nearby AA or NA meetings, and then hit the gym for some cardio and free weights followed by a steam or a sauna. He came home exhausted, mentally and physically, and often took a midafternoon nap in order to still be upright for a quiet dinner at home with Carly and me. We watched the news or a movie after dinner while Carly did her homework, and sometimes we had a late night snack before we turned in. It wasn't very exciting, but considering the alternative, I counted my blessings every single day.

I tried to write in my journal and usually found time to squeeze in yoga or an aqua jogging class at the gym. I was decades younger than most of the other women in the pool, though most of them could swim circles around me. But it was a great workout, and I didn't have time to think about anything else in the pool.

We found Marie, a part time housekeeper who came by a couple of times a week and kept the place neat and tidy, but I was doing most of the cooking. Simple stuff like stir-fries or hearty soups and stews. On the rare nights we had guests, I usually would order in, overwhelmed by the idea of entertaining the way we used to. Some days I felt like an impostor, like someone could just draw back the curtain to reveal the real me. "Halt," they might demand. "Who goes there?"

Who indeed? Devoted mom, loving wife, and happy homemaker? All of the above, but some mornings I could barely summon the strength to get out of bed, and even when I did, it was a struggle to get dressed and out the door. But I usually pushed myself to do my errands and gym visits in the mornings while my house was being cleaned and my laundry was done. Then I could enjoy a late lunch in front of the TV, in my clean, quiet home with a cup of last night's soup or some cheese and crackers. After watching a home improvement or cooking show, I was ready to write for an hour or two before James got home.

My 'journal' those days was a slim laptop computer. I didn't use all of the bells and whistles, but I kept up with emails and ventured into social media just a bit as well. My favorite site was Carly's Facebook page, where she posted scanned images of her artwork and photographs. She had always been pretty artistic and has quite an eye behind the camera, from what I can tell, and she really seems to enjoy it. I hadn't seen James with a guitar for almost a year and I would have been thrilled if he could find a way back to his music. Take away my pen or Carly's paintbrush, and we would be lost. Without a guitar pick in his hand, James was too. I kept telling myself to suggest it to him, but I was so afraid to rock the boat, especially when he was doing so well.

He got a call one day out of the blue from a producer that he used to work with, and he was excited to be offered a chance to tour again. He quickly rejected the idea when he found out that it was going to be promoted as an oldies show, featuring a roster of artists that no one heard from anymore. The "Where Are They Now?" Tour was launched without James 'Jamie' Sheridan.

**2008**

## Chapter 45 - *Truly Madly Deeply*

After a 2½-year hiatus, James went back into the studio! He was no longer under contract with the label, but after all those years in the music industry, he had enough contacts to allow him to sit in on other artists' sessions whenever he wanted. Jamie Sheridan was still considered to be somewhat of a legend, despite the fact *Guessing* was released 16 years before, and his only follow-up LP was both a critical and commercial flop. I was just so glad to see him doing something that he clearly loved, and it gave him a reason to get up in the morning, besides Carly and me.

Carly turned sixteen that summer and swore she had no interest in obtaining a driver's license. For me, that was such an important rite of passage. I remember getting my learner's permit on my sixteenth birthday, and then begging my folks to take me out driving. Being able to drive was a critical step if I was ever going to escape from Jericho Road. My father had delegated the responsibility of teaching me to drive to my mother, but since we had one car and he usually was driving it, opportunities to practice were few and far between. Plus she was a nervous wreck who was convinced we would crash and die a horrible death if I drove over fifteen mph.

Finally my sister Susan, who was living a few towns away at that point, took pity on me. A couple of times a week, she would pull into our driveway, beep the horn until I came out, then slide over onto the passenger's side and command me to drive. Some days we headed toward the highway, other days she would have me practicing parallel parking and making sudden stops in the high school parking lot. I got really good at both, but when my driving test required me to demonstrate neither of my newfound skills, I was crushed.

But Carly was a city kid, and since we didn't even have a car for her to drive anyway, it was probably just as well. I had wanted to celebrate her 'Sweet 16' in a special way, so we ended up taking her and a few of her friends to see Katy Perry at the Garden. I still have a picture that I took that night backstage. Katy was beaming, surrounded by five of her biggest fans, including my darling Carly. Carly and I still talk about that night. That young woman can sing!

I kept busy song writing after we moved back east. One of the songs got used in a movie, and although it was only an indie release, my song got nominated for a Grammy. A few months later, I was called up on stage to accept my award. I was seated way in the back of the auditorium with the other 'artists who probably didn't stand a chance in hell' of winning. After freeing myself from the proud embraces of my husband and my daughter, I made my way down to the dais and mumbled a heartfelt 'Thanks, everyone', before I waved and was led away to meet the press.

What a thrilling night! I posed next to Carrie Underwood (what a cutie) and I swear John Mayer winked at me. Also a cutie. My thoughtful daughter had recorded the whole ceremony on our VCR, so a few days later, I watched the replay and saw the camera panning back to James as he stood clapping for me. Tears were running down his face, and the text on the screen identified him as 'Husband, Grammy Winning Music Legend Jamie Sheridan'. I can count on one hand the number of times I saw James cry, and it really touched me. He could be such a sweetheart!

By the next day, the demand for my song-writing skills had quadrupled and Ari joked that her assistant needed an assistant to keep up with the offers coming in for me. There was still no word from Tom Jones or his people, but virtually every other A-lister was looking to collaborate with me. Even Katy Perry! One day Ari called, wanting me to plan a trip out to LA in order to 'take meetings' with several of the artists at the top of her list. She filled me in on the comings and goings of a few of our mutual friends, and then asked to speak with my other half. As James no longer had the need for full-time representation, Ari had been working with him on occasion. I put down the phone and went looking for James to tell him to pick up. But as I wandered down the hall, I heard him opening the front door and shouting that he was going out for a newspaper, and he was gone. I shook my head as I picked the phone back up.

"Ari? You just missed him. He had to run out for a second." A newspaper? A likely story. In eighteen years, I had never seen James so much as open a newspaper, and I knew that he had recently started smoking again on the sly.

"Okay, toots. No worries. I'll talk to him in a day or two. Hug that gorgeous girl of yours for me, will ya? Later."

I hung up the phone chuckling. Freakin' James. After everything he had been through, a few cigarettes wouldn't have bothered me, but he was sneaking them anyway, maybe for Carly's sake. I decided I would have to tell him that it was okay. And that I loved him very much.

I never got that chance.

## Carly Speaks Up

*Losing my dad? It was like the sucker punch you never saw coming. I mean, who gets hit by a bus on the Upper East Side of Manhattan? Guess he hadn't seen it coming either. What? Too soon?*

*So after 25 years of rock 'n roll, the tours, the drugs, the booze, the women... he's living a clean and sober life, waking up next to my mom every morning and kissing me good night every night and Bamm, just like that, he's gone. He takes a walk around the block from our apartment, tries to sneak a cigarette when everyone knows he's smoking again, apparently hunkers down to try to light it despite a strong breeze, steps off the curb and that is all she wrote. I loved him. I miss him. I can't even imagine living without him. Someday, I'll be able to listen to his music again, but not yet.*

*A couple of years ago, when he went to rehab, I was pretty mad at him. I didn't understand his addictive personality, and I couldn't figure why he would pick the drugs over my mom and me. But I was only 13 back then. It's taken me a long time, but now I get it, get him. And if I am certain of anything, it's that it wasn't a decision that he ever really made. I have already sworn that I am never going to drink or do drugs. I probably have enough of my dad's DNA to just about guarantee that they would be a problem for me, too.*

*My mom thinks I blame her for my dad's death. Like if only she wasn't so controlling, he would have been able to light up at home and not on the street. I actually heard her telling my Aunt Beth on the phone, "It's all my fault." She thinks that's why I* decided to move in with my Uncle Alex and his wife last month, because I'm mad at her. Everyone keeps telling me that they understand why I would want to go live with my dad's twin brother. Because it must be so comforting to be with Alex, like he's a stand-in for my dad or something. They are all so wrong! I sure didn't move to freaking hot and humid Nashville to be closer to my dead dad's twin! It's actually just the opposite. My uncle doesn't remind me of my dad in the least. I mean besides some of their shared physical attributes. They are both tall and dark-haired, but my dad had kept his hair short as long as I've known him and was usually clean-shaven. Alex, who is rapidly going grey, sports a long straggly ponytail and beard. Alex's voice is higher, nothing like my dad's deep baritone. Alex is a weed-smoking vegan with very liberal beliefs, while my dad was a conservative Republican who liked nothing more than a juicy steak after a power walk around Central Park. So, no, I didn't move in with my uncle because he reminds me of my dad. I moved out simply to get away from my mom!

Not that I don't love her-I do, more than I can ever tell her. She's actually my best friend. It's just that being with her makes the loss of my father so painful and real, I couldn't take it anymore. I can't look at her without seeing him, too. They were closer than any couple I know, certainly more than any of my friends' parents. I know they have had their differences over the years, and neither was all that easy to live with, but they were joined at the hip. They finished each other's sentences, shared their own private vocabulary, and when they looked at each other, the look that passed between them was so hot and steamy that I wanted to turn the hose on them sometimes. I know you're not supposed to think of your parents doing it, at least except for the one time nine months before you were born, but I knew that my parents' love life was still pretty spicy. My mom would actually blush when my dad walked into the room, and they were constantly touching each other. Not in a gross, pervy way or anything like that. Everything I ever witnessed was strictly PG. But neither missed the chance to brush by the other, exchange a quick hand squeeze or a light kiss on the top of the head. So when I see my mom sitting at the table, I can't stop myself from imagining that my dad is walking over to pour her a cup of coffee or sitting next to her, stealing her fries. It hurts, all those reminders. My mom still has the greeting on the landline phone that we recorded a couple years before Dad died. I know, because I still call the number whenever I am certain that my mom is out of the house. I bet she wonders about all those hang-ups. But I can't help it. I was really ticked off at both of them that day (although for the life of me, I can't remember why), and the last thing I wanted to do was to record a cheery greeting for the handful of people who don't just call our cellphones. We were all trying to say the same thing; my mom had written the stupid script on a post-it note. It's easy to make out my dad's deep bass, and my mom's voice, kind of breathy and almost like she's surprised, and me sounding like I'm in grade school or something. What you don't hear is how I yelled at them, "We're such a bunch of dorks," as soon as the recorder clicked off, or how my dad responded by picking me up and swinging me around, telling me "Take it back, we're the coolest family EVER," and my mom smiling and reminding us, in case we had forgotten, "I sure love my family."

So being down here with my Uncle Alex, my Aunt Melissa and my cousin Ryder is a break from all of that. They are a close-knit family, and they all get along. The laughter that I had grown up hearing back home wasn't all that common, but that was okay too. It's quieter down here. One day, I took the phone from my uncle's hand and spoke to my mom for the first time in a few weeks. Just hearing her voice hurt. She and my dad even sounded alike, at least to me. Our conversation was pretty strained.

"Carly bear, I miss you."

"I know, Mom. I, um, miss you too."

"Sweetheart, don't you think it's time to come home?"

"Not yet, Mom. I'm not ready."

"But why? Carly, I don't understand…" The rest of what she said was muffled by the sound of her tears.

"Mom, I just gotta… Mom, stop, Don't cry. C'mon, Mom, you're gonna make me…" And I broke down and cried right along with her. Finally, I dried my eyes, and I promised to call her in a few days. I told her I'm looking forward to seeing her.

I just needed this time away. I have to figure out how I'm going to make it work when I go home. How to get used to that big gaping hole in our lives that my dad used to fill. I didn't bring any art supplies with me, so the only creative thing I do these days is to bake with Melissa. Yesterday it was lavender shortbread cookies. She is amazing in the kitchen, making vegan fare something I could almost see myself eating back in New York. Then I picture my dad and those big juicy cheeseburgers he used to take me for on Tuesdays when my mom had her creative writing group and I think, no, probably not.

I guess it's time to go home. I miss my mom.

Jill's Journal


Send thank you notes to Ron (Martha's
Vineyard address?)

    & Ed (label) new address?

Call

    Tiki

    Ari

    Marnie/Teddy re: Christmas in
California??


Write Beth, thank you Jesse!!

Carly's flight??

Call/check on Kathy & Mike

Fruit basket (organic) & thank you to Alex
& Melissa

*July 26, 2008*

*Dear Beth,*

*I really appreciate all that you and Jesse did for us during this most difficult time. My mom enjoyed riding with him back and forth to the service that horrible day. I was so grateful; I couldn't have done it myself obviously. She says he's a very nice young man, so you've done well, my friend. I was so glad you were able to stay here with me for a few days. Even with James' folks and Alex and Tiki all here, it was you making the coffee and answering the phone, ordering takeout and accepting all those floral arrangements. Thanks for having them sent over to that retirement home. My house still reeks of lilies!!*

*Carly will be coming home soon. She's down visiting with Alex and his family for a while. Probably good for her to get away, but I miss her so much!! Maybe it's different with a son. She and I are just soooo close we even finish each other's sentences. What would I ever do without my Carly Bear?*

*Oh and the weirdest thing? Susan found me on Facebook!!!! Yes, my sister Susan. No one in my family has heard from her in like 15 years and one day, there's a message on Facebook. She heard about James and she's all saying how sad it was and how she hoped I was doing okay. Guess she's been living in Canada all this time. Thank goodness for socialized medicine or whatever they have there that is better than here. She's on meds for her bipolar issues, is married and has three kids!!! I called my mom who cried and cried. I would love to pull together some sort of family reunion, but I guess I should get reunited with my own daughter first, huh??*

*Do you believe we're turning 40? Think of something fun to do or someplace cool to go. How about a cruise? After all, we're not getting any younger. As Carly says, you only live once!*

*Thanks for being my best friend and always being there for me.*

*Love, Jill*

An Excerpt from *Jericho Road*

Lyrics by Jill Griffin Sheridan

I couldn't go back there, even if I tried

And you know why that's true

I always said I would, but you know that I
lied

Something I said I'd never do

Only way this makes sense is you by my side

I'm not sure you ever knew

I needed you here, not to run and hide

If it's not me, then who?

## Jill's Journal

Everyone seems to want to know why I stayed all those years. I don't fully understand the question. James was the love of my life! I mean, don't get me wrong. I thought of leaving a bunch of times. After Sharon and Amber and the drinking and the fighting. The thing with Leah could have ended it for us, if James hadn't been a stand up guy. Even with a tiny baby to take care of, I swear I would have kicked him out if he had been unwilling to settle with his ex. Then the drugs and rehab and the need to move away from most of our friends and the comfortable life we had been living. To have to start over, to say goodbye to Tiki? I knew I would see Ted and Marnie again, and I still had a professional relationship with Ari, but the day we left LA, I felt my heart break when I said goodbye to my trusted friend and confidante. When I saw her at James' funeral, I bit my tongue to keep from once again begging her to relocate to NY. I understand why Tiki wants to stay out there. She's building a whole new life for herself and I have to respect that. I have to do the same for Carly and me.

Through it all, I loved James and I know that he loved me. Our lives together were pretty messed up at times, but we raised our amazing Carly and won Grammys and stayed best friends until the end. I just assumed we'd have more time, you know? Looking back, I guess I was pretty lost when I was 21. Dead-end job, one room dump in a crappy neighborhood, no direction, no clue. James may very well have saved me way back then in that motel lobby. But my songs and my love ended up saving him too. So maybe *Jericho Road* is a song about salvation after all!

## Jill's Playlist

What I Got- Sublime

Say My Name- Destiny's Child

Friday, I'm in Love- The Cure

Got My Mind Set on You- George Harrison

I'll Be Missing You- Puff Daddy

Baby, One More Time- Britney Spears

I Don't Want to Miss a Thing- Aerosmith

Every Rose Has Its Thorn- Poison

Two Princes- The Spin Doctors

Bitter Sweet Symphony- The Verve

Only Wanna Be with You- Hootie & the Blowfish

Torn- Natalie Imbruglia

Hard to Handle- The Black Crowes

Everybody Hurts- R.E.M.

Walking on the Sun- Smash Mouth

Right Here, Right Now- Jesus Jones

You Get What You Give- New Radicals

Linger- The Cranberries

Crash Into Me- Dave Matthews Band

Come As You Are- Nirvana

(Everything I Do) I Do It for You- Bryan Adams

Californication- Red Hot Chili Peppers

Losing My Religion- R.E.M.

One Headlight- The Wallflowers

Something to Talk About- Bonnie Raitt

One Week- Barenaked Ladies

Un-Break My Heart- Toni Braxton

When I Come Around- Green Day

All I Wanna Do- Sheryl Crow

More Than Words- Extreme

You Oughta Know- Alanis Morissette

The Boy is Mine- Brandy & Monica

I Try- Macy Gray

Give Me One Reason- Tracy Chapman

One- U2

Daughter- Pearl Jam

Killing Me Softly- The Fugees

Ray of Light- Madonna

I Believe I Can Fly- R. Kelly

What's Up?- 4 Non-Blondes

Lose Yourself- Eminem

End of the Road- Boyz 2 Men

Closing Time- Semisonic

Truly Madly Deeply- Savage Garden

Did you enjoy *Guessing at Normal*? I hope so, but I would like to hear from you either way. You can find me on FaceBook (Gail Olmsted Author), on Twitter @gwolmsted or email, gwolmsted@gmail.com . Watch my website www.gailolmsted.com for news on upcoming releases. I hope that you will take the time to post a review on a website of your choice or a rating on Goodreads. Authors live and die by these reviews, so please give some feedback. It is much appreciated.

My first novel was *JEEP TOUR*, a light and breezy read about the path not taken and what can happen when you get a do-over in your life. Jackie Sullivan is a woman who most readers can relate to and you'll cheer her on as she attempts to navigate the rocky road to romance in Sedona, Arizona. Here's the first chapter for your enjoyment!

Best for now,

*Gail*

P.S. Are you wishing for a 'happy ever after' for Jill Griffin? Check out *Second Guessing*. Available now in print, kindle and audio versions.

## JEEP TOUR

### Chapter 1

"Need a hand?" Our tour guide looked down at me. I was the last one to board the brightly colored Jeep.

"Yes, thanks," I mumbled as he took my hand and helped me into the open back seat.

"You dropped this," he told me as he handed me my water bottle. Glistening with condensation, it slipped from my hand a second time and rolled under the Jeep.

"Sorry," I apologized when he bent down to retrieve it. When he stood upright, I really saw him for the first time. I gave a small gasp. God, he was gorgeous! Tall, built and tan, with a shock of blond streaked hair and dazzling green eyes.

"It's Okay," he said. "I always end up crawling around under the Jeep for one thing or another." X-rated images of him crawling around on me flashed before my eyes, but I quickly dismissed them. I'm a middle-aged tourist, not some sex-starved guide groupie. But could I be both? *Don't be ridiculous*, I told myself. Obviously, my lustful thoughts were not reciprocated. Mr. Hunk patted my hand rather absentmindedly, then swung himself into the driver's seat. He turned the key and the Jeep roared to life.

"Okay then, ladies. Before we set off today, I'd like to introduce myself, find out a little about you and go over a few ground rules. I'm Rick and I'll be your tour guide. Have any of you been on a tour of the desert before?"

I looked over at the other two inhabitants of the Jeep, my colleagues Kate and Linda. Linda spoke for the three of us, since she was riding shotgun and since she was Linda. "No, we haven't. You're our first, Rick," she replied.

Oh, grief, was she flirting with him? We've been there before, Linda and me. She gets this southern-fried thing going on and although she's never lived further south than Rhode Island, it somehow works for her. But it's wrong on so many levels.

*Not now, Linda*, I begged silently.

"So Rick, is this *really* the best tour in all of Arizona?" she drawled.

"Why yes, ma'am," Rick replied. "You ladies have come to the right place." He beamed at Linda, who smiled back at him like they were sharing a secret. Leave it to Linda. She always spoke up first, always got noticed and always took center stage. Bitch.

"I'm Linda," she said as she extended her hand to Rick.

"Well hello there! And who are your friends, Linda?" he responded, still grasping her hand.

"That's Kate and her camera and this is Jax," said Linda, pointing to me.

"Hi Jack," said Rick shaking my hand, before turning to Kate.

"It's Jax," I said.

"What?" said Rick, turning back towards me.

"It's Jax," I murmured. "Not Jack."

"Jax?" he questioned. Knowing I should just shut up, I found myself explaining how I had been named after former First Lady Jacqueline Kennedy. What can I say? My Irish American parents came of age in the 60s, okay? But as a toddler, I lisped and referred to myself as Jackth, and the name stuck.

"But you can call me Jackie," I finished rather inanely. Sensing my discomfort, Linda chimed in "and you can call me Linda," and then she started chattering away about how we had been attending an academic conference in Phoenix and had decided to visit Sedona for some R&R and a quick overnight visit. Rick listened patiently as Linda told him that all three of us were faculty in the School of Business at a small private college in New England, Linda in accounting and finance, Kate in management studies, and me in marketing. At that, Rick turned and looked at me.

"Marketing? I took a class in marketing. I remember the 4 Ps."

I smiled. "Yeah, I get that a lot," I said. "But it's really more about..."

"Okay, ladies, we're off," Rick interrupted. "I'll go over the ground rules on our way to the desert."

Rick drove through the lot and turned right onto the busy surface road. As he weaved his way through the heavy midday Sedona traffic, he began explaining some of the sights that we would be seeing. I vaguely remember him talking about keeping our arms inside the Jeep and how we should stay belted in. Something about the need to drink lots of water and that he had a cooler with plenty of cold bottles. He may have said more, but I honestly don't remember. What he was saying was pretty inconsequential. I was still blown away by how good-looking he was. Shallow, I know. He could have been reading from a phone book for all I cared.

From my current vantage point, I could only see the back of his head and the gold streaked hair that grazed the collar of his khaki tour guide shirt. And his massive tanned right forearm as it maneuvered the steering wheel. Yikes. I couldn't see his left hand and I wondered if he wore a ring. Hmmm. Confident that I had seen all I could for now, I started to pay attention, to listen to him. He spoke clearly and it was pretty easy to hear him over the road noise and the midday traffic. I struggled to place the slight accent that I detected. I am an amateur linguist and I have a knack for identifying where someone might have grown up. But I also know that it's not always accents that identify your place of birth, sometimes it's the words themselves or the phrasing. For instance, if someone says their hair needs washed or their pants need pressed, you can just about guarantee that they were raised in the Pittsburgh area. It's true. But I digress. Struggling to focus, I heard Rick ask Kate about her camera and promise her some amazing shots that afternoon.

"This really is the best tour," he boasted. "Everyone loves it!"

"How long have you been giving Jeep tours, Rick?" Linda asked, accent-free.

"Almost three years," he replied. "I came here on vacation and fell in love with the blue skies and red rocks. Went back, quit my job and here I am."

"Where?" I piped in.

"Where?" asked Rick hesitantly, without turning around.

"I mean, where are you from?" I added.

"All around," Rick replied casually. "I went to college for a couple of years in Pennsylvania and lived in Ohio for a while. I worked as a computer tech, but I was miserable working in a little cubicle. I love it out here in the desert. I can't imagine ever leaving. Okay, ladies, we're going off road here, so hang on. This is where the pavement ends and the adventure begins!"

Over the next hour or so, Rick showed us the sights. We traveled up steep inclines and down narrow trails. We bounced over an old wagon road that used to be a cattle trail. I loved how enthusiastic he was about everything, how he seemed to delight in all the beauty and unique qualities of the desert. Also he was very knowledgeable—he really knew what he was talking about. Rick identified the unofficial state flower—the prickly pear cactus.

"It's edible and is used in so many different things. You should try the prickly pear jelly. We can barely keep it in stock in the gift shop," he assured us.

"Hmmm. Sounds nummy," Linda purred. Honestly!

At one point, we got out to stretch our legs, and Linda and Kate hurried off to take more pictures. Actually Kate was taking the pictures that Linda was telling her to take, but whatever their dynamic, it allowed me to get to know Rick a little more. Just a little bit.

Rick was a better listener than a talker, so I ended up doing most of the talking. They say nature abhors a vacuum? Well, so do I! At even a hint of a potentially awkward silence, you can count on me to jump in to save the day. I told him about how I was up for tenure and that the decision would be announced any day now. I may have flirted a bit in my rather awkward yet endearing manner. I may have hinted that as a college professor, I had summers off. I may have even suggested that I had access to a boatload of frequent flyer miles. I was trying to subtly communicate my potential availability without being too forward. Hey, use what you've got, right? To be truthful, those miles had been racked up by my jet-setting ex, but I'm pretty certain that I had some coming to me as part of last year's divorce settlement. So I talked and Rick smiled and looked thoughtful, and said things like "Is that right?" at all the appropriate moments.

A little while later, we left the mesa somewhat reluctantly, as the views were stunning for miles, but Rick assured us that there was plenty more to see. I was becoming more comfortable around him and hopefully more appealing as the afternoon wore on. He was receptive to my chatter and we really seemed to hit it off. Linda and Kate had already clambered back into the Jeep and I saw that Linda had relinquished her seat up front to me. I was thrilled to be that much closer to our engaging tour guide. And the amazing vistas. And the tour guide.

"C'mon, Jackie. We've got places to go and rocks to see," Rick called out.

"Okay, Rick. I'm coming," I responded with probably a bit too much enthusiasm. I could get used to agreeing with him, if you know what I mean. He waited for me and took my arm to help me into my new seat upfront. It was like a date. Okay, so not a date but I felt a tingle, a really strong reaction to his touch. I think he felt it too. He smiled at me and wait, was that a wink? Was dating a tourist allowed or was it frowned upon by the official tour guide conduct code? And if allowed, how and when would we manage it? And if not allowed, would he be willing to sneak around or even give up his job for me?

*Hold on, hot stuff*, I cautioned myself. *Don't get ahead of yourself. He's just flirting to get a bigger tip.* But still.

The second half of the tour was even more thrilling. In between explaining why canyons exist (apparently rivers cause erosion—who knew?) and identifying scrub live oak and mistletoe, Rick shared bits of his life with me. Okay, with us, but honestly? I was the only one paying attention. Rapt attention! I learned that he lived alone in a cabin in the woods, loved hiking, was a vegetarian and that he had been working down in southern Arizona when he first visited Sedona.

"Where in Arizona?" I asked. I'm in marketing, okay? Curiosity comes with the territory. It's an occupational hazard, as it were.

"Winslow," he replied. My face brightened. Winslow, Arizona? I couldn't help it. This was too easy. I began to sing a line from that Eagles song,

"Well, I'm standing on a corner in Winslow, Arizona." Self-conscious since I am a terrible singer, I was relieved when Rick chimed in and sang with me. "I'm such a fine sight to see."

"You two make quite a pair. You should consider a lounge act," Linda called from the back of the Jeep.

Ignoring her, Rick turned to me. "Yeah," he said, gazing at me appreciatively. "Such a *fine* sight to see."

Whoomp, there it is! I blushed and almost dropped my water bottle again. I gulped down a large swallow before I managed something like, "Oh I bet you say that..." when he reached across the Jeep and wiped a drop of water from my chin.

"No, actually, I never say that," he admitted candidly.

What? Our eyes met just for a moment and I knew that what I had been feeling wasn't just in my mind or my other body parts. The attraction was mutual. We had chemistry and it was the good kind! We were off again and Rick was deep into a lecture about tectonic plates before my breathing returned to normal. It had been awhile since I had felt such a strong reaction to anyone. Since splitting up with my husband, there hadn't been anyone else of note, not until now.

"Hang on, ladies," Rick called out and I looked up just in time to see a guy in a 4-wheeler barreling towards us. Rick expertly turned us out of danger and muttered "Effin' rental" under his breath. "These guys come up here and think that they can handle these vehicles. Like it's a game or something," he complained. Linda leaned forward. Had she been listening the whole time? When she winked at me, I knew that she had been.

"How much training do you need to handle one of these babies?" she asked. Rick explained about the process of becoming a tour guide. He really seemed to take it seriously. He ended with how you weren't able to take a tour out on your own until you had passed all kinds of on and off road tests.

"What about the rest of it?" I asked.

"The rest of it?" Rick was confused.

"I mean, you know, all the soft skills. The people skills, the knowledge of the desert and what guests would be seeing."

"Oh, yeah sure," Rick smiled. "Being outgoing helps. You gotta be a people person. They look for someone with some life experience. Someone who has been around a bit. Seen things. Done things. Anywhere else, my resume would be a liability. But not here. And of course, there's classroom training too, and lots of books."

"That would be right up our alley," Linda assured him. "We love being in the classroom, especially Jackie. She's a *really* good teacher." I colored at the sound of my name. Rick looked at me again and spoke in a voice that was only meant for my ears.

"I bet you would be good at *anything* you put your mind to, Jackie," he told me. In spite of the blazing mid-afternoon sun, I shivered. This *really* was the best tour ever!

"Oh yeah, you too," I responded. Have we established yet that I'm just a bit of a novice when it comes to flirting? I never got the knack. It would actually be kind of funny, if it were not so pathetic.

Rick turned our attention back to the path that lay ahead of us. The last hour of the tour was relatively uneventful, I guess, if you call watercolor vistas and harrowing descents uneventful. We drove back through the surface streets towards the tour office and were about to turn into the parking lot when Rick spoke up again.

"How long are you in town?" he asked.

"We're not," I told him apologetically. "We drove down last night and spent the morning shopping and then here. We're heading back to Phoenix now and flying home tomorrow." Rick actually looked disappointed.

"I've got another tour in a little while but, maybe..." I didn't get to hear whatever "maybe" might entail, because Kate broke in.

"Another tour? Wow, no rest for the weary, huh?" Great timing, Kate. Rick told us how 3-4 tours a day was standard in season. After we pulled into the lot crowded with Jeeps, and started to unbuckle our seatbelts, Linda piped up again.

"Can you request a certain guide? Is that possible?" Linda asked with more than a little flirt in her tone.

"Oh yeah, we get that a lot." Rick nodded.

"I bet you do," Linda chuckled and discretely handed him some cash (I later found out it was $40) and promised, "Well, if I ever come back to Sedona..."

Tour duties over, Rick got busy in his role of consummate company professional and he handed her one of his cards.

"I hope you ask for me. And please, tell your friends. If you want to fill out a quick survey on our website, that'd be great!" he replied enthusiastically.

"Terrific. Thanks again, Rick," Linda concluded just as Kate went in for a hug. Everyone loves Kate and she gets and gives a lot of hugs. She looked so tiny next to Rick and I think she caught him a bit off guard but he recovered quickly and hugged her in return. I have never been so jealous of anyone in my life, not since my best friends all went bra shopping back in seventh grade, but didn't think to invite me, citing my apparent lack of need at the time. Not much has changed, but I wished right then, that I too could pull off a hug.

But, no. Sadly, physical displays of affection are just not in my skill set. I would have to settle for a handshake or something equally lame. Note to self: learn to flirt and learn to hug! Basic survival skills especially for the newly single. But for now, the tour had ended. It was time to go and my travelling companions appeared ready to depart.

"Hold on a second, Jackie," Rick said and disappeared around the counter. He returned just seconds later and handed me a card as well. "Hey, I really enjoyed meeting you. Have a good trip back East. And really, if you're ever out this way..."

"I'll look you up," I assured him. Would I? Boy, would I! He grasped my hand in farewell and I thought he might be leaning in for a hug or something, when Kate grabbed my other arm.

"C'mon, Jax. Traffic is gonna be a bear." Vowing revenge on perky Kate and all of her well-intentioned but poorly timed interruptions, I turned to wave at Rick and he smiled back at me.

"Take care," I called out. "And thank you!"

He waved and then turned and disappeared through an open doorway into what looked like a break room of some sort. Sigh. Oh well, it was fun while it lasted.

Linda and Kate were already walking towards the back of the parking lot. I hurried along to catch up, but I was too late. Kate was already in the driver's seat and Linda had claimed the front seat of our tiny rental car by the time I reached them. I was going to be squished in the back with my knees up around my ears for the two-hour ride back to Phoenix. But somehow I didn't care all that much. The warm glow I was feeling had nothing to do with the temperature. As I struggled to make room for my long legs in a backseat designed for a toddler, I looked at the business card he had handed me. Beneath a brightly colored logo was 'Rick Bowers, *Professional Tour Guide*'. The office number and website address were listed as well. When I turned the card over, I gasped. There were the digits that would change my life. He had written in a cramped hand what could only be his cell phone number, with a note. "Call me," it read.

Order your copy of JEEP TOUR today!!